DIRTY DANCER

82ND STREET VANDALS
BOOK TEN

HEATHER LONG

Dirty Dancer/Heather Long – 1st ed.

ISBN: 978-1-956264-90-6

For Carol and Gina, I miss you ladies each day.

SERIES SO FAR

82ND STREET
VANDALS

FOREWORD

Dear Reader,

Welcome to the tenth, bonus book for the 82nd Street Vandals series. If you have not read the first nine, stop. Do not pass Go. Grab book one: Savage Vandal, and start there.

Seriously.

This is a series that really must be read in order.

While it might be beneficial to read Bay Ridge Royals following the other books in the Vandals series, you are not required to other than the introduction of Theo who features in this book began there. Also, the tale of how Milo, Lainey, Adam, Ezra, and Bodhi formed their own dynamic. The key thing to know is that Theo is a younger sibling to Em and Milo via King. A younger sibling they didn't know about previously and he had a hard life before they found him.

Now, Theo is living with the Vandals and you'll see some of his story playing out in these pages. You will also see threads from the very beginning of the series being revisited. While the main happily ever after was wrapped in Fierce Dancer, there were still pieces of the story left to tell.

Pieces that didn't fit into the framework then. I can't tell you how great it was to reconnect with Em and the boys. Even more to see where they were in the lives they are growing together.

The timeframe covered in Dirty Dancer stretches from before the last scene in Fierce Dancer, through Bay Ridge Royals, and then beyond. You'll see the time jumps.

Please note that while the Vandals includes 7 MMCs and a loving bond between them all, Dirty Dancer narrowed the focus to the pieces of the story we needed to explore. You'll see what I mean, particularly because this title is the marriage of Dirty Devil and Fierce Dancer.

Please be aware this book contains content with dark themes and intense situations intended for mature audiences only, including but not limited to: sexual assault, mentions of grooming, underage/childhood sexual assault, physical violence, emotional and mental abuse, as well as kidnapping, stalking, manipulation, addiction and other potentially triggering topics.

And now, as always, the housekeeping notes:

For those of you who have never read a why choose, or reverse harem before, first let me thank you for picking this up and giving it a shot. Second, the heroine will not make a choice in this book or any other between the guys in her life. It may take her a while to reach that conclusion, but it's the journey that drives it. There are many ways to frame this kind of relationship, currently why choose fits it very well.

This is a bonus book to the overall series in order to explore facets that I knew would happen, but that I thought you might want to see.

Finally, one last note. Thank you.

Thank you for reading. Thank you for rooting for the Vandals. Thank you for being so invested in their story.

I'll see you on the flip side.

xoxo

Heather

P.S. Yes, at the very end are the collected bonus scenes from the rest of the series that were originally posted on my website.

THE VANDALS

82nd Street Boys
   Jasper "Hawk" Horan
   Kellan "Kestrel" Traschel
   Rome "Hummingbird" Cleary
   Vaughn "Falcon" Westbrook
   Liam "Mockingbird" O'Connell
   Freddie "Shrike" Cleary
   Milo "Raptor" Hardigan
   Mickey "Doc" James aka Vandal
   Emersyn "Dove, Sparrow, Starling, Swan, Little Bit, Boo-Boo, Hellspawn, Ivy" Sharpe

Other Characters
   Theo Hardigan
   Andrea Reed
   Levi Cavendish
   Elaine "Lainey" Benedict
   Adam Reed
   Ezra Graham

Bodhi Cavendish
Ms. Stephanie

DIRTY DANCER

PROLOGUE

MONTHS AGO...

EMERSYN

I gripped the silk, winding it around my forearm as I did the slow roll up the fabric. The climb took skill to make it appear effortless. Training and discipline made the motions a reflection of muscle memory.

If I moved one way, the silk would fold over the forearm and I would then shift my weight so I could roll upwards. Action. Reaction.

Action.

Reaction.

While my muscles and I both still remembered how to perform the most basic of tricks, the scars and residual trauma to my forearms themselves created impediments.

The actions weren't smooth.

I lost my grip more than once.

A slip sent me rolling downward before I could catch myself. Then I started all over again. Movement below snared my attention and I locked gazes with a pair of stunning blue eyes.

Paint flecks decorated his cheeks. Red, purple, and blue stained his forearms and his shirt. Using my own weight as a counterbalance, I shifted until I was holding all of my weight on my damaged forearms.

The scars would never be fully gone, but the feathers Vaughn tattooed on them for me transformed them. No longer did they represent my brokenness. Broken wasn't bad, but having my wings clipped *hurt*.

Head up.

Wings out.

My arms trembled as I maintained, and then began the arduous climb again. I would nail this movement. Much of my performances on this tour involved new choreography and new routines.

For the past twelve weeks, I'd been playing it safe and avoiding the possibility of a tumble that could end with me hitting the stage itself.

Below me, there was a net spread out. It was just six feet above the floor, but it was also pulled tight. The tension would help catch me if I dropped. When I told Vaughn what I wanted to do, he'd given me a long measuring look then nodded.

Two hours later, he told me the stage was ready for me to rehearse. The net had been here. I'd yet to actually fall, and if I could help it—I wouldn't.

But if I fell, it was also okay.

I would get this. I would fly again.

"Did you finish?" I called to Rome and he gave a careless shrug.

"Mostly."

"Can I see yet?" After seeing some of the backdrops at our last few venues, he'd decided he wanted to do our own. Liam and Rome disappeared for a day and then came back with a lot of work for Rome.

I wasn't allowed to see them until he was done.

It was a surprise.

"No," he said, one corner of his mouth curving up.

"Aww," I complained. He'd been working on the art for a week while we were on this break. Not that I'd been resting, so much as reworking some of my solos. Which was exactly what I was doing now.

"Tomorrow."

I slipped, and dropped a few feet, but caught myself like I'd meant to and my body arched. One arm in, one arm free. I was balanced against the silk, the wrap, and just one arm.

A grin worked its way over my face. When I glanced at Rome, he nodded.

"Closer," he said. "Stop thinking."

He wasn't wrong, but... "Easier said than done."

"Yes. But you can do it." His absolute faith wrapped around me.

I drank in the certainty in his voice and his eyes. Head tilted back, I took a deep breath. Rolling down, I landed on the net. For now it served as my "floor."

Rolling my head from side to side, I shook out my arms. Stop thinking.

"Will you start the music?"

Just do it.

Head up.

Music filtered through the speakers. It was the opening number for a solo I hadn't performed in over two years. It harkened back to a time when all I had was the music, the flight, and when we could see each other, Lainey.

I had so much more now.

Stop thinking.

The second refrain began and I caught the silk...

CHAPTER 1

TODAY

EMERSYN

*M*y right arm trembled faintly as I adjusted my stance. The warmth of Liam at my back with his hands on my hips shifted my position a bit more, then he flattened a hand between my shoulder blades.

"You're out of practice," he said, though there was no recrimination in his voice. The noise suppressing headphones muffled his voice, but I could still hear him. "Kel was worried that too many weeks without practice would throw off your aim."

It wasn't an unfair assessment. Shooting, it turned out, was like any other skill. I needed to practice it regularly to keep my muscles in shape and the skill itself honed. To my own surprise, I'd turned out to not be a bad shot. While it wasn't my favorite task, my skill made the boys feel better.

There wasn't much I wouldn't do for them.

"Easy," Liam continued, the pressure forcing my shoulders back. It wasn't quite a relaxed position, but it eased some of the strain on my right arm. With his left hand on my hip and his right hand on my back, he braced me. "Now, sight, relax, breathe, squeeze the trigger on the exhale."

I knew *how* to do it. Kellan had taken it as a personal challenge to prepare me to defend myself using three different types of guns. I favored the smaller one that was easier on my hand, but I could fire both Kel's and Liam's guns nearly as well as my smaller caliber preferred weapon.

Breath control was as much a part of dance as the muscle discipline, so I slowed my breathing down as I sighted the target at the end of the gallery. The targets were different, depending on the shooting range we used. This one had people shaped targets, with the rings spreading out from right over the heart.

Liam and Kel both insisted body shots were good, but go for the head if you wanted to make sure they didn't come back. Think of targets like zombies, Kel had suggested once and at my wrinkled nose, he'd *laughed*.

I hated zombies or zombie movies. So imagining them was not really conducive to my peace of mind, but it worked real well to shoot them and make them go away. One more deep breath and on the exhale, I squeezed the trigger.

One.

Two.

Three.

Four.

Five.

Six.

Six shots in rapid succession. I didn't close my eyes once. That was one of the first habits that Kel drilled out of me. *Protecting yourself is a natural instinct. You are tempted to look away from what you're shooting at—don't. You know it's going to be loud, so you'll brace at the last second, which can pull off your aim—don't. You may not want to keep firing even as you adjust your aim, but you have to trust your training.* The weight of the gun and the action of firing it will affect your targeting, so use it to your advantage.

I'd taken the rules and the techniques, and made them my own. I didn't need anyone to repeat them to me, I was already doing it. So while some of it was muscle memory and training, the rest had to come from putting my experiences to work for me. I would never be an expert shot and I'd rather never be in a position where I had to fire a gun again...

Shots streaking through the darkness. The pops accompanied by muzzle flashes as lights around me exploded. The guys were hauling me up on the emergency line, but the theater in Prague where I'd been performing turned into a nightmare of screams as gunmen raided it.

We'd planned for almost everything, even the full assault that we faced, and it still left me dangling, heart racing, and a little panicked until I had confirmation that all of my people were safe. My guys. Lainey. My brother.

Everyone.

"Hey," Liam shifted his hold to slide his arm around my middle and he pulled me back against them even as he braced my right arm with his hand on my wrist. "Where'd you go?"

He studied me with flinty eyes. The severity of his expression and the fierce mask he wore would convince everyone of what a hardass he was. Liam could be an absolute dick if he wanted to be, but he also loved me with a kind of all-encompassing possessiveness that shielded me as much as it embraced me.

Me and his twin were his two favorite people. They were definitely two of mine. Like every other relationship I'd forged with the other Vandals, ours was unique. Liam loved to bait me and give me hell. He also taught me how to kick his ass and the ass of anyone else who needed it. His words.

"Nowhere," I promised, resting my head to his shoulder. The warmth of him surrounded me, buffering against the aches from all the shooting. "Just..." I paused when he tugged off my ear protection then his own. Fortunately, Liam had rented the whole range to give us privacy. He nudged me forward, and I kept my grip on the gun until he was ready to take it. Once he had it unloaded and on the table in front of us, he turned to face me.

"Want to try that again, Hellspawn?" He locked those stunning blue eyes on me, depending on the light they could go almost blue-green. They always reminded me of the Caribbean in some ways. As identical as he and Rome were, their eyes reflected different facets of their personalities. I loved just staring into their eyes, as silly and swoony as that sounded.

"Nowhere I needed to be," I amended, but at his continued stare, I sighed. "Just—thinking about Prague. The shooting..."

His expression went grim. "Why are we thinking about that?" He didn't tell me I shouldn't or why I shouldn't think about it. In fact, he didn't tell me how I should behave or react at all. He asked.

"I love you," I murmured and that earned me a curve to his lips and a faint softening around his eyes.

"That's not why you were thinking about Prague," he chided me, but his eyes remained gentle. "C'mon, Hellspawn, tell me what is upsetting you so I can fix it."

"It's not upsetting me," I protested and when he cupped my chin to search my eyes, I met his gaze unflinchingly. "I promise, it's not. I just dangled out there when the shots started firing and I didn't freeze, but—I couldn't do anything.

It was a horrible few minutes to not know if everyone was okay or not."

"Vaughn and Jasper had you." Absolute confidence infused every word.

"Yes, they did," I agreed, leaning my cheek into his hand when he shifted his grip from my chin to my face. "Vaughn pulled me up so fast and they covered me on the catwalk. But those people were firing wildly. Later, they said they'd deliberately started firing at me to distract all of you."

Which just pissed me off.

"What makes you angrier? That you were used as a distraction? Or that it worked?" The blunt honesty in his voice demanded the same from me.

"A little bit of column A and column B." I shook my head. "I hate when you guys are put into danger because of me."

He snorted. "Hellspawn, if you took a bullet one of us could prevent, none of us would forgive ourselves. You'd take a hit for us if you could and you *have*," he continued, stressing that last word without allowing me to interrupt him. "You know it, I know it. Trust me, the guys know it too. The last thing I ever want is for you to be hurt again."

"But it's okay if you guys get hurt because of me?"

"In my opinion? Yes." He made no apologies for it either and I sighed. Not because we were disagreeing but because it was the last thing I wanted. "Look, if I take a hit and you don't, I'm okay with that. I'm more than okay with it."

"If Rome took that hit instead?" I dared him and the corners of his mouth tilted a little higher. "It's not funny," I added with a scowl and thumped his chest.

"It's not funny, but you are adorable."

I rolled my eyes and pushed away, but he just dragged me back. "Liam…"

"Shh," he hushed me then dropped a kiss on my lips.

When I just glared at him, his smile deepened. "Hellspawn, it just makes me hot when you get mad."

I scoffed but the comment managed to burst the bubble of my temper. "You're impossible."

"For you, I am anything but." He winked. "Now, if Rome got hurt protecting you, I'd be pissed—at the people who were trying to hurt you and then hurt him. I'd be just as fucking mad if you got hurt. Like I was when you two were taken and they were threatening you to keep '*me*' in line."

They'd made Rome take a beating by threatening me. "I stabbed that guy."

"Yes, you did," Liam said, his smile growing, the pride evident in his expression. "Just like you shot the guy who had the drop on me. Or went after that bastard at the hospital who was trying to hurt you. You're a fighter, Hellspawn. I've known that from day one. So... you can be pissed that someone targeted you to distract us so they could get to Lainey. I'm pretty fucking annoyed by it too. But none of us are going to regret putting you first."

"And that's that?" I tilted my head back to study him and he slid his hands down to cup my elbows and tugged me forward.

"Not the answer you wanted?" He pressed his lips to my forehead and I closed my eyes, drinking in his nearness.

"It's not about the answers I want," I said. "It's about the ones I can live with..." But I slid my arms up around his neck and he lifted me right up and hugged me close. "I just want to keep you guys safe."

"Same," he reminded me. I buried my face against his throat, and took a deep breath of him. He had that crispiness of fresh autumn leaves, sunshine, and amber. I could just detect the notes of his coffee from earlier too. The rest was just him, gunpowder, and the smell of the range. "That's why we practice, so we know you can protect yourself if we just don't happen to be there."

"And so I can protect you too," I reminded him and he chuckled. I pulled back to eye him, but he had me lifted clean off the ground, which was fine. I liked being nose to nose with him. "What's so funny?"

"Just how fierce you are, Hellspawn. I will never make the mistake of thinking you can't handle something or you can't protect us. You do a damn good job of it."

"But?" I prompted, not quite trusting the devilish little twinkle in his eyes.

"This ass of yours is just fine," he teased me, squeezing one cheek playfully. "No other buts about it."

A real laugh escaped me and his expression softened.

"Better?" That question was packed with so much meaning. Was I feeling better about what happened? Could I handle that their answers weren't likely to change? Did I know how much I meant to him?

"Yes," I said, dipping my head to press my lips to his. The connection was instantaneous. It had been from the beginning, even when he irritated me. Or I irritated him. I couldn't help my smile as I lifted my head. "So does that mean we can call practice finished and go actually spend our time doing something else fun?"

Liam didn't spend as much time on the tour. He couldn't, but he visited every chance he got. I understood the absences from him, from Jasper and Kellan. Even Mickey had to go back periodically. Didn't mean I didn't miss them, and I went back to Braxton Harbor so we could all be there together as often as possible.

"Nope," he told me, his smile growing. "Need at least another thirty minutes, so I can tell Kellan honestly that you're getting your practice in."

I groaned and let my head fall back as I stared up at the ceiling. "So mean to me."

He nipped my throat. "I can be meaner, Hellspawn. We haven't had a good sparring session in a few months."

Lips pursed, I eyed him. He was only *partially* kidding.

"Fine, we can wrestle when we're done as long as you have to be naked."

"If I'm naked," he informed me. "You will be too, whether you start out that way or not."

"I'm not really hearing a downside here." I bit my lower lip as he groaned. The heat flashed into his eyes and he landed a slap against my ass that was all sting and a little heat. Another wave of laughter burst out of me. I really wasn't hearing a downside. I mean, I got why he wanted to practice. "Promise you don't have to leave tonight?"

He'd just gotten in this morning in the very early hours after taking a red eye flight.

"I can stay for a couple of days," he promised, then set me on my feet before he reached back and got the gun reloaded. "So, show me what you got…"

The temptation to take off my shirt to tease him was right there, but I decided to save it for later. He didn't offer me the gun until I put the ear protection back on. Then he put on his own.

He got the new target set up and it was back ten feet from where the other had been. Right… thirty minutes and then we could "play." I braced myself and used both hands this time to steady my arm.

I didn't need to be perfect, I just needed to be accurate.

The next six shots went center mass and I caught Liam's wild smile of approval.

"Next?"

CHAPTER 2

FREDDIE

The last of the gear had been packed into one of the trucks. We'd brought three of our own to handle all transport of the equipment, gear, and extras in case we needed to repair or replace any of it. The drivers had all been heavily vetted. Jasper offered them a separate contract for handling these routes, including bonuses for each city, and paid time off when Boo-Boo took breaks.

Considering the guys would be on the road more than home in Braxton Harbor, it seemed a reasonable exchange. All three were more than committed and we had two backup drivers amongst us if anyone got sick. Vaughn could handle one of the trucks, and Jasper would fly out to take over the other if necessary. I was almost dead certain Rome knew how to drive one, but he didn't say and no one asked.

Then again, if Rome wanted to drive one, he'd just climb up in the cab and get it started. A laugh escaped me because that really did fit. One of the outer doors to the practice theater we'd been using for this break creaked as it was opened letting in street noise, the faint stink of exhaust, along with Vaughn and Rome.

I frowned at the sight of both of them, but Vaughn just waved off my concern. "She's sleeping in with Liam this morning. Since he has to leave after lunch, we're giving them the day."

Relief crashed into me and I blew out a harsh breath. Rome bumped my shoulder on the way back. The guys limited contact most of the time. I'd known, but I hadn't really noticed until we were on our way back from Pinetree and taking care of Boo-Boo was the priority.

The guys never crowded me, never started wrestling with me. Hell, they'd have those wrestling matches all the way around me, but I wasn't involved unless I involved myself. The only one who actively didn't hold back to grip my shoulder or give me a hug was Jasper. Somewhere in my brain, Jasper had been marked firmly "safe," even if I trusted all of these guys with my life.

Rome paused to look at me even as Vaughn stayed where he was. He hadn't moved away from the door yet. Fuck...

"I'm being weird," I admitted and Vaughn shrugged.

"Not really," he said in an even tone that insisted I believe him. "But you look worried."

"Not worried," Rome countered, and when I glanced at him, I found him really studying me. He even held my gaze for a long moment. He wasn't one to stare, but I didn't withdraw. "What's wrong?"

I opened my mouth to say nothing, but then swallowed the lie unspoken. Maybe not a lie so much as a distinct untruth. "I'm worried about Boo-Boo." It was wrong to talk about her when she wasn't there to defend herself and at the same time, I didn't think she'd admit to this one.

Fuck, I wouldn't. That thought crystalized for me exactly

why I was worried. Boo-Boo was a beautiful mirror, she was all the good things even with the shadows and the cracks, of survival and rising above it all. I wanted to be those things but...

"What's up?" Vaughn asked, bringing me firmly back to earth and I folded my arms.

"It's hard to put it into words," I admitted. It was an instinct, a gut feeling. They could go with that sure, but I wasn't sure that would tell them what they needed to know in order to do something about the issue.

"Do your best," Rome said and he turned to grab one of the wooden crates that we weren't taking with us. We'd consolidated. So he dragged it over and sat on it.

"Need coffee?" Vaughn offered. It was kind of funny, we all brought coffee in the mornings that we knew Boo-Boo would be right there, but I didn't expect her to be here so I hadn't...

Shaking off that thought, I scrubbed a hand over my face. The need to fidget was there, but I didn't have anything to chew on or smoke or snort. All good things to not have, cause they usually get me into trouble. I settled for flicking my knife out and letting the blade dance over my fingers and began to pace.

Restlessness invaded every muscle. Rome waited, an oasis of calm on one side while Vaughn settled in to lean against the wall. Where Rome was calm, Vaughn seemed almost peaceful—no, it wasn't peace. It was patience. He could, and would, wait for as long as it took me to figure out what to say.

It helped that the theater was quiet, the darkened stage areas offset by the low lighting in the backstage area. The smell of sawdust and sweat, that was how Boo-Boo described it. Back here was where the magic rested and prepped to be on the stage. It had to be a little dirty, a little grimy, and very *real* because when she was out there, she wasn't.

Her little laugh when she'd explained it held a note of apology. Not that she had anything to be sorry about, but she worried I wouldn't understand it. On the one hand, I hadn't —not fully. But I didn't need to be the one who understood. It was always about her and what she needed.

But right now? Right now, her words resonated as they whispered to me from the past.

"Back here, it's the most real it ever gets. You see the running makeup, smell the sweat, and taste the hot lights and feel the sawdust where it clutters the corners. It's reality, in all the ways that reality *makes it a little dirtier, a little grimier. Then I step out there... and all of that melts away as I become the fantasy and I fly. It's the yin and the yang of the theater. I love it so damn much."*

"I'm going to be real with both of you right now, and I accept that you may not see things the way I do and that's cool. But I know you don't see what I do and I think—no, I *know* you need to at least hear it. She needs all of us."

I cut a look at Rome, and he nodded once. "You see Starling differently. We know."

No questions or demands for proof. Just quiet, perfect acceptance. I raked a hand through my hair. It was getting longer and I needed to get it cut, but the one barber I trusted was back in Braxton Harbor. Maybe Boo-Boo could give me a hand...

Still dancing the blade, I continued my pacing. "She's pushing herself really hard. Our last two breaks weren't really breaks for her."

Not that they weren't aware. The three of us were the primary ones on this tour with her. We went city to city, Vaughn inspected every installation of her equipment. He went over it with a fine-tooth comb before every performance and if even one thing was off, he made the techs do it again.

No accidents on our watch.

Rome and I took turns being with her backstage throughout the prep and performance. There were a few other dancers on the tour. Most of whom she'd interviewed herself or had worked with in the past. The history with them helped, but I didn't know them and I wasn't trusting them with her.

More often than not, there was a line after a performance when we were leaving whether we had breakdown or not to get ready to move on. She always made time to talk to her "fans," particularly the kids. Those she gravitated right toward and I got it. I just hated the crowd.

"It was worse in the beginning," I said. "I think she had something to prove to herself." As much as she loved the performance, I wasn't so disconnected that I didn't see the hours and hours of work she put in. One of the other dancers, one of the guys, asked if she wanted a partner like she used to work with and she said no so fast, I didn't even have time to think about that question until now.

Back and forth I went, aware of the two of them listening, and at the same time, just letting my thoughts go where they needed to go. There was something here and it had been chewing on me for weeks.

"She's doing better—I think. Or maybe I should say, she *was* doing better until we went to Prague." Going to Prague was something we all absolutely had to do. I'd never had a passport before, much less left the country. But we'd all gone, it had been a group effort. We went to help Ball-Cracker and Milo find their siblings.

Fuck... a new sibling. I was still rolling that fact around in my head. Doc had called to say that the kid had shown up in Braxton Harbor with Milo and Lainey. He wanted to stay with us. Right now that didn't mean on tour, but it could mean on tour.

I'd met Theo, briefly. He was—he didn't look like Em or Milo—and fuck that wasn't the point right now. My thoughts kept going scattershot. I stopped mid-pace and scowled at the floor. The path I'd cut through the dust reminded me that maybe getting someone to sweep up these places needed to be a priority, or would that mess with how it smelled?

"Wow," I said aloud and then shook my head. "Sorry, apparently I'm all over the place."

"We're fine," Vaughn said. "We have at least four hours before someone will be looking for us."

The delivery was so droll and dry that I laughed. "I always forget that you can be a dick."

"Happy to remind you," Vaughn said easily enough.

I snorted, then blew out another breath. "I think she is better about some things, but she's pushing herself again. I want to tell her to take a real break, not one where she tries to do everything in the few days she's supposed to have off or be everywhere for everyone."

There it was, it *clicked*.

"The last break we took at home, she didn't slow down for a day. She went on the road with Jasper. She went to the mechanic's shop with Kel. She even took turns to go with Doc to the new houses. Liam came in on that flying break and she left with him for meetings. By the time we got back on the road, I don't think she had a real day off."

That was also not counting all the hours she spent in her studio. At least two hours every single day, whether she was training a routine or just training. She argued she had to because that was what it took. But what was that cost to her?

"After Prague, I think she needs it more than ever. But even if we plan to go home, Theo is going to be there now." If I was Boo-Boo's baby brother, I'd want to know her too. I'd want her attention, hell, I wanted her attention now but she had so many demands.

"You think she's spreading herself too thin." It wasn't a question. Vaughn lifted his shoulders. "I don't disagree, but Freddie—she misses the guys and I think she needs that time with them even at the cost of *not* taking a break."

"I know she misses them." She never hid that from any of us. Her excitement when she saw them was so genuine. I also knew she didn't relax as well as she did when we were all home. One of us was with her every night on the road, sometimes it was all of us. I didn't like to hang out through the sex part. Sometimes it was fun, but other times...

Right not about me.

"But I think she's demanding more of herself and now she's adding new routines." Which was what this break had been about. "She wants to challenge herself."

For some reason, those five words scared the piss out of me. They had from the moment she said it aloud this week when she'd been testing a new routine on a pole that dangled with no silks.

"Challenge herself," Vaughn repeated and he cut a look past me to Rome and when I glanced at him, I found him wearing the same expression.

"That's what she told me." It wasn't betraying a confidence. I'd cut out my tongue before I did that to her, but she'd mentioned it in passing and I needed to not be the only one who *heard* the problem present in those words.

Vaughn blew out a breath.

"I'll talk to her," Rome volunteered and I raised my brows. At my skeptical look, he shrugged. "I can be blunt."

Yes. Yes he could.

"If she needs a partner to challenge herself," he continued. "I can do that too."

The profound relief that crashed through me had me flipping the knife closed. He put the two parts of it together and that was the part that had been haunting me. I got that she refused to let fear dictate her life, but the last partner she had when she performed had been a brutal, abusive piece of shit that should have suffered even more than he did before we killed him.

"Better?" Vaughn asked and he made no effort to cover his own relief. "Also, Rome, if you're going up there too, we need to work out new engineering so it's safe for both of you."

Since my next step had been to call Ball-Cracker or Milo or both, yes, I felt a lot better. "I want to help her too."

"Let her teach you to dance," Rome said as he stood and straightened. "I want coffee now." He was heading to the door and I stared after him. Vaughn chuckled but pushed the outer door open for Rome.

"C'mon, Freddie. Coffee and food. Then we can plan the next few days…"

Let her teach me to dance?

CHAPTER 3

EMERSYN

"Sully!" Surprise fountained through me when the familiar figure turned toward us. We'd just arrived at the theater in Miami where I was scheduled for a couple of weeks of performances. It was in part to make up for the dates I'd canceled to go to Europe, and then we'd added more dates to accommodate the demand and to hold onto the theater we'd wanted.

The shift in the schedule only moved some of my down days and the guys were okay with it. It was utterly worth the trade-off. We'd been there for Milo, Lainey, and the others. We succeeded in closing off wounds we hadn't even realized were there and now...

I shook off that part as Sullivan Donner dropped off the stage and made his way up the aisle to greet me. It was an old opera house-styled theater that boasted seating capacity for up to two thousand people. It wasn't the largest venue I'd performed in, but damn it was close.

Skipping ahead a little, I threw myself into a hug at Sully. He caught me easily and chuckled.

"Long time no see, Sprite," he said, giving me a squeeze before he set me on my feet. He flicked his dark eyes over my head to look behind me so I pivoted to hold out a hand toward Vaughn. "Your escort has definitely improved," Sully commented.

"Be nice," I told him as Vaughn slid an arm around me. He didn't tend to loom over the other dancers, even if he was the tallest guy in the room. Where Sully was concerned, he was definitely a whole head above him. Sully was barely two inches taller than me. Another reason I'd always been comfortable with him. "Sully, this is Rome, Vaughn, and Freddie. Vaughn handles all the rigging, and equipment. If he doesn't sign off on it, it doesn't happen."

That was a bit of warning for him because this was his first time meeting my guys. They were all mine and I'd been clear about that when I spoke to him on the phone. I didn't spend an unnecessary amount of time explaining my personal life to anyone. Sully Donner, however, wasn't just anyone.

"Rome knows my routines better than I do and when I need a partner for practice or support, he's my guy. Freddie handles all my backstage security before, during, and after performances. You don't get into my dressing room or quiet room without getting cleared by him."

I didn't miss the flash of surprised pleasure on Freddie's face at my description. It was true. I never worried about going backstage or resting in between sets. Freddie picked which of the dressing rooms would be mine and he *always* changed the locks. It was such a thoughtful thing to do and it always reminded me of my first real encounter with Jasper.

At least the one I remembered, when he was changing out the shitty lock on my dressing room at the theater in Braxton

Harbor. The security and peace of mind that offered then hadn't changed now. With that, I pivoted to look at Sully and let Vaughn pull me back a couple of steps to tuck under his arm.

"Guys, this is Sullivan Donner, the choreographer I told you I wanted to bring in. He helped to design some of my bigger set pieces a few years ago and he was always one of my favorite people in the business." Reminding them didn't seem like such a bad idea, because all three were stonily silent during my introductions. "Also known as Sully, and he's graciously agreed to help me punch up some of my older pieces and help me with new ones."

I wanted fresh challenges, fresh dances, and fresh movements. It was so hard to explain that now that I was mastering my older routines once more, they didn't feel like they fit as much. If anything, most of them were more ill-fitting than a polyester suit. They were Emersyn, lost and broken girl hiding from her family on the road and in the dance.

They weren't *me*. They weren't the me I'd become, the Hellspawn or Starling or even Boo-Boo. I'd become a Vandal and I wanted my shows to reflect that.

Vaughn extended a hand to Sully. "Dove has told us about you. It's interesting to meet you, but to be fair, we did a background check too."

The latter didn't even surprise me. It would have been far more astonishing if they hadn't.

Sully raised his brows then gripped Vaughn's hand easily. "Glad to hear you're looking after her. I take it, I passed muster." It wasn't a question or a joke. But Rome merely shrugged without answering.

Freddie, on the other hand, smirked. "You're here and you got to hug her." In other words, if he hadn't, this conversation wouldn't even be happening. "Just to be clear, do anything to hurt her and it won't matter what your background check said."

Vaughn sighed. "I was going to put it a little more politely."

"I wasn't," Rome said. "Blunt is better."

"Agreed," Sully said and a flicker of surprise rippled over the guys' faces. Well, over Freddie's and Vaughn's. "I like to know where I stand." With that, however, he met each of their gazes individually. "Just to keep us all on the same page, *I'm* the choreographer and *she's* the performer. All final decisions on set pieces will be made by her."

"With consultation," I amended before he incited a riot. "Vaughn has to know the equipment demands. Previously, there were near misses and close calls. No one wants those."

"As long as *you* are satisfied with that caveat," Sully said. "Then I can work within it. But you're asking for some new routines to start training when you're only four days out from an opening *here*. That's a lot of pressure, Sprite."

I grinned for real this time. "I like that kind of pressure. I need to be pushed again. It's been a long time since someone pushed me."

Rome was the closest to pushing when it came to dance and performance. But he didn't push so much as offer such unwavering support and faith. He didn't let my fear dissuade him, and his steadfastness kept me from giving into that fear.

If I failed and I fell, I'd get back up again.

He *knew* it and his knowledge meant I didn't forget.

But Sully was different. He wouldn't hold back on his critical appraisal of my abilities and he'd also push me if he thought *I* was limiting myself.

"Be careful what you ask for," Sully warned. "I tend to be a bit of an asshole when I train."

"It's okay," I assured him. "I still like you."

"Fine, then get into some training gear and warm up. We're going to do some ground runs before we go aerial."

We hadn't even begun the bump in yet. "I thought you'd want to review my current shows first…"

He held up his phone. "Been catching up since you called. I already have some ideas. Now, move your ass. We have a limited amount of time to get you at least one new routine before this series of shows opens. No sense in wasting it."

My mouth popped open a little. I'd just said I wanted to be pushed, but I hadn't expected him to take me so literally. Snapping my mouth closed, I glanced at Freddie. I didn't have a dressing room yet.

"I got you, Boo-Boo." Then he held out a hand to me. Him asking for contact was always a huge thing. I had my own duffel with practice gear in it so I shifted the weight then slid my grip into his. "We'll be back in fifteen."

"Make it ten," Sully said. The shifting temperature made me bite my lower lip even as I trotted along with Freddie toward the stage itself. The guys would be doing a full sweep, but Freddie would get me a dressing room sorted and guard it so I could change without any concerns.

"You'll take fifteen," Freddie said over his shoulder. "Or I'll make it thirty." He sounded positively smug about it.

"You're going to make fetch happen, aren't you?" At my question, Freddie shot me an amused smile.

"You want fetch to happen, Boo-Boo. Then we'll damn well make fetch happen." He was so damn serious, it made me giggle. Once we reached backstage, he shifted his grip from my hand. "You got your gun?" The last bit was asked in a low voice.

I patted the holster on my hip that was hidden by Vaughn's huge sweatshirt. Liam had been working on getting me a carry license and a concealed carry license in every state I could possibly need it. I wasn't even sure if Florida was on the list yet, but the guys were firm, I was armed at all times unless I was actually on stage or in practice.

Even then, I always had backup.

"Good. Stay behind me." He took point. The backstage area was quiet, lights on and while there was a crew who worked at the theater, they weren't going to be working on my equipment or bump-in. We brought our own people. So unsurprisingly, the backstage was mostly empty.

As quiet as it was and decorated in puddles of light from the overheads, a peace rippled over me. I loved the feeling of a theater at all stages of a performance. From now, when it was in resting mode. Then when activity picked up during bump-in and rehearsals, to the night of performances when the energy thrummed through the building.

Freddie led the way down the hall. He had his phone in one hand, but his attention wasn't on it so much as the doors along the hall. Without consulting for directions, he led me right to the stairs that took us down to a lower level. A blanket of silence enveloped us as we descended.

The stairs opened out into a wider hallway with signs pointing toward different stage access points, including an elevator that would take me right up to the rafters. Freddie inspected each door along the hall, but he angled to put me closer to the elevator. It meant when I came down or went up, I'd be right here.

I liked that. He did a full scan of the hall before he opened the first of the doors and I moved to put my back to the wall next to the door. It let me watch both ways down the hall. It also meant I could warn him if trouble came looking for us.

In the room, Freddie grunted. At his snort, I suppressed another smile. A long sigh accompanied his reappearance. "Don't like this one. Next." Three more rooms were inspected, but it was the fifth one we visited that made him happiest. "C'mon in, Boo-Boo."

I slipped inside to see what had finally met his requirements. There was a sofa, a makeup counter, a separate bathroom and a closet. Pretty standard, well for the headliners. The chorus performers and the supporting players might have to share a room or they had to use one of the bigger makeup areas. Private room or not, they had communal bathrooms.

That used to never bother me. Just like nudity didn't bother me. Particularly after Eric though, I liked the ability to lock a door and pee in peace. The guys were even more particular. They didn't pay a lick of attention to any of the dancers walking around in partially dressed or undressed states. But Vaughn didn't care for them being able to see me, and for Freddie?

Well, for Freddie it wasn't even a question. He didn't want to see them and he didn't want them seeing me. It was just easier for him all the way around. That was worth more to me than all the rest combined.

"I like it," I said. "Will you make sure they set up my gear in here?"

"Yep," he said. "You want me to stay or go while you change?" Normally, in an empty theater, he would just step out without asking. He only asked when others were present in the building.

"You are always welcome," I assured him as I stripped the sweatshirt off. I'd need to take off my gun and holster. Freddie would take it while I performed until my gun safe was brought in with the rest of my equipment. I had a tank top on under the sweatshirt. "Are you okay with staying?"

He scratched at his jaw, then shoved a hand through his hair. The blond locks were getting longer again and I rather liked the length on it. He hadn't gotten a haircut since we got on the road. Vaughn had and so had Rome, but not Freddie.

"I want to stay," he admitted and I locked gazes with him

in the mirror. A quick frown tightened his brow. "That's okay, right?"

"Of course it is," I said, pivoting to face him. "You just—you never tell me when you want something lately. You always have me choose unless it's really about security." In those cases, it was never a question for any of us.

"Maybe it's time some of that changed," he said and I couldn't stop my smile. "I don't know what it will look like, but I want to find out." The uncertainty in him was still there and I wanted to...

"Can I hug you?" Contact was still on his terms, period.

With a sheepish expression, he opened his arms and met me more than halfway. I crashed into him and wrapped my arms around him tight. He smelled like my shampoo and soap. He'd taken his shower this morning right after me. I loved it when he used my products. It was stupid, but it just let me feel close even when he was holding himself apart.

"I really am trying, Boo-Boo," he admitted in a low voice.

I fisted his shirt and kept my face pressed to his shoulder. Some things were just easier to address when we couldn't see each other. Honesty sometimes required anonymity. "You don't have to do a damn thing you don't want to do. Ever. The only thing I need from you is for you to be happy."

"But you want more." It wasn't a question. At that, I leaned back and met his troubled gaze. "I know you do." With care, he raised his hand but he didn't touch me without me nodding. Then he cupped my cheek so gently it made tears burn in my eyes. "The thing is—I want it too. I want to touch you and have you touch me, so the only things I feel and see are you."

"If only it were that easy," I murmured and he let out a long breath. "Of course, I understand. I will always understand it and that's why in this—it's about what you want and what you need. You set the tone and you set the pace. I'm good with everything. You want me to get on my knees and let you fuck my mouth while I don't touch you? I will do that."

His pupils dilated at the statement and his lips parted.

"You want me to bend over and let you fuck me from behind while I can't see or touch you—I will do that too. I mean it, Freddie. You touching me is not a bad thing. It will *never* be a bad thing. So if that's what you need to do to touch me, my answer will *always* be yes."

The stroke of his thumb over my lower lip sent tingles shimmering through my system. "I may take you up on that."

Oh, my heart bounced at the suggestion.

"I heard that sigh," he said with a faint grin of his own. The fatness of his pupils betrayed his arousal and there was a hint of a flush to his own cheeks. "I share it…you still have the prettiest pussy I've ever seen and ever will see."

"Thank you. I rather liked your dick the one time I felt it."

That earned me a dry stare before he started laughing. Then he pressed his forehead to mine. "I adore you, Boo-Boo."

"That's cause I'm *fetch*."

He laughed harder and gave me a gentle squeeze. After, he steadied me before he stepped back. "While we're working on this touching thing, I have one more request."

"Tell me."

"Teach me to dance?"

I blinked.

"I know you'll have to touch me when we do that and we'll have on clothes and stuff, but I'm asking you to push me a little that way. Teach me how to dance with you."

"Yes," I whispered. "I'd say we could start right now…"

"I know," he said, then gave me a slow smile. "You'll also have kept him waiting thirty-five minutes by the time we get back up there."

He was so damn pleased with himself, I burst out laughing. "One more hug?"

"How about this?" He dipped his head and pressed his lips to mine. It was a there and then gone again kiss but it sent another cascade of warmth through my system. "I'll save you a hug for after your first practice with him."

"That's definitely something to look forward to!" I hurried to change, because he wasn't wrong. I was going to have kept Sully waiting and I didn't even care. What I cared about was that Freddie didn't take his gaze off me as I changed. "Freddie?"

"Hmm?"

I glanced over my shoulder at him. "I can't wait to dance with you."

"Here's hoping I don't suck," he said with a shake of his head.

"You won't, but you will still have to do one thing for me," I informed him as I pulled on my leotard. Once I was in it, I pulled my hair back and Freddie eyed me with a hint of apprehension.

"What?"

"You're going to have to pick your favorite song," I told him as I pivoted. "Fast. Slow. Hard. Gentle. Rock. Rap. I don't care what it is, you pick the music and then we'll dance."

He blew out a long breath. "I can do that."

With a grin, I finished pulling on my ballet flats so I didn't go barefoot all the way through the back. Freddie locked up behind us as I began to half-dance, half-jog down the hall to the stairs. I was a mess of wild energy and as excited as I was to work with Sully again, nothing could top the last thirty minutes.

Nothing.

CHAPTER 4

VAUGHN

S hawn Mendes *In My Blood* played over the sound system that the techs continued to tweak. Bump in started an hour earlier, but Em had been on the stage working for the past three. *Sully* had only allowed her a brief fifteen minute break for water and to discuss corrections before he put her back to work.

The song was on repeat and while I actually liked it the first time I'd heard it, I was beginning to question my taste, though I would never get tire—

"Stop," Sully bellowed out abruptly and the music cut off as Em slid to a halt. She'd been mid-transition, everything about her flowed. The choreographer's interruptions grew more frequent and more irritating.

"Is it bad that I'm picturing stabbing him right now?" Freddie asked from where he was kicked back in an audience seat with his feet up on the row in front of him.

"No," Rome responded in a dry voice. His attention

remained riveted on the stage. He'd been closer when they started. Yet, after several of Sully's interruptions, he'd retreated to join us.

One of us should go supervise the bump in, but none of us moved. Sully was an unknown. Yes, he passed muster on a background check Liam had run. Doc had his friends pull another one, but everything came back green lights.

Still, that could just mean he'd never been caught. Background checks on the uncle never revealed his disgusting and brutal predilections where she was concerned. The only thing that had me holding still and *not* interrupting was the sharp focus in *her* expression.

If he was irritating the shit out of her like he was us, it wasn't on display. We were close enough to hear him when he yelled with all his wild hand gestures. Not close enough to hear everything when he spoke as he did now, quiet and intense.

I couldn't see his expression, but I could read the focused intensity on Dove's. Whatever he was saying, she seemed to be absorbing. Sweat soaked through her leotard, and her brow was wet. She'd long since coiled her ponytail up into a bun that crowned her head.

As much muscle as she'd put back on, she was still tiny. The strength she housed in that slender body of hers was a thing of wonder.

"Huh," Freddie grunted and I refocused my attention to the stage. Sully used a remote to start the music and then he began to move on the stage.

Rome straightened and I leaned forward. He was repeating every step Em had done, only there was something…

"It's predatory," Freddie said. "When she dances, she's not the aggressor…"

That was definitely the difference. Sully was repeating

her steps but there was just a serious amount of violence in his movements. At the one minute mark, he cut off the music and faced her again, arms spread like—*see?*

Head tilted, she put her hands on her hips. Her gaze drifted to us then snapped back to Sully. I had to bite back a smile at the instinct she had to check in with us, but she was right... This wasn't *our* decision.

I stretched, the taut skin along the back of my left arm and shoulder where I'd been burned ached. The scars had left ripples in some of the tattoos. I'd fixed most of it, blended it in to hide the distorted skin. Most of my scars were external, and while Em had them—I flashed a look at the inside of her right arm as she raised it while talking to Sully.

The scars left by the bastard who'd cut into her had been deep and vicious. It had damaged muscle and tendon as well as skin. The butchers who sutured it hadn't done much to mask the damage, if anything, they'd made it worse.

Doc treated the scars and helped her rehab the muscles and the skin trauma. They were never not going to carry the darker marks of that past, so I put feathers along it on each arm. Her *wings*.

Every single piece of art on her was my work. I soaked in the sight of her as she repeated the steps without the music or emotion. It was more a question, a pause here or a pause there as she looked at Sully. He would replicate a motion, make some alteration, then she would repeat it and change it more.

They walked through the whole thing, making adjustments. For the first time since they started, I saw her wings coming out even as she raised her chin. There were very clear moments where she said *no* to him. No argument, just *no*.

The firmness in the response and the snap in her manner made me glad I couldn't hear the question. Might have made me want to hit him. I used to be the guy with the most even temper, now I pictured rearranging his face for thinking he *might* upset her.

Even the mental head shake didn't clear away the image. Violence was not my first choice. Or it didn't *used* to be my first choice. The last few months...

The music kicked on abruptly and pulled my attention back to the present and the stage. Em and Sully were both dancing, both snapping arms out, then crossing the stage at speed. Their mirrored motions were sharp, violent, and between one breath and the next, I saw what he'd been going for.

"Wow," Freddie exhaled.

"Yeah," I said slowly.

While the choreographer mirrored her steps and followed her across the stage, it wasn't his steps that held me captivated. Emersyn went from hesitation to action, she controlled that stage and every movement was a deliberate provocation. That was what he'd been wanting her to do. Stop questioning the music and motion, tear it up and just own the stage.

It was erotic as hell and I blew out a slow breath. Sully slowed as she finished the song and ended on a stomp with one hand on her hip and tossing a glance over her shoulder. I adjusted my pants before I shifted to lean against the seats. Soaked in sweat, flushed, and panting—she was absolute fucking perfection.

"We're going to need more security," Freddie said abruptly. "Better locks too."

I got what he was saying and at the same time, it was just one number. A number on the ground. Most of her work was in the air. Still...

"Better," Sully said when the music cut. "Much better.

Walk it off, hydrate, then again. Let's nail this one down and we'll start on something new after that."

I shook my head, then checked my watch before I glanced at Rome. "You got this?" While Freddie had her backstage security down to an art, Rome stuck with her anytime she was out in public as well—particularly if she was on stage.

Every once in a while, one of the chorus dancers decided to make a move and see if they could audition to be her new partner. We'd disabused a couple who'd decided to push it when she turned them down. One guy tried to intimidate her into letting him *audition* and I removed him from the chorus that week. I sent him out with a wrenched arm, a healthy sense of fear, and some newfound respect following the apology he owed her. He was lucky I didn't break both of his legs.

"Yes," Rome said. "Bump in?"

I nodded. "I'd rather watch, but I don't want there to be anything that slips through the cracks." I trusted our drivers. I trusted the majority of our crew. Didn't mean I was willing to let them do everything without my supervision. There were too many opportunities for accidents if the gear had been damaged in transport. I inspected it when we took it down and packed it up. I inspected it again on bump in.

Once we got the primary and secondary sets of silks hung, we'd do a test run. Her weight was negligible, but I didn't want there to be even a suggestion of possible failure. Minimizing the risks to her let her focus on her performance.

"Remind her to eat," I said, then lifted my chin to Freddie. "You staying or coming with me?"

It could go either way. He glanced away from where she was doing circuits while downing water to look at me. "Need help?"

"I can do it," I said.

Freddie grimaced. "Nah, I'll help." Then he shot another look at the stage, she and Sully looked like they were debating something. I couldn't quite read her expression and based on Freddie's frown, I don't think he could either. Rome, however, didn't seem bothered at all.

"We'll do this as fast as we can. That way, the sooner we're done, the sooner we can see her again."

With a grunt, Freddie passed a key to Rome for her dressing room. We weren't leaving the building but it was better if we all had keys. After Rome pocketed his, Freddie passed another key to me.

We'd just made it to the doors to go out front when the music resumed, Em was in the center of the stage, the kinetic energy seemed to swirl around her and I caught her eye as she looked right toward me and Freddie. We were a little far to be absolutely certain, but I'd bet she just winked at us.

Rather than guess, I just blew her a kiss and savored the smile she wore before her expression went all business.

"You make that shit look so easy," Freddie said as I shoved the door open and he followed me out into the lobby. We could have gone via the backstage, but I wanted to get a good look at the whole building inside and out.

"Blowing her a kiss?"

"Yeah," Freddie grumbled and I had to swallow a chuckle at how irked he sounded. "You just—do that shit and she lights up."

"She lights up for you too," I reminded him before shoving open the exterior doors and letting the humid air chase away the suggestion of chill from the interior air conditioning. It wasn't *that* much of a temperature differ-ence. I pulled out my phone and scrolled for the facilities contact for the theater.

"But I don't do any of that romantic stuff you guys do." He

trailed behind me, head on a swivel even as he shoved his hands into his pockets.

I cut him a look after I sent the message to have them check their units. She was sweating up there now without a full house audience, and the only difference I could feel between interior and exterior was the amount of humidity. "You do your own thing, Freddie, it's not a competition."

Sometimes, we all needed to be reminded of that. Jasper and Liam loved to wind each other up, particularly cause Liam could afford to drown her in gifts. Thing was, Dove didn't give a damn about the presents. She gave a damn about us and the way we made her feel.

Jasper building her a dance studio or Kel teaching her to drive or even Rome taking her out to paint with him. "She treasures the moments, Freddie," I reminded him as we headed around the building. "She treasures the things we do with her, not just what we do for her."

If anything, she didn't need our money. She had plenty of her own. Granted, the source was someone she wanted nothing to do with, but Liam had taken her inheritance and cleaned it, bit by bit, he was wiping away the blood money and investing it in the things that mattered to her.

Things like Kel's new mechanic's shop and rehabbing some of the properties around it.

"I want…" Instead of finishing the thought, he let it drift off as we came around to where the trucks were beginning to back to the loading docks. I paused to glance at him.

"You want?"

"Yeah," he said with a long sigh. "I do. I just don't know how to do what you guys do."

"You don't," I said, and at his frown, I shrugged. "You don't. You be Freddie. That's who she needs you to be. Who she wants you to be. She doesn't want us to be anyone else. So just be you."

"But..." His frown deepened. "What if I want to be more romantic for her?"

I didn't laugh. In a way, it was funny, but not in a humorous way. Freddie was so goddamn hard on himself. "Freddie, you had yourself committed to a place that tested your sobriety and could have killed you, to be there for her and to get her out. Trust me, you could write the book on romance."

"It's not the same thing," he argued.

"No," I said. "Maybe not. But you showed her in far more than words, that there is nowhere she can go that you won't follow to be there for her and you're willing to go through hell with her. It's better in some ways. Don't beat yourself up —that's my job." With a light bump of my fist to his shoulder, I left him to chew on that and headed toward the lead tech.

We had a lot to do.

CHAPTER 5

EMERSYN

The sound of the alarm going off penetrated the shroud of sleep with an annoying amount of chirpiness. Groaning, I swam up through the drowsy layers of comfort and warmth wrapped around me. An arm tightened around my middle, tugging me back and then another arm reached past me and the alarm silenced.

Oh. *Much* better.

I sank back into the pillows when a second alarm jarred my eyes open. Rome stretched past me again. This time, he yanked the whole alarm off the nightstand, unplugging it from the wall, before he sent it flying. It landed with a thump somewhere across the room.

The sudden silence landed like a heavy blanket and I groaned. As much as I did not want to get up, I needed to shower and stretch or I wouldn't be able to move today. Sully had spent the last four days being the most grueling of taskmasters. I'd spent between eight and ten hours each day creating, adjusting, and then fine-tuning three new routines.

Despite his statement that we would probably only have time for one, we'd actually tackled five. The last two weren't ready yet, but they would be for the next tour stop and I couldn't wait to perfect the final one—it was a secret even from the guys. Rome hadn't cared for the idea and Freddie had liked it even less, but after three days with Sully, they were a little more trusting.

Pushing upward, I forced my eyes to open. Every muscle in my body ached. With a groan, I made it halfway before Rome curled an arm around me and dragged me backwards. He curved his body against my back. That elicited another groan from me cause he was so warm. I just wanted to burrow into him.

"I have to get up," I told him, though my eyes closing and the fact I was rubbing his arm made a bit of a liar out of me. I wasn't even sure where Vaughn was. He'd been in bed the night before when I'd crawled up between them to watch the movie, and Freddie had been sprawled in one of the chairs the suite boasted.

Lifting my head, I swept a squinted glance around. They weren't in here. Ugh.

"Sleep," Rome said, flattening his palm against my abdomen. The drowsy notes in his voice gave it a huskier quality.

"I have to train."

"No," he replied.

"No?" I tried to twist to face him, but he locked his arm and slid a leg over mine. "Rome…"

"Rest. You are tired."

"The show must go on." This was what I did. We opened in three days. I had just this week to train before we would be doing performances every day and twice on the weekends for the next two weeks. I would cycle the crew in and out. The other performers, however, were like me, we were used to the longer stretches.

And honestly, the performances weren't eight to ten hours, so those days were actually lighter than training.

Skating his hand up my abdomen, Rome slid it right under the tank top I'd gone to bed in. He cupped one of my breasts and my nipple went taut at the contact.

"Rome..." I groaned as he massaged my breast before he caught the nipple and gave it the barest of tweaks. I went from struggling to get up to waging a battle with the desire he ignited with a few gentle strokes. He pressed his lips to my bare shoulder and when I twisted this time, he let me roll over.

"Starling," he said, bracing a hand on either side of me as he blanketed me. I shifted my thighs to cradle his hips automatically. Someone was naked already and the thick weight of his cock was teasing along the seam of my panties. Maybe I should have gone to bed naked. I did more often than not, but I'd fallen asleep while we watched movies.

All thoughts of getting up fled as I stared into his gorgeous eyes. The sun was up already, the light filtering through the curtains though we were still mostly in shadow. "Rome..." I cupped his cheek. The bite of stubble stung my palm.

"We're taking a day off," he said.

"We are?"

"Yes." Then he dipped his head to kiss me. The massage of his lips was a question and an entreaty all at once. Morning breath was absolutely a thing, but I didn't care as his tongue swept in to tease mine. The scrape of his stubble on my cheeks left a trail of electric heat as he made a path from my mouth to my throat. His hand glided beneath my tank top again.

The warmth of his palm on my breast had me arching my hips. I was still stiff and sore, but I'd rather grind against him and my body was more than happy to get on board. "Can we afford—"

My thoughts splintered. Holy shit, he'd locked his mouth around my nipple through the fabric of the tank. The heat and dampness hit me even as he sucked my nipple to his teeth. The combination of suction and the muted pressure of his teeth made me squirm. Arching my back, I rolled my hips wanting to caress him but he was moving too.

The sinuous length of his body pressed down on me, his chest against my thighs now as he pushed my shirt up. He replaced his hand on one breast with his mouth. If he was trying to drive me mad, it was working. I wiggled to tug the tank up and over. As Rome had with the phone earlier, I threw it toward the end of the bed.

He lifted his head from where he was kissing my breasts. He pushed them together and stared at me as I stretched. "We're taking a day off." It was what he said earlier and for some reason, the declaration came out an order.

Licking my lips slowly, I studied the heat in his eyes. I loved it when he stared at me like this. He never avoided my gaze. Yet, when he dipped his attention to my lips, I smiled. "I'm having a hard time remembering what my argument was."

His eyes softened. "Good."

At the same time, I needed to—

"No," he said, pushing upward to kiss me again. He cupped my face, holding me tight as he devoured my mouth. "No to practice." Kiss. "No to worrying." Kiss. "No to anything except me."

Laughter swarmed through me, but he swallowed the sound with his devouring kisses. Wrapping my arms around his neck, I locked my legs around his hips. With a twist, I rolled us over and sat astride him as he went flat on his back. His hands glided down to my shoulders, then my breasts and further still until he settled them on my hips.

The only thing separating us was the thin fabric of my panties. He rocked my hips, letting me grind down on him as I leaned forward and this time, I braced one of my arms against the bed before I nuzzled a kiss to the corner of his mouth. "Just you?"

"Just me," he confirmed. "Vaughn and Freddie are busy." He ground me a little harder with each word and the steel of his cock rubbed along my clit. The panties kept the friction from doing what I wanted.

"You're not busy?" I ran my fingers over his chest, tracing the tattoos. He really was so beautifully inked. Fine lines with little hidden features. My favorite was his cock where, he'd inked me. I couldn't quite wrap my mind around it when I'd first seen it, erect and straining. He'd tattooed *me*, dancing in the silks, along his cock and there was no mistaking it for anyone else.

"Yes," he countered. "I'm busy with you."

My smile grew and I arched my hips, pushing up with my knees. It forced me to lose contact with that beautiful work of art he'd created and I trailed my fingers down to his waist then to his groin.

There I was, one leg twined in silk and If I wrapped my hand around him like I did now, I could see the other side. He let out a harsh exhale as I stroked him from base to tip. "Busy with me…"

"Yes," he said, bumping his hips upward as my grip on him loosened. I flexed my fingers and stroked him again. "With you."

"All day?" The more I turned this idea over in my head, the more I liked it. I was stiff and sore.

"Yes." He squeezed my hips. "We need to play."

Another squeeze of his cock had him thrusting against my palm again. Rome telling me what he needed, that could be addictive. "Do you need to play?" He always asked me what I needed and did what he could to fulfill it.

"Yes." Zero hesitation as his eyes locked on mine. "So do you."

I opened my mouth to argue the point, then closed it again, I shifted and then slid the gusset of my panties to the side so I could tease him against me. I was soaking and as much as we'd kissed, we'd barely touched. My breasts ached from his earlier attention. Then as if reading the direction of my thoughts, he stroked his hands up to my breasts.

Every light touch teased. He alternated between those and actually pinching, pulling taut, then releasing my nipples. The pattern had me leaning forward as he studied my breasts and kept playing with them.

"Rome..."

He flicked his blue eyes upward, settling his attention on me. Heat unfurled inside me. As our gazes locked, I sank down on him and took his full length with one thrust. His beautiful mouth opened in a soundless little cry. The dampness on his lips had me stretching along him and kissing him softly.

Little butterfly brushes of my lips to his as I rolled my hips. It eased him out and then back in again. Slow, teasing motions that denied us both any real friction. He clasped a hand to my ass and another to my face as I kept lifting my head away. No long, wet kisses. A groan vibrated in his chest as he tried to increase the friction.

In some ways, it was like dancing where he matched my steps and pursued me. Each time I changed the pattern, he was right there and not once did he take his eyes off me. The feel of him thrusting left me shaking almost as much as trying to control the rhythm.

I loved that he knew how to move with me and when I dropped my hands to rest on the bed on either side of his head, he wrapped his hand around my nape and dragged me down for a soul deep, wet kiss that chased all other thoughts from me. It was just Rome and how he filled me. He rolled us over again, setting the pace to something far more delicious.

Every thrust rocked me up the bed, but he hooked his hands under me, holding my shoulders so I couldn't slide away. I wrapped my legs around his waist, arching my body to let him hit deeper. Then he was stroking that spot, striking with every thrust. The deep wet kiss turned to a biting one and then he lifted his head to stare down at me.

I added a swirl to my hips, a sway that increased the friction of the cotton against my clit as he ground himself against me each time he sank to the hilt. My breasts rubbed against his chest, and the increased sensation just added a little more madness to my morning.

"Come?" It was an invitation, not a command. If I wanted to go like this for hours, he'd indulge me. The heat of his cock seemed to pulse inside of me, but he wasn't releasing. No that was just *Rome* and how fucking good he felt to me.

I slid a hand between us and into my panties. The grind was wonderful, but I needed just a bit more pressure. The movement seemed to be the encouragement he sought. I began to swirl my fingers against my clit, when he eased upwards and pushed my legs higher.

The stretch burned along the backs of my thighs. A groan tore out of me. This was pleasure and pain. It was perfect. He braced my legs higher, pushing them up to his shoulders and then he covered my fingers with his.

The pressure detonated the ropes of tension, expanding them outward as I went rigid chasing that pleasure, then he tipped me right over as he sank into me again and again. His low shout as his pace stuttered warned me of his release. Yet even as that heat filled me, he kept teasing my clit until I was sobbing.

It was too much and not enough. Then he dragged my shaking fingers upward to suck my fingers clean. My whole body trembled, and he was still inside me. Softening, but stiff enough to stay in place.

When I was able to catch my breath, I said, "What are we doing next?"

His smile was breathtaking. Then he was sliding down my body, kissing a path to my cunt before he went to work on my swollen, sensitive clit. I had no other thoughts after that save for just one.

Rome.

CHAPTER 6

EMERSYN

*R*ome and I didn't leave the bed until nearly noon and only after we ordered room service. Then he sent me to shower while he waited for the food. I half-wished he'd come with me and at the same time, the break was probably something we both needed. My earlier muscle soreness seemed to all be located in my cunt now.

Once beneath the hot spray, I closed my eyes and just let the water beat relief into my muscles. Funnily enough, I felt so much better and it had nothing to do with stretching. Or maybe it did, Rome had certainly gotten creative. All traces of my earlier aggravation were absent.

Instead of hurrying through the shower, I languished and washed my hair before soaping down the rest of me. If we were taking the whole day, we were in no hurry. It was only the second time in a few weeks that I didn't have to be *somewhere* on a prompt schedule.

The last time had been with Liam. A smile curved my lips

and that had been what? The week before? Or was it the week before that? Rinsing off, I sighed. Time began to bleed together on the road. I was so glad I had Vaughn, Rome, and Freddie with me.

At the same time, I missed Mickey, Kellan, Jasper, and Liam. They had other demands on their time. I didn't have to do this tour, and at the same time, I really wanted to do it. I wanted to reclaim my love for the stage.

It had been love that drew me to dance, and the desperate desire to escape that kept me on the road. It was the very best and worst in equal measures. On the road, I was far away from friends even as I made other friends amongst the performers. I was also stuck with my horrible chaperone, but she preferred to ignore me and I was okay with that.

This tour was entirely different. I wasn't running away from anyone. I brought my home with me on the road and returned home as often as possible. I didn't join another troupe, I built one. Liam vetted the performers with background checks and security sweeps, Rome and I both watched their performances and vetted their personalities.

Rome had an excellent head for casting. He could also identify a problematic personality in a single glance. We'd built a good crew and I really liked them. They'd come with us to Europe without a single hesitation and they'd been in that line of fire just like me. Instead of quitting or telling us to get fucked after everything went down in Prague, they brought their enthusiasm and loyalty to the stage and just asked what was next.

Shutting off the water, I pushed open the door to find Rome waiting for me with a huge bath sheet. His hair was also damp and his face freshly shaved. "Took a shower without me, I see." I stepped right up to him and let him wrap the towel around me.

"Yes," he said. "Food is here. We have plans. If I showered with you... we'd be late."

He wasn't wrong. We had plans, apparently. "Do I need to wear anything special?"

"Comfortable." Then he brushed a kiss to my forehead before he headed back out.

Comfortable could be a lot of things. I squeezed the excess water out of my hair then added some leave-in conditioner, brushed it through and left it to air dry for a bit. I'd braid it before we went out. Fifteen minutes later, I walked out of the bedroom into the sitting room of our suite.

The smell of burgers and fries hit me like a sledgehammer. My stomach let out a gurgle that turned into a lusty growl. Rome glanced at me as I padded barefoot out of the bedroom. The food was set up on the table near the sofas. The suite was lovely. There was a proper sitting room and a dining table. We'd actually used that a couple of times when it was all four of us.

"You didn't have to wait for me," I told him as I settled on the sofa. Rome followed with a pair of cold water bottles from the fridge.

"I wanted to," he said before handing me one of the bottles. He didn't automatically open it for me and I appreciated that. I didn't mind when the others did it. It was so natural for them to. But I'd said something once about being able to open my own bottles and Rome never presumed. If I asked, he would.

I leaned over to press a kiss to his cheek. "Thank you."

He pulled the silver dome off one of the plates. "You're welcome."

There was a *huge* burger under there. Two giant patties, cheese, tomatoes, onions... My mouth was watering before he even passed me the plate. The french fries were crispy, and still on the hot side of warm. We didn't say much, or at least I didn't, as I devoured my burger. The fact I was ravenous probably had more to do with not eating since dinner the night before and that had been a little early.

Sometimes when I was overtired, or exhausted like I had been the night before, I didn't eat much. Unlike in the past, however, I wasn't on such a restrictive diet. While I might get by with skipping a meal if I was genuinely not interested, they always made sure I ate the next day.

I caught a glimmer of Rome's smile as I took another huge bite of the burger. It left some grease dribbling down my chin. He held out a cloth napkin before I could even ask. Then I was covering my own smile and wiping up my mess with a laugh. Then with a wink, I took another bite.

It was almost one by the time we finished our lunch. We really had slept in late. Well, maybe not that late. We'd definitely been in bed late. I cleaned up the plates and put them back on the rolling cart while Rome grabbed our phones from the bedroom. He also came out with a pair of my sandals. Most of the time, I was either in boots or sneakers.

Sandals sounded nice. I tucked my feet into them and grimaced at my toes. "I need to get a pedicure before the show opens." Most of the time, people didn't see my feet. They were often bruised from the work. But the current polish was chipped on three of my toes and utterly missing on the others. "Or do it myself."

"We can go today if you want," Rome offered and I grinned at him.

"Nope, you wanted to do something else and we still have a couple more days before the show opens." I double checked the messages on my phone. The family chat with all the Vandals had a few messages, including one from Rome telling them I was asleep. I sent them a good morning or afternoon, depending on their time zone.

Then let Vaughn and Freddie know Rome and I were

heading out. My phone shared its location with them at all times and I had a tracker. Oh, I glanced down at myself. "One sec, I need to get a different purse." 'Cause I couldn't wear a holster in this outfit.

The cross body sling bag was perfect. My gun fit right in it and the holster secured. All I had to do was slide down the zipper to get it out. My phone went in the front pocket with my hotel room key. My wallet was in the middle pocket. I wore it across my chest so no one could lift anything from it.

Ready, I grinned at Rome.

He watched me with the most adorable expression, then tilted his head as I braided my hair without looking away from him. It was still damp, but it would dry and if it was braided back, it would be out of the way.

Before he could say anything, his phone buzzed and he glanced down at it. He typed in one word, hit send then turned the screen off before he pocketed it. The guys knew where I was and they could find me.

When he held out his hand to me, I clasped it and let him lead the way. The Florida sun blazed down at us as we exited the front of the hotel. The humid air left sweat dotting my brow, but the breeze chased it away. We were staying at a hotel not far from the beach. Where Braxton Harbor had chilly water lapping at its shores, the Atlantic was much warmer down here.

I wasn't sure if we'd grab a rental car or get an Uber, but instead Rome led the way down the path. The area was popular with the tourists and there was a whole string of hotels along the beach. A mall wasn't much farther away, and there was plenty to see and do.

For a brief moment, I wished we were home and he had his backpack loaded with spray paint and we were on our way to do a project. It would be colder there and the wind would have more bite, but even the gray and chill days, I loved the city. For now, I just soaked up the area around us. There were plenty of other pedestrians. Music blared from passing cars. A wide variety of bars and eateries boasting indoor and outdoor seating cropped up as we passed.

It was just a colorful swath of humanity, populated with a wild array of culture, music, and art. I slowed when I spotted a mural and Rome halted so I could look at it. He didn't seem that interested but I kind of had to know...

"What do you think of it?" It had the look of the water itself, the waves rolling in and there was sand and seashells visible. Even the sun rising in the distance had been added to the painting. It was—almost too serene.

Rome turned to the painting. "The water is off. It's low tide—because you can see the sandbars, but the waves look like high tide."

Oh.

I studied the image and it seemed to rob it of some of the serenity. When he gave a light tug, though, I forgot about the mural and moved with him. He paused at a street vendor and bought me a floppy hat. The sunglasses helped to shield my eyes, but the hat would protect my face.

The longer we walked, the happier I was that I'd gone with shorts and a light shirt over a tank top. Rome was in cargo shorts and a t-shirt. With his sunglasses, and easy stride, he blended right in with the locals. I didn't worry about where he had a weapon hidden.

Rome was *always* resourceful. The longer we walked, the more tension melted away. The soreness in my muscles was still there, but it wasn't the primary thing on my mind. My steps were looser and I spent as much time watching some of the street performers as I did the various musicians, artists, and vendors along the way.

At one kiosk, I found a seashell necklace on a leather strap. Rome paid for it then tied it around my neck for me. It wasn't a choker, but it also didn't dangle. When I picked out one for him, he studied it for a moment then said yes. So I paid for it and he shifted lower so I could tie it around his neck. His shell was longer, more of an oval where mine was a fanned out pattern.

It looked elegant on him.

"Do you like it?"

He touched it with two fingers then gave me a light kiss. "Yes."

Clasping hands again, we continued toward a boardwalk area that kind of reminded me of Southern California and the pier in Santa Monica. Kinda. But Rome diverted toward a different hotel. When I frowned, he just gave me a little tug.

"Trust me."

Of course, I trusted him. He led the way through the sliding doors and we crossed the Arabesque Spanish Mission red-tiled lobby and along a long passageway that opened out onto a huge swimming pool. It was more like a lagoon than a pool. The size of it really did give it a lagoon feeling. Actual music came from the speakers and there were plenty of pool chairs and tables.

Most of them were empty. I'd have expected it to be much busier here, but only a few people were moving around the pool area and they seemed like staff. Rome headed toward a side of the lagoon-like pool where a man in a polo shirt and white shorts waited for us.

And yes, he was absolutely waiting for us.

"Mr. Cleary?"

"Yes," Rome said and he handed him a card.

The man flashed us a grin, then he motioned to the water. "We're set up to trial here if you're ready."

Trial what?

"Once you're comfortable, we can head over to the bay."

"Thank you." Rome squeezed my hand once, then he

moved toward the board that was sitting next to the water. He stepped into boots and clipped them on. He glanced at me. "Watch?"

"Always," I promised.

"Just take a couple of steps back, miss." The man in the white shorts circled around Rome to a piece of equipment and he got it started. I retreated a couple of feet and water began to jet out of the—

Oh.

It was a flyboard. I'd seen a video of this and Rome went from being right there on the ground to rising. The steady stream of water gave him lift and there was a hose attached to the flyboard but he moved out over the water. Then twisted and turned and...

He was dancing on the water and I pressed my hands together against my mouth as I watched him do a couple of flips. Had he been practicing this while I'd been training? There was a flush to his cheeks and a hint of a smirk on his lips as he lowered slowly toward the edge. Even expecting it, my heart did a little fist bump to my ribs when he held out his hand to me.

Without an ounce of hesitation, I moved over to step onto the plate that was between his feet and then I tilted my head up to look at him. I could see my own wild grin reflected in his sunglasses. He wrapped an arm around my waist, took my right hand in his as I put my left hand on his shoulder.

Belatedly, I realized the music changed and then we were rising and weaving in the air. A whole new kind of dancing as we flew.

CHAPTER 7

ROME

Starling's laugh filled the air with a music all of her own. The songs I'd asked them to cue up were based on one of her favorite playlists. We'd had to replace a number of the CDs after the attack on the clubhouse. I didn't mind so much, it let me involve her in the musical selection and now I knew all of her favorites.

Since then, we'd added to the collection. The current piece was one she'd discovered a few months earlier. After, she'd downloaded and listened to every single song by the group. I didn't mind it so much, but her attention to it, and subsequent licensing for the current show had earned the Wolfe Pack top spots and more fans.

The jet board twirled as I spun us up and then down again. The current setting wouldn't take us above twenty feet over the pool. The water was deep enough to cushion any possible fall. While I could go faster once we were on open water, speed wasn't the goal.

Flying was Starling's joy. It had been her escape, then it had become her prison—a gilded cage where her wings had been clipped and jesses tied to shackle her in place. Those were all gone now and this tour was about recapturing her joy.

Remaking it.

Rebuilding.

Whatever it took. If she needed a year or ten, she would get it and find every piece she needed. I spun us around as she laughed and then lifted her. It took concentration to balance the shifting center of gravity. I'd practiced every single day this week. Two hours a day while she'd been hard at work in her rehearsals.

The distraction helped. She wanted different. What pleased me more than anything was the way she relaxed into my grip as I raised her up. When her gaze latched onto mine, I said, "Fly."

Bracing her strength with my own, I was ready when she elongated her legs until she was holding herself almost horizontal. Then I did another spin and laughter spilled out of her.

Her hug was everything. Then she tilted her head back and trusted me to balance her as she went loose like one of her own silks.

The shift in her muscles told me when she was ready and I braced her with a grip on her waist as she planted a hand on my shoulder. She released me with the other arm and we soared over the water with her body curved like one of the doves Vaughn named her after.

For the next hour, we played. She twisted and writhed around me like I was her silk and I kept us airborne. A deep satisfaction filled me at the laughter erupting from her as we wound our way over the water.

Our audience was a handful of techs who were just

keeping an eye on the equipment and a pair of security guards hired to keep people out of the pool area. This surprise had been created for her and her alone.

Another laugh escaped her as I held her arms and let her spin out floating on the air and then she was wrapping her arms around me again to close the distance.

"I love this," she promised, a golden light in her deep brown eyes that made them look lit from behind. Even better, her smile reflected in her voice and her words. There was a effervescence that had been missing over the past few weeks.

"Yes?" I confirmed, slowing the pattern from spinning to more like skating over the air. The swish from side to side reminded me of Liam on a skateboard.

"Absolutely." She punctuated the promise with a kiss. "Thank you."

She never had to thank me, but I nodded. Liam told me once that people needed to express their gratitude and it was important to let them. Ms. Stephanie always stressed manners and they were important to Jasper.

It wasn't something I needed to think about with Starling. Sometimes, she understood without the words at all. Other times, the words brought her comfort. "You're welcome. I wanted to make you smile."

"Mission accomplished." The sigh in her voice could have carried a lot of different meanings. I just trusted her earlier smiles and the words themselves. Starling didn't lie to me. She might tell me she didn't want to talk about something, but she didn't lie.

"Good."

"I want to learn how to do this though," she said, then glanced down at my feet in their boots. "I can't believe you got lessons."

"You said you liked it." She'd watched the video so many times. "It would be different."

"It is different, it's flying on water and I love it. Can you imagine if we were both on the boards?"

I turned the idea over in my head. "Yes," I said eventually. "But I couldn't hold you like this."

"That is definitely a con," she agreed. "But I'm also imagining the way we could chase and play…like when you and Liam were tossing me back and forth that day and I was trying to fly again."

She'd trusted us even when she hadn't trusted herself. So the idea had merit.

"Maybe we do both," I told her. "You learn to jet board too. Then we can do both types."

"Oh!" Her expression brightened. "Yes. Might take us time."

"We have time," I promised. "We will make the time too."

"Can we waltz on the water?"

"Yes." We could do anything she wanted. I turned us back toward the tech supervising. "Second playlist."

He gave me a thumbs up as I took her left hand in my right and settled my left on her hip. She smiled up at me and then the music changed. It was another instrumental she'd been considering for her show, and based off a song she adored from Torched.

I followed the beats of the music, swishing back and forth over the water in a twist. When I did a spin, she kicked up her legs and floated before landing perfectly back in place.

More than once, I spun her out like I would let her go to spin away. It took muscle control from both of us, but she never faltered. We spent another hour on the water and we tested so many dances. Most were just fun, but others had her looking thoughtful.

"Maybe," she said after we'd returned to the ground and I

was removing my boots. The air around her was positively electric. "Maybe we look at putting together some elemental numbers for a future show? Even if we never perform them for anyone other than us?"

Once I was out of the boots, I studied her. "Do you want to perform them or just play?"

"Play *is* important."

I nodded. It was. She paused when the tech came over to take the fly board. He also handed me a card. "For future lessons. Or set up." Another nod, then I shook his hand before pulling away, to hold out my hand to Starling.

She clasped mine easily and there was a skip to her step as we headed back inside. They would be opening the lagoon soon to the other guests.

"Not everything needs to be about performing," she admitted as we made our way through the hotel and across the lobby. We had another couple of hours before Vaughn and Freddie would be back.

It was pizzas, beer, and movies night to cap her day off. They would have finished set up and inspection. The final dress rehearsals would be over the next couple of days and then opening.

"I know that," she continued as we stepped out into the sunshine again. Her hat had slid down while we danced on the water. I paused to set it back on her head again. "I mean, I know that in here." She tapped the side of her head. "But my heart still feels like everything should be about the performance."

Not seeing the problem yet, I guided her toward the boardwalk. When she focused on one of the carts, I followed her glance and then guided her toward the ice cream vendor. She was allowed to have treats.

Her happy little bounce when we got there told me it was the right choice. I let her inspect the offerings. "Can I get a double scoop on a cone of chocolate and strawberry?" When she glanced at me, I nodded and just held up two fingers to the vendor.

He scooped out hers first, then mine. I paid for it and passed her the cone. When she tipped hers to me, I frowned.

"An ice cream toast," she informed me. "Just tap our scoops together."

I touched mine to hers and she grinned again. Then we headed back in the direction of our hotel, hand in hand, while we enjoyed the ice cream. She seemed focused on devouring hers, but I didn't think she was wholly thinking about the ice cream.

"Anyway," she said, chasing a melting drop of strawberry up from the chocolate with her tongue. "Like I was saying, I know in my head not everything is about the performance. This tour has been amazing, but it's been missing something…"

I waited for her to work it out.

"Before, the tours were always about getting away from Uncle Fuckbucket and not going home. Don't get me wrong, I loved performing, but I just didn't want to be around him."

"You never have to be again."

Another quick smile chased the shadows from her eyes as she glanced at me. "I know. I'm glad."

So was I. Maybe we should have made it hurt more. I wanted him gone though. I wanted to erase him thoroughly from Starling's life.

"But I don't want to escape home now," she said. "Home is with all of you and I love the performing—or maybe I should love it more than I am." She frowned. "It's kind of jumbled."

"Is that why you wanted to learn new sets?"

"Yes," she said, then shook her head. "And no. Sorry." She made a face. "I think I'm making it more complicated than it is. I love performing, but I don't know that I've ever been allowed to *just* love it and not need it desperately."

I could understand that. "What do you want to do?"

"I don't know," she admitted. "I called Sully because I thought that I needed more challenging routines. It took me a while to master the old ones, but I don't—"

When she cut herself off, I waited and just worked on my ice cream. We were walking slowly back to the hotel. The breeze from the water cooled the hot sun, but it was hardly chilly. The brightness made for vibrant colors everywhere, but they didn't stand out the way they did in the harbor.

We passed more art, but Starling wasn't looking at it as much as she was studying her ice cream cone. That was the problem with some of the works. They were bright colors, but they blended here. Too much light saturated the paint and it lost some impact. There was a stark black and white cartoon done along one side of the beach wall.

That intrigued me because it stood out.

"I want to push myself," she said, then looked up at me. "I want to take more risks with the dances."

"Then we take more risks." I touched my ice cream to the tip of her nose. It left a strawberry smear and I used my finger to wipe it off. She caught my hand and licked the ice cream from my fingers. "But we do it safely."

"Yes, or Vaughn will be cross." She scraped her teeth over her lower lip. "But pushing it means, pushing boundaries and taking risks means actually risking the falls to master the new skills."

He'd be far more than cross. "I'll talk to him."

We could still make it safe.

"You don't mind?"

"Why would I mind?" I wanted her to be happy. She couldn't see herself when she flew. I could. Flying made her happier than she knew, but she didn't trust it yet.

She trusted us and that was enough. She needed to trust herself and she was learning to do that.

"Because I make things complicated," she said and I tilted my head.

"No," I said. "You don't. The past makes it complicated. Vaughn makes it solvable. You make it beautiful."

"Thank you."

This time, I did ask, "What for?"

"For being you. You're—you make me believe everything is possible."

"I like being me," I said. "Liam's terrible at it, but I'm not bad at being him."

For a moment, I could feel her staring at me and when I smiled, she burst out laughing.

CHAPTER 8

EMERSYN

J checked my stage makeup in the mirror before glancing at the time on the wall. Tonight marked our last weekend on the road. We'd close the tour for eight weeks, take a break and go home.

Excitement unfurled in my belly. I couldn't wait to be back in Braxton Harbor and at the clubhouse. Even as the anticipation surged through my veins, I forced my breathing to regulate. We were close, but we still had these last three shows to get through.

Freddie lounged in a chair on the other side of my dressing room. Head back, his eyes were half-slits like he was dozing. I stole a look at him.

"Stop worrying, Boo-Boo," he said without shifting his position. "I had a bad night. It happens."

I stuck my tongue at him. "I could just be looking at you cause you're all sexy and sweet."

"Sweet?" That earned me a real snort, but the corners of

his mouth curved. He gave a gentle rolling motion with his hand. "You may proceed to look at me for as long as you like."

Not rolling my eyes took everything cause I was touching up the liner. It needed to be dramatic and I didn't want it to melt off after the first set. Smiling, however, I could do. "Do you need to talk about it?"

Neither of us ever wanted to talk about the bad dreams. I still got them too. The nightmares came and went, dark memories that crept out of the rotted floorboards of the past. Didn't matter how often we tore them up, something could trigger them.

A smell.

A sound.

A touch.

Shivers chased up my spine and I gave myself a little shake. No, I never *wanted* to talk about it. Need, however, was a pesky little beast.

Sighing, Freddie sat up and clasped his hands together loosely. His blond hair had gotten longer on the tour. It fell in waves, like those poets from the old movies and it always reminded me of Renaissance paintings.

Instead of looking at me, he was staring down at his hands so I gave him space as I straightened and studied my appearance. The body suit was one of the new costumes we'd ordered and it would stand out against the chorus. The past few weeks with Sully had me changing a number of my routines.

Tonight, we were going to show off a company wide number since these last three showings were all for charity. They'd reached out to Liam who brought it to me. The organization raised money and awareness for the survivors of human trafficking.

Despite the worry in his eyes, Liam put the choice and the

call in my hands. My answer was an immediate yes, but I ran it past all of them first because it meant one more week on the road past when we'd planned to stop, because we needed the rehearsal time.

"I think it's some of the stories we heard from the director yesterday," Freddie admitted in a quiet voice. "I know she didn't know about me. How could she?" He spread his hands out and exhaled a long sigh.

I debated between pivoting to face him or just letting him talk. When he lifted his head and his gaze locked on mine in the mirror, however, it decided me.

"At the same time, she could have been describing some of my childhood. The parts I remember anyway." He grimaced, but he didn't look away from me when I faced him. "Most of it is shadows and monsters. Pain. Pain and enduring. There was nothing to do but endure because complaining and sobbing just made more pain. Then came the drugs."

Now he looked at his hands again. He flattened them out, his fingers were rock steady. That—that was a good sign.

"I thought I was fine," he continued. "The people she was talking about, they weren't me and I hated it for them. I'd cheerfully cut up everyone involved with hurting them. No one gets to do that to kids or anyone else. No one should."

Agreed.

"I was angry. Anger is good. Anger is healthy." A faint smile flickered over his face, one I understood on such a primitive level. "Anger is a feeling I can embrace, cause it's not... sadness or despair or crushing guilt."

The desire to wrap myself around him and shield him from the rest of the world burned through me, but I had to keep myself in place. Touch could trigger Freddie right now, particularly when he was being so vulnerable.

"So I thought, sucks for them and I was feeling kind of

proud to be a part of this—helping them." Now he slumped back, elbow on the arm of the chair and two fingers against the side of his head as he stared up at me. "Then I went to sleep."

The struggle playing out across his face was so real. It hurt to see him hurting.

"I don't know if I was just picturing myself in all the different stories she told or if those things happened to me too. I mean, they could have. I know there was a lot. The drugs used to keep it all away."

No they didn't.

"Ugh," he grumbled. "No, they really didn't keep it away but they could numb me, you know? Sometimes, it's just better to not feel at all, but if I don't feel, I miss out on stuff with you Boo-Boo and stuff with the guys. Now, I'm all up in my head and I've been jonesing all goddamn day."

Anger surged through his expression as he rose.

"Fuck, I wasn't going to dump this on you."

"Excuse me," I said, pointing a finger at him. "I'm *your* Boo-Boo and you're *my* Freddie. There is no *dumping*. If you need me, then I'm here. If you want me, then I'm here. You listen to me, I listen to you. I can take a lot of things you say, Freddie, I will never not hear you. But you can stuff the dumping comments up your butt where the shit belongs."

He blinked, surprise rippled through the anger and the worry. Like lightning dancing in a storm, his lips quivered with suppressed laughter. "Anyone ever tell you that you're scary when you're bossy?"

"Not that I've heard," I said, head tilting. "Though Liam does call me Hellspawn." I'd earned that name after I punched him in the nose for calling me *princess*.

"True," Freddie agreed, then a real laugh escaped him. It was quiet, a little ragged around the edges and dipped in tears, but it was a laugh. Bit by bit, the sound escalated and then he opened his arms. I flew across the room and wrapped around him even as he lifted me.

He buried his face against my throat and I stroked my fingers through his hair. The dampness against my skin warned me of his tears, but I wasn't going to melt.

"I'm always here for you," I promised. "Always."

"I don't want to fall," he whispered.

"I know," I answered in the same soft tone. "I know you don't. If you need to, hold onto me. Hold onto Rome. The guys. None of us will let you fall, Freddie."

We couldn't *fix* it for him. We couldn't erase the addiction or the reason he'd descended into it in the first place. But as long as he was willing to reach out, we would always catch him.

Frankly, even if he wasn't, still wasn't going to abandon him.

A brisk knock hit the door. "Five minutes!" The techs were summoning us. The new opening number required me to be up there with them. It was a surprise for the guys too.

Freddie let out a wet laugh. "You need to go."

"No, I need to be right here," I told him. "They can do the number without me."

"Absolutely not," he said, pulling back to look at me. With careful fingers, I swiped away the tears on his cheeks. "You've been working on this all week, *I* want to see how great you look."

I searched his blue eyes, then brushed a kiss to his jaw. I didn't quite make the contact because he was already pushing himself so much. I also didn't want to leave a lipstick smear on his chin.

"I promise," he continued in a sobering tone. "I'm not going to slip off and get high. I'll be right there on the side of the stage. I want a front row seat."

"I'm not worried about that." I really wasn't, though his

surprise made my heart ache. "I never want chasing my dreams to hurt you."

"They don't hurt me," he told me. "Bottling this shit up? That hurts. I know better and I know I can tell you anything." He pressed a finger to my lips. "I promise you, *I know* I can tell you anything. Doesn't always make it easier."

"That's the truth." I kissed his fingertip as he cut his gaze to the clock on the wall.

"Three minutes, Boo-Boo. Let's go wow the world with this new routine."

"I want pizza tonight," I said as I let go and retreated a couple of steps. Freddie was asking for normalcy. I couldn't possibly tell him no.

"Done. I'll tell Rome so we can grab it on the way back to the hotel." He already had his phone in his hands as he fired off a text. I gave him the time to get his walls back up.

One more glance in the mirror and then down at my outfit. I snagged the suit jacket that went over it and picked up the bowler hat.

At two minutes, Freddie and I were striding up the hallway to the stage. The other dancers moved ahead. The curtains were down, the hum of the audience invaded the backstage.

The air was electric as Freddie squeezed my hand once before I stepped away from him and out to the stage. With the curtains down and the lights low, I took my mark from memory.

The other dancers set up around me. The hush of anticipation threaded through us.

"Sixty seconds," came the whisper from stage right as a tech began the countdown. The lights were darkening everywhere. Even beyond the curtain.

Eyes closed, I dropped my chin. Ahead of us in the dark, the curtains rose. The opening number was six minutes long and it involved every single dancer in the production. Men. Women. Me. I would blend in for the first three minutes because we were united.

The music began as the lights came up abruptly. The sharp notes of Beethoven Scherzo by David Garrett required us to hit our marks in unison. We danced as one. Everyone moving in sync until we broke into two groups then we danced in and around each other.

The three minute long piece filled with verve, performed by a man with such musical genius that it was impossible to not move when it was playing. The colors lit us up as we traded places, dancing in between each other, then in rounds.

Every strike, a stomp. Every sweep, a twirl. On the finish of that piece, every member of the chorus hit the stage, dropping in a circle around me as the light narrowed to me alone. The applause rolled through the audience.

David Garrett's version of Viva La Vida poured out of the speakers. The beautiful strings flooded me and I sent my bowler hat flying as my suit jacket dropped and then I was leaping to catch the black silks that dropped toward me.

From the corner of my eye, I caught Freddie's wide grin and that made me soar higher than even the music.

This was just the start.

CHAPTER 9

KELLAN

*D*oc pulled up in his truck out front as I closed down the work bays. The new shop had been bringing in a brisk business. I had three cars in for work right now. Two were waiting on parts, a third was parked out back because it wouldn't be picked up until the following day.

Currently, I was doing all the work myself. I needed to bring in a new crew but I wasn't ready for new people in here yet. Liam had popped around a couple of times recently to give me a hand and Jasper had started spending his Saturdays when he was in town helping out.

With Sparrow on the road so much, I liked keeping busy. We'd been working with the locals a lot over the past few months. More businesses were opening, and some of the local kids were volunteering to help clean up empty lots and repaint defaced buildings.

No one touched Rome's art, but I'd noticed an aspiring

artist starting to decorate some of the freshly painted buildings. That said, Liam and I had a bet on how long it would
take Rome to track down the new creative.

I figured it would be three days tops once he was back.
Liam said twenty-four hours from *when* Rome noticed. The
funny part was if he didn't notice until he'd been back two
days, we both won.

"Hey," Doc said as he strolled up. He had a light jacket on
over his t-shirt and jeans.

His dress code had grown more and more relaxed since
he retired from his clinic. While he helped out periodically,
particularly on free immunization days, he devoted most of
his time to the safe houses he was managing now. An
endeavor we all supported.

"Hey," I greeted him. "Give me ten more minutes, if you
don't mind. I got caught up working on that Mustang GT."

"That's an old one," Doc said as he studied the black and
red 1985 classic muscle car.

"Yeah," I said on the exhale, not quite grinning. "The kid
who brought her in said he got her for a song, but he wanted
to make sure she would still run and his grandfather would
pay for the assessment."

"You're in lust, aren't you?" The soft laughter underscoring his words didn't offend me in the slightest. I was in
lust.

"Probably the second or third sexiest girl I've seen in a
while," I told him. The body was a classic, but it was what
was under the hood that had me preoccupied.

Shaking his head, Doc chuckled and followed me inside
as I closed the last bay. The office area was cleaner, it had
new floors, new furniture, and a fresh paint. The kitchen in
the back was also decked out in amenities, including an
espresso machine.

Sparrow had purchased the property and finished

knocking down the burnt out shell of the building that had been left after an explosion gutted it. The new shop resembled the old in size, and design but that was all on the surface.

The interior had been upgraded across the board. New equipment, new tools—we had to replace most of mine, and I'd brought some of my favorites from the clubhouse. Frankly, as brand new as the shop was and it had that "new" smell to it still, I couldn't complain. We'd get to the lived in, worked in feel, eventually.

But it was ours. No one was taking it away again and I didn't work for anyone that wasn't us. As gifts went, I could still paddle her ass for spending money on me, but she'd just given me that impudent smile and said she was going to do what she wanted to do and I could do whatever I wanted to with the building.

She had a point.

Doc dragged a chair over and settled into it while I moved behind the desk. I had a handful of work orders to review. I was only charging the kid and his grandfather for any parts needed. Labor was totally on me.

Suddenly, Doc's solo presence registered. "Wasn't Theo supposed to be with you today?"

The arrival of the sullen, difficult fourteen-year-old had presented its own set of challenges. Milo had traveled with him. We'd met the kid in Prague, briefly. He'd returned to the States with Milo, Lainey and the rest of them. But his stay in New York proved exceptionally short.

The distance between Milo and the newly discovered younger brother couldn't have been clearer. Nor could the animosity. The kid seemed to relax once he was *here*, but some tension resumed when he realized Sparrow was not actually here but on the road.

Doc's arrival had settled him once more. Since then, Theo

had been attached at the hip with Doc, which Doc didn't seem to mind. If anything, he'd been even-tempered if *firm* with the kid, particularly when Theo's belligerent attitude reared its head.

It was weird how alike, and at the same time wildly different, from Milo he was. Then again, the only commonality they had was their sperm donor, a man Milo despised and I had no idea how Theo felt about the guy. Then again, I didn't think Theo had ever met him.

"He's with Jasper," Doc said, one corner of his mouth twitching upwards in the suggestion of a smile.

I straightened. "Is that a good idea?"

"Eh." Doc shrugged. "Theo wanted some 'freedom,' or so he said and Jas had a run up to Pennington. He'll be back by dinner, so it was an easy run."

"Let's hope he doesn't try to test himself against Jas' temper." Theo had been testing all of us. Doc more than most, but he'd attempted pushing my buttons a few times. If we were younger, I'd have probably popped him more than once.

Jasper definitely would have. The only one who ever seemed utterly unbothered by him was Doc. Then again, he'd put up with all of us for how long?

"He'll be fine," Doc said with a kind of confidence I envied, but then in the great grand scheme of things, a reckless, and challenging fourteen year old punk was hardly the worst thing he'd ever had to deal with, and he certainly had way more patience now than he'd had back in the day.

"You know what," I said, double-checking the invoices and making sure the inventory had all lined up. I was waiting on three more parts and the last time I checked, they were on their way but it would be Monday or Tuesday before they arrived. "I'm just going to go with it. I promised Sparrow and Milo we'd keep an eye on him and we're doing that. Course, we still need to get him into school."

"We will," Doc said. "Liam's got a tutor coming for a few weeks so we can do a full assessment and see what he needs before we drop him into a school. He doesn't want private school, but he might have to suck that up for a while."

It wasn't like we couldn't afford it. "Has anyone told Theo that yet?" The longer this conversation went on, the more amused I was by all of it.

"Nope. One battle at a time." His half-sigh made me shake my head. "It's a push and pull right now, he'll grow out of it eventually."

"You sure about that?" Cause I wasn't. His history wasn't quite the same as ours. It might be closer to Freddie's... That was a thought I didn't want to contemplate or pursue any further. We could only hope whatever had happened wasn't *that* bad. Freddie's past haunted him to this day and Theo might be a punk but no one deserved those experiences.

No one.

"You guys did." Doc shrugged then glanced at his watch. "Finish wrapping up."

"In a hurry?" I didn't smirk but he just gave me a bland look. It wasn't that late in the day. I liked shutting down around four unless I had a client coming in later. There was a dropbox for anyone leaving a car overnight for me to work on the next day.

"Hungry," came his droll response. "I didn't pause for lunch today since Theo was tied up with Jasper, I wanted to visit as many of the shelters and safe houses as I could."

Made sense, he wasn't all that comfortable with putting Theo into those situations when we were still trying to sort out his own history. I could almost *hear* Ms. Stephanie suggesting therapy but none of us had followed up on that idea at all.

I talked to my guys if I needed to work shit out and so did they. Sometimes, I worried about Freddie but the handful of times he'd been "forced" into therapy had just not gone well at all. The less said about Pinetree, the better. So, no, we'd pass, thanks.

At least for now.

"Right," I said, and slid the last of the papers away into their files. I might be my only employee, but I wanted everything in its place before I shut down for the night. I turned the phones off so it would provide the general message and a place for customers to record a message and then I was ready. "Let's go. I could use something that isn't pizza."

Doc chuckled as he rose. "The kid likes it."

"I used to," I admitted. "But I like other foods too."

I headed for my car as Doc diverted to his truck. "Follow me," he said, over his shoulder. "I know a good place."

Sounded like a plan. We could always grab takeout for Jasper and Theo. Liam came and went on his own schedule. Running his family business took a lot of time and energy. Course, it also meant travel and he took time to see Sparrow as often as he could.

I wanted to go and see her too, but that meant leaving her after a couple of days and I hated that more than just making myself wait for her to come home. Sometimes, I worried we were all just a little too fucked up.

But I'd take on every single damn challenge for Sparrow *and* my guys. Doc waited for me to start the Charger before he pulled out and I was right behind him. Instead of heading toward the Clubhouse or even one of the places we liked over on fiftieth, he took us uptown.

There were a few restaurants here I liked. Most of them were overpriced with small portions and stuffy service, but the food was worth it—*sometimes*. I could go for straight bar food at the moment, my stomach had started grumbling the moment I got behind the wheel.

Doc wasn't the only one who hadn't eaten much today. I'd ignored it while I was working. We didn't stop at any of those places. In fact, he took a turn that put us on the East Bay Road and heading toward the bridge.

It was almost forty-five minutes away from the shop, but the Hearthfire Grill, which opened up on the point, was not a location I thought about that often. We'd managed a few meals here over the years, special occasions mostly—like when Milo got accepted at law school.

Was that the last time we'd come up here? Doc had an excellent idea, definitely time to change that. The sun was gradually descending in the distance, when it was down, the lighthouse would raise it's own glow and the restaurant overlooked the rocky shore below as well as the turbulent waters from the channel.

Across that channel on its own rocky outcropping was the lighthouse. We'd actually made it out there once with a paddle boat. Insane didn't begin to cover it, but we'd all been what? Fifteen?

Maybe sixteen at the most.

It was the same year we'd also taken those jobs at the resort. No risk was too big to take and no dare too insane to try. The more I thought about those days, the more I considered that I should probably cut Theo a break.

The lot wasn't full, which was fine. It wasn't even five yet so barely even happy hour. I was fine with a quiet beer, some food, and excellent view. I slid into a spot right next to Doc's and climbed out.

He led the way up the steps to the front of the building. It was a combination of coastal New England charm and Victorian aesthetics, but that was just the facade. The interior was almost cozy despite the upscale nature of the place.

Doc pulled the door open and waved me inside. I didn't even make it three feet before a shout of "surprise" went up and there were so many familiar faces from Milo and Lainey to Jasper and Theo—so much for their run—to Freddie, Vaughn, Rome, and Liam. Where was...

Before I even finished forming the question she was skipping across the open space and I caught her as she threw herself at me.

"Happy Birthday, Kel!"

CHAPTER 10

EMERSYN

$\mathcal{T}$he party had lasted well into the night, the pure surprise on Kellan's face when he arrived at the restaurant had been worth all the secrecy that involved us returning to town in time for the surprise party. Mickey had waited until we said we were there before he went to get Kellan.

"Hey," Kellan said, his voice low and husky with sleep as he snaked an arm around my middle and pulled me back to him.

It had been late when we got back to the Clubhouse and we'd celebrated until I was yawning so hard I couldn't see straight. Then Kellan scooped me up and said, birthday privilege and off we went to his room. Curling up with him wrapped around me had been—divine. I'd missed them so much.

"Where are you going?" He nuzzled a kiss to my throat as he tugged me back into him.

"I need to pee," I told him, a yawn smothering my laughter even as he snuggled me closer.

"It can wait." The sleepy notes in his voice were endearing, even more, the hint of plaintiveness.

"I wish it could," I whispered, stroking his forearm. "I will come right back, I promise."

Another butterfly light kiss to my throat and a huffing complaint. "Hmm…" Then he lifted his head and seemed to be squinting toward his door. "Right, I locked it. Okay. Off you go, pee and come right back."

He delivered the last line with a swat to my ass and I couldn't help the giggles that escaped as I rolled off the bed. Kellan was always so in control, so calm, and direct. The demanding petulance was refreshingly sweet.

I hurried into the bathroom, peed, then washed my hands and face before I brushed my teeth real quick. Then grabbed a glass of water to take back out with me. Kellan lay on his back, one arm behind his head like a pillow. The drape of the sheet did nothing to hide his morning wood.

He was shirtless, but I was also wearing one of his shirts and I hadn't bothered with panties when we got back in here last night. As it was, I enjoyed the way he studied me through half-lowered lids.

"You're too far away, Sparrow," he said in a voice still rough from sleep and maybe from laughter. The night before had been amazing. Liam arranged for us to have the whole restaurant to ourselves.

Lainey and Milo had been there. Ezra and Adam showed up a little later, and the only one who hadn't made it was Bodhi, but Lainey said he was with his brother. Andrea had tagged along and that had made Theo happy. They'd been thick as thieves all night until Andrea had to leave.

"I've missed you," I told him, abandoning the bathroom

door to cross to the bed with the glass in hand. I walked up onto the bed on my knees and made my way up to him.

He dropped a hand to my hip as I straddled his hips before I took another drink of the glass of water before I offered it to him. He pushed up and took it before downing a long drink. Then the glass went to the nightstand and his gaze came back to me.

"I missed you too," he said, tracing his fingers down my cheek. "Seeing you in Prague was almost too much and not enough."

It had been wonderful to see him there, despite the reasons that had taken us there. "Agreed," I said, sighing as I leaned my cheek into his hand. "I wanted to spend more time with you... with all of you. There was so much going on and then we were leaving and there was Theo..."

Theo added so much more of a new wrinkle to everything.

"Have I said thank you about him yet?" I covered his hand on my cheek as I gazed into his blue eyes. Even in the dim lighting, it felt like his eyes glowed. Then again, I'd memorized everything about him over the past few years. Everything about all of them.

"For Theo?" Kellan raised his brows as he slid his hands under my shirt to rest against my bare hips. "You don't have to thank me for that, Sparrow. He's family."

The easy acceptance in his voice and his tone made me sigh. "I don't think he knows what to think about me."

"He knows you're his big sister and that you brought your whole show to Prague to save him and the other kids." Despite his calm certainty, I still frowned. "Right now... He's struggling with a lot of things. From the way he was raised to his identity to who he can trust. As someone who was once a fourteen year old boy, if I had a big sister like you—I'd have treasured every moment with her."

"He doesn't know me though."

"He wants to know you. That's as important. He's not demanding the time with you or trying to get arrested daily for attention."

I grimaced at the description, but Kellan chuckled.

"Trust me, we've all been there. Me. Vaughn. Even Jasper and Freddie."

The mention of Freddie brought another sigh out of me.

"He's one of us, Sparrow. Whether he knows it or not. Whether he's ready to hear it or not, he's a Vandal. We'll keep him safe."

I knew that. I'd known that from the beginning. Stretching down, I brushed my nose to his. "Sorry…"

"If you apologize to me because you're bringing me what you're worried about and letting me address it, I'm going to spank that gorgeous ass of yours until it's shiny and red."

My cunt clenched along with my thighs at the description. "Well, technically, I wasn't going to apologize for that."

"Uh huh." Amusement populated his voice. "Then what were you saying sorry for?"

Busted. Still, I didn't mind anything Kellan wanted to do to me. The man held my heart and my soul, and he'd done everything in his power, along with all the other Vandals, to help me reclaim my body and my mind. "For getting distracted from you and going back to sleep."

His snort was worth the playful tease. He tugged me forward, then wrapped a hand around my nape. "I don't care if I haven't seen you for five minutes, five days, five months or five years—though if it's five years, trust me when I say you and I will have a lot of words about that—if you need to talk to me about anything, Sparrow, I am here for you."

A true giggle escaped me. "No way would I let it be five years. I don't even like more than five weeks."

Personally, the longest we'd done was six weeks, then a week of downtime, then back on the road again.

"The tour has been extended twice now, but this is a longer break." We hadn't really had time to discuss this the night before. "The crew is taking a well-earned break. I released the dancers for a month, so they could take their own breaks or do other gigs in the meanwhile, then we'll meet up back here in Braxton Harbor to train for the next leg."

"Four weeks?" Kellan's smile deepened. "That's a whole month, Sparrow. I like your confidence and I'm glad everyone is here, but I hope you aren't planning on a lot of sleep."

That made me laugh harder. The guys always put my care far ahead of their own. I wasn't concerned. "Good thing for all of you that being back in peak performance means I have loads of energy."

"Yes," he said slowly, stroking his hand down to my ass. The shirt had slid up and he took the time to rub one cheek and then the other. It was gentle petting interspersed with deeper massaging squeezes. Once upon a time, even the suggestion of it would trigger me.

The only thing it made me want to do right now was stretch out like a cat. Particularly with his cock firmly set between my thighs, though a sheet still separated us.

"Are you really enjoying your tour, Sparrow?" The quiet question brought my mind to the present and up from where he was touching me.

"I am," I said slowly. "I told you about making changes, right?"

"Yes," he said. "I want to hear more about those while you're here. It's not just about the silks, but the stage work, and you're adding more challenges."

I smiled. Yes, he always listened to every single word. I

soaked up the admission to store away for when self-doubt plagued me. "Yes, Rome is going to perform with me. I want to do more partner work again, some of these I can totally do on my own and I'll be good at them."

Cocky? Maybe, but I was pushing my own limits and there were a couple of these I had coming up that would give everyone pause. I truly couldn't wait.

"I need to be pushed out of my comfort zone though," I confessed. "This isn't about sex so much as trusting outside of the bedroom, trusting on the stage and in the air."

"Rome will never hurt you," Kellan said, not that I needed the assurance.

"I know he won't. He also knows my routines better than I do sometimes. I worried when he first volunteered that he was only offering because I wanted someone to partner with."

"But you don't think that's the only reason now?" He was drawing circles against my hips while I rested my chin on my forearms. I draped him like his favorite blanket. There was something utterly magnificent about being together like this.

"No, I *know* it's not. I think he wants to push himself too. And I get the feeling he *wants* to perform with me."

"Good," Kellan exhaled the word. "He's been your biggest fan forever. I know he used to watch every single recording, picked up the discs when they were released and more than once, if he got to see you perform, he recorded it himself. He loves to watch you move."

I knew that. "I love to dance with him too. I'm looking forward to those rehearsals. I just want to make sure it's not too much, you know?"

"You'll listen to him," Kellan said, brushing a stray strand of hair away from my face and tucking it behind my ear. "You'll look after him the way he looks after you. The two of you have your own language."

Did we? I frowned.

"It's like Liam and Rome, the twins always understand each other. I get Rome most of the time and even when I don't, I've learned to just accept him as he is. But you hear everything he doesn't say."

"I hear you too…" I didn't want him to think that I didn't.

"Shh," Kellan said, pressing his finger to my lips. "You loving Rome, or any of the other guys, takes nothing away from me. It never has and never will. You share a connection with each of them that is unique and vital. Just like what you share with me is about us and not them."

I blew out a low breath. "You all matter to me."

"I know we do," he assured me before leaning up to press a kiss to my lips. "Now tell me what else is worrying you, because you're dancing around it Sparrow, and I can't fix it if you don't tell me what it is."

I turned that description over in my head. Was I really dancing around it? As soon as he pointed it out, however, I saw the truth in the sentiment. "Freddie asked me to teach him to dance."

There were things about each of them that they would never confess to the others. The secrets they confided in me, they were to be protected. Even if they already knew them, just as they shielded me the same way. We needed to trust each other.

"Okay," Kellan said. "That's good, right?"

"Yes," I said swiftly and then added, "But I don't want him to hurt himself. Before you scold me and tell me I need to support him in making his own decisions, I absolutely plan on it… but I want his lessons to start while we're here on the break. Somewhere he feels safe and secure."

"Ah," Kellan said then began to nod. "You want me to buy you time with the guys?"

"I absolutely want time with all of you. We all need it."

Family time was paramount. "I need to spend some time with Theo, but I don't want anyone to feel neglected if I focus on Freddie for a bit."

"Particularly because Freddie is on the road with you." Kellan nodded again. "I get it, Sparrow. I'll take care of it."

Relief spilled through me, easing the tension I hadn't even realized had knotted me up. "You know I adore all of you."

"Yes," he said, giving me another kiss. "I do and so does everyone else. We love Freddie too, and if he's asking you for what he needs, Sparrow and you're telling me what you need —then we'll take care of it."

I had no idea how much I needed that reassurance before he told me and I kissed him. The pressure of my lips to his wasn't as much about passion or desire as a fierce declaration of the connection between us.

"Thank you," I whispered.

"It's going to be my pleasure," he told me, and then he flipped us so I was on the bottom and the sheet slipped away. "And yours." He nibbled another kiss before he paused to raise his head and study me. "Unless there's anything else you'd like me to fix?"

"Can we get burgers later?"

His laughter was its own reward. "We can get anything you want." Then his mouth fused to mine and I wrapped my arms around his neck. I had nowhere else I needed or wanted to be.

CHAPTER 11

JASPER

"Why do I have to talk to this guy?" Drawing himself to his full height, Theo glared at me.

I scratched the side of my nose before I turned to the coffee pot and poured myself a large cup. While I liked an espresso now and then, there was nothing to replace the feeling of pure industrial brew first thing in the morning.

When I turned, coffee cup in hand now, I found Theo still standing there in all his self-righteous fury. His eyes blazed and his mouth compressed. There was just something unimpressive as fuck about a kid with peach fuzz trying to stare me down.

"Well?" he demanded, in a voice that held more anger than petulance, but the petulance was still there. Fuck me, what a little asshole. "Are you going to answer me?"

I took a swallow of the coffee. The too strong brew ripped through my system and promised to clean all the pipes. Just what I needed. Lowering the mug, I met Theo's pissed off gaze. "No."

Coffee in hand, I headed over to the fridge and opened it. Leftovers had been stored in there, along with danishes that were perfect for the microwave. I debated just grabbing some Pop Tarts, but Doc stressed we needed to set healthier examples for the asshat currently trying to intimidate me.

Danishes had fruit, right?

I grabbed the box with the apple ones in it. Another swallow of coffee gave me life on the way to nuke. I slipped two of the danishes onto a paper plate and right into the microwave. The rest could sit on the counter and begin to warm.

"What do you mean, 'no'?" Theo snapped. Oh right, he was still in here.

"Kid, I'm tired and I'm on my first cup off coffee. You need to sit down, shut up, and stop your bitching until I've at least finished the first full mug." I considered the fact I'd already drunk half of this mug. "Maybe wait until I'm done with the second."

We'd been up really late the night before, first with the party at the Hearthfire, then coming back here for pool, shooting the shit, and hanging out. It had been nice to have everyone here for a while. Theo had been fine until Lainey, Milo and the others left with Andrea in tow. Then he'd gone all sullen and pissed off teen again before he vanished down to his own set of rooms where Milo's and mine used to be.

Were all teenagers so goddamn dramatic?

"I just want to know why I have to talk to the Reynolds guy."

Reynolds... Who the fuck was Reynolds? I was still mining for that information from my sleepy brain when the microwave beeped. "Oh, the guy from the learning center."

"Yes, the guy from the learning center. Some old dude with a receding hairline and he smells like bad candy."

I needed way more coffee for this. I downed the rest of the mug before I took out the heated danishes and handed them to Theo. He stared at the paper plate then at me.

"Look, take them or starve. I don't really care which at the moment." I was a little hungover, running on not enough sleep, and fighting all the desire I had to break into Kellan's room and steal time with our girl. I *could* be patient, didn't mean I had to like it.

Theo huffed out a breath, but took the plate before he stomped over to the table and sat down. Thank fuck for that. Time for more coffee. I slid two more danishes in to heat and then filled my mug to the brim with more coffee. Then I started another pot brewing.

I was halfway through the second cup before I carried it and my danishes over to the table. "You need assessment tests." It had actually taken me that long to remember what the hell we'd scheduled the appointments for. Liam had made the arrangements on Doc's recommendation.

"Why?" Hostility vibrated off the syllable.

"Because you don't remember the last time you actually attended a school. You speak English pretty well, but you don't *read* it very well. You're good at figures in your head, but when we were tallying something up on paper for weights on the truck, you didn't know what to do with them."

His expression remained mutinous.

"You also need to go to school, you need to get an education, but you need to get the one *you* need. Before we dump you in a school, we need to know what you need to work on and where you need more help." I took another swallow of the coffee then set the cup down and reached for the first of my danishes.

"Nobody bothered to even ask me about it," Theo snapped. "What if I don't want to do it?"

"You'll be shit out of luck." I could play the *because I said so* card. But I wasn't the one saying so. In fact, I was pretty sure it was Doc who talked to Liam after I mentioned the thing with the numbers. "You don't have to like getting an education, but you need one."

"It's not like I need it for a job," he snarled. "My brother and sister are clearly loaded. So was my father, if they are to be believed, so tell me again I why I need to go to school?"

Oh, this kid. For a moment, I considered calling Milo and telling him he was a dick for sending Theo to us. I hated school. Hated the hours. Hated the restrictions. Really hated most of the teachers. I skipped every chance I got and the minute I could get my diploma and get out, I was gone.

You couldn't pay me to go back to school. I got my CDL license and took some night courses for business. That was practical application only.

"You don't want to have this argument with me," I told Theo. Maybe he didn't get it, but I did. "Like I said earlier, you don't have to like it. But you want to be in charge and in control of your life. You don't know enough to be left to your own devices. So, that means you do things our way until you get there."

"I'll just go back to New York." The hollow threat just sort of dangled out there.

"Don't let the door hit you in the ass on the way out," I told him. "You'll be going to school there too."

"It's such bullshit," Theo swore as he flung himself back in the chair. Anger just shimmered in the air around him. Man, it was like looking in a dirty mirror reflection of me. I'd been this little punk.

A headache pulsed behind my eye and I stuffed the rest of

the danish into my mouth to keep my next comments to myself.

"I could just leave."

"Yep," Freddie said as he wandered in. "If you keep shouting like that while we're hungover, I'm going to say someone is going to help you get the hell out sooner rather than later."

He wasn't quite staggering. Nor was he hungover. The clarity in that blue-eyed gaze wasn't focused on me, however, but rather on Theo.

The little shit in question frowned. Probably didn't think the argument would turn this direction. Grateful for the backup, I washed down the rest of the danish with some coffee and rose to refill my cup.

"You don't even know what we're arguing about," Theo finally settled on a new course of battle. Ugh, I owed Ms. Stephanie so many apologies. I really hoped I'd never been this bad to her.

"And I don't care," Freddie said. "You don't want to do something. So you're sitting here whining like a little bitch about it and demanding someone else fix it so you don't have to because you think no one else should be in charge of you."

"So?" Right, time to antagonize Freddie apparently. I debated stepping into it, but Freddie didn't seem angry. Hell, he didn't even look particularly annoyed. Instead of addressing Theo's demand, he opened the fridge and took out the orange juice.

"So," Freddie said. "If you don't want people making choices for you, stop demanding they fix your shit too. If you don't need the help, prove you don't, and move on. Or here's a thought... *shut up.*"

Theo's mouth fell open and it took everything I had not to laugh my ass off at the stunned look on his face. While

Theo searched for a response, I pulled another mug out of the cupboard.

"You want coffee, Freddie?"

"Not yet," he said. "I'm going to wait for Boo-Boo to get up and then we'll have lattes. I could eat though."

"There's more danishes there," I told him. "Didn't grab donuts yet. Figured we'd do that tomorrow."

I carried my mug back to the table where Theo was still staring at Freddie, who opened the cap on the orange juice jug and downed about a third of it. Since the only two people present were me and Theo, I didn't say anything.

After pulling out a couple of the cold danishes, Freddie carried them and the OJ over to the table. "Think we should make breakfast for Kel when they get up, too?"

"Only if you're volunteering," I said, before taking another bite of my own. Kel liked cooking and he really liked cooking for our girl, so I wasn't taking that away.

"Point," Freddie said before he finally focused on Theo "So, you going the shut the fuck up route?"

The kid scowled. "I don't want to be assessed."

"Well, nobody does." Freddie shrugged. "But you don't want to be stupid or helpless either. So, get assessed, figure out your weak points, then strengthen them."

"Great, so now I'm stupid?" Was that hurt in Theo's voice?

"Did I say you were stupid?"

"You just said I don't want to be stupid and helpless. I'm *not* helpless. I'm *not* stupid either."

"Okay," Freddie said, almost too agreeably. "So, why are you so scared of meeting—who is he supposed to be meeting?"

I almost snorted a laugh at that bland delivery. "Educational assessment from the district learning center."

"Ugh," Freddie said, making a face. "Right. Is it here? Or does he have to go to them?"

"Pretty sure we decided to take him there, but that's just cause we don't need anyone else hanging out in here. We want to give him as clean and safe an opportunity as possible." I shrugged. "Liam made the arrangements."

"He's some creepy old guy," Theo admitted. "I saw him last week when Doc swung by the learning center to discuss the testing options. I told him then I didn't want to do it."

"What did Doc say?" I had my own ideas, but I didn't assume with Doc anymore. I'd learned that lesson.

"Just that assessments weren't about passing or failing. I shouldn't worry about it and I wouldn't be alone."

"So Doc picked up on the fact you didn't like the place." Freddie scratched at his jaw. It wasn't a question. "Is it because it's a guy and not a woman?"

I didn't say anything, just sipped my coffee and kept an eye on Theo over the rim.

Theo folded his arms almost defensively and shrugged. "I just don't want to do it."

"I get it," Freddie said. "I had to get tested every year, but it worked out. Meant I got the right classes. Ms. Stephanie always went with me though, she sat through the assessments. She promised to be my backup and she always was."

Freddie hated to be alone with strangers. Maybe Theo did too.

"So," Freddie continued. "If you want, I'll go and hang out for your assessments and I'll be your backup. I can't really help you cheat or anything, cause my grades were never that good anyway." He waved it off like he didn't have the intellectual capacity. Freddie was a hell of a lot smarter than he pretended, but he liked to keep what he could do to himself.

I respected it.

"Think they'd get pissed if I asked for someone different to do the testing?"

The almost cooperative meekness in his Theo's tone

almost knocked me over with a feather. The anger and belligerence drained away and now he just sounded tired.

"Nope," I said. "I'll call Liam right now and ask him to get it changed." Then because the kid was talking, I said, "Do you want to go to the learning center and meet the other counselors and candidates, see who you click with?"

Theo rubbed at his lower lip, a deep scowl settling on his brow. "I don't know. I don't… I don't know any of them."

Fair.

"That's why you take backup," Freddie said. "I got no problems tagging along. We'll check out who is there and who looks good and if they all suck, Liam can figure out another way."

Discomfort reflected in Theo's eyes. "Just like that?" Disbelief underscored the words.

"Kid," I said. "Let me tell you what being a Vandal means —it means you don't have to do shit alone. It means we will have your back every step of the way. If the path needs to be cleared, we clear it. If you need a hand, you get it."

"It also means if you need a boot to the ass, you get that too," Freddie said, self-deprecating grin in place.

"But I'm not a Vandal." The emptiness in that statement cut me.

"Sure you are," Freddie said easily. "You're family. That makes you a Vandal."

The hungry look in Theo's eyes at Freddie's statement answered the last question I had. Theo was fighting us to make us prove we were here and wouldn't abandon him. He wanted to be here. He wanted his brother and his sister, whether he was willing to admit it or not, and he wanted to be a part of something.

"What he said," I told him. "Also, I am the boot that is going to be up your ass when you need it. Now, eat your food. I'll call Liam."

"Should I go with…" Theo started to rise, but I waved him back to his chair.

"Emersyn will be down soon and I think you wanted to see her."

He tried to cover up the flare of interest, but he couldn't hide it fully.

"She's going to want to see you too," Freddie said, giving him an out and I bumped Freddie's shoulder with my fist as I stood. I caught his eye as I turned and he lifted his chin.

He had this.

Cool.

I would get with Liam and we'd put our heads together. We needed someone who could work with Theo, but not threaten him. We were gonna find him someone we would trust to work with Freddie.

CHAPTER 12

EMERSYN

*E*ach time we came home it took me a few days to reacclimate. I loved traveling, training, and performing. It was a constant flow of energy output. Our days were mapped out and scheduled. We might wake up in one city and go to bed in another, but there was a familiarity to the routine that I craved.

Coming home meant an entirely different routine. Time with the guys, resting, getting a bit of a break from the daily grind of performance and training. Not too much of a break because the last thing I wanted was to get sloppy, or worse, out of shape.

This was the first break I'd taken with Theo in residence. He'd been present at Kel's birthday party, and I'd earned a quiet hello from him and a couple of words before Lainey arrived with Andrea. After that, he ignored me and Milo both.

Milo hadn't cared for it, but accepted that we had to be

patient. After all, he'd been patient with me. His snort had been pretty amusing at the description.

"Hey," I'd reminded him with a little jab of my elbow. "I was worth it and so were you." That earned me a kiss to the top of my head. Theo was a tough nut. If not for Mickey, Jasper, and Kel promising me that he was coming around slowly and talking to them, I would worry more.

For now, I trusted their thoughts on the matter. Rome was waiting for me as I descended the stairs. I'd gone to sleep with Mickey in my bed, but he was gone when I woke. He never stayed the whole night, he was always too worried about bad dreams and losing control.

"Hi," I said, greeting Rome as he lifted me right off the steps and I wrapped my arms around his neck.

"I'm going out today. But I waited so I could tell you before I left." That was huge for Rome. When we were home, he kept his own schedule. It had been a while since he got to paint anything.

"Okay," I said, stroking my fingers through his hair before I dropped a kiss on his lips. "I'll be at the Clubhouse all day. Jasper is on the road, but I promised him a date tonight."

Rome nodded. "Liam will be back tomorrow."

I sighed.

"Are you well?" Quiet intensity underscored his inquiry.

"Yes," I said. "I promise. I love being home, but we're all so busy. I like it when we're all here, and it's noisy and chaotic."

"Jasper and Liam like hitting each other too," Rome said and I grinned. That wasn't quite what I meant by chaos, but it fit. "Tell them you want family dinner."

Family dinner when we were all together. I chewed my lower lip. We'd make adjustments for Theo being here, but maybe if everyone was present, he'd relax more.

They were always asking me what I needed or wanted. I tried to do the same for them. "I'll tell Kellan, but I think he is going with Vaughn to look at possible sites for his new tattoo place."

It wasn't a done deal, not yet. He didn't want to make any decisions until we were going to be home longer term. That said, as much as I loved having him on the road with me, I didn't want him to give up his interests for mine.

"Starling," Rome said, recapturing my attention. His expression held a combination of understanding and curiosity.

"I'll be okay," I said. "I just worry about Vaughn."

"You worry about everyone." Rome pressed a kiss to my nose and then put me on my feet.

"I suppose I do." Then again, they all worried about me. "It's kind of what we do."

"Yes," he said before he shouldered his backpack. "Do you need me to stay?"

The offer made me sigh. If I said yes, he'd change his plans just like that. "No," I said. "Go make something beautiful, and then show me when it's done?"

"I will." It was a promise. Then he gave me another kiss. "I have my phone." For a moment, he studied me. I met his gaze without looking away.

At his nod, I smiled. "I'll see you later?"

"Yes." Then he was heading for the door and letting himself out. The downstairs was quiet, but it was also still early. I'd come for coffee, but I diverted to my studio instead. What I needed to do was get out of my head, that meant stretching and dancing for a little while.

After, I'd shower and then roust anyone else who was here to have breakfast with me. The studio was exactly as I left it, although maybe a bit cleaner. They didn't let it get dusty and I appreciated that. Someone had also organized all the CDs.

It took me a few minutes to punch up the boxes on my

toe shoes, and then to stretch. Once I was ready, I slid in a playlist and moved to the center of the studio. It was a thirty minute set. More than enough to warm up and exercise without overdoing it.

Eyes closed, I got into position and when the first note left the speakers, I was ready.

FREDDIE WAS SITTING ON THE FOOT OF MY BED WHEN I CAME out of the bathroom. I'd pulled on a tank top and panties after I toweled off but I carried the lotion out with me.

"Hey," I said, smiling at him as I dropped to sit on the edge of the bed to apply the lotion to my legs. "Good morning."

"Hey, Boo-Boo," Freddie said. His hair was pulled back from his face into a loose ponytail. Dressed in jeans and a t-shirt, he looked relaxed. "You have any plans?"

"Not until tonight." I ran the moisturizer over my arms and then up to my neck. My hair was still damp, but I'd run a comb through it and it fell in straight lines. It would dry eventually. "Jasper and I are going out."

"He told me," Freddie said, one corner of his mouth quirking up. "But you're free until then?"

"Liam says I'm very expensive, especially when I keep making changes to the show." He'd said with as much laughter in his voice as there was exasperation. "Course, he also complains when I don't spend money so..." I spread my arms. "What are you going to do?"

"Make fun of him," Freddie said with a chuckle.

I wrinkled my nose, but I couldn't hide my own smile. "That's fair." I went over to the drawer and opened it. Since I wasn't performing today or going out until later, I could dress in the comfy clothes.

"I know you just danced…"

I looked over my shoulder to find him staring at me with a nervous air shimmering around him. "Yes."

He blinked. "I haven't asked you anything yet."

I pulled out a pair of leggings and then opened a second drawer to pull out a shorter, workout skirt. "My answer is still yes, but I will hold it in reserve until you ask the question."

Clothes in hand, I turned to face him and leaned back against the dresser. The corners of Freddie's mouth curved upward into an adorable smirk. "You will, huh?"

"I can do pretty much anything for you," I said and all at once his expression softened.

"You know that it's the same for me…and I'm working on the rest."

"You're perfect the way you are."

He snorted. "I'm a lot of things Boo-Boo, but I'm not perfect."

I shrugged. "You're perfect for me."

Freddie saw me and my damage long before any of the others did. He seemed to resonate with me and when I needed someone to truly understand, he was right there. If I could give him anything in the world, it would be the freedom from what happened to him. Since I couldn't do that, I would treasure that he understood me and I would be with him every single step of the way.

A flush touched his cheeks and his ears went a little red. When he ducked his chin, I had to smother my own smile. I hadn't meant to embarrass him but he deserved to hear how much I appreciated him.

He deserved so much more.

"I adore you," I reminded him. "You can get away with anything you want, but you don't get to talk bad about you. I'll fight you on that."

A huff of laughter escaped him. "What am I going to do with you, Boo-Boo?"

"Like I said, anything you want. Now, ask your question so I can say yes and figure out what I'm wearing."

That earned me another chuckle. "Very gracious of you."

"I have manners," I said, almost primly. "It was one of the things Jasper liked about me."

His actual guffaw tickled me. "One of the things..." The humor sparkling in his eyes chased away the shadows even as the flush in his cheeks cooled. "Boo-Boo, never leave me."

"Cross my heart and hope to die," I said, miming the motion. "Stick a thousand needles in some bad guy's eye."

Lips pursed, he straightened and raised his eyebrows.

"What?" I said, spreading my hands. "I don't want to stick needles in any of our eyes."

"You know," he said. "Let's just go with it."

I beamed and he pushed up off the bed before he crossed to me.

"Up for giving me dance lessons today?"

"Absolutely," I told him. "Can we grab food first?"

"We can do anything we want." He glanced at the skirt in my hand. "Though if you're wearing that, I need to go get more knives." With that, he dropped a kiss to the tip of my nose. "Meet you downstairs?"

"Absolutely," I said and when he pivoted to leave, I let out a little whistle. "I need to make sure I'm armed too."

He cut a look back at me from the door. "Besides the obvious, why?"

"Cause those jeans are really working for you."

The flush on his face returned and he pressed his forehead to the edge of the open door before looking at me again. "Then I better put a little sway in my step."

"You won't hear me complain." Then I winked. The rush

of color deepened but so did his laughter. It didn't take me long to change.

Since he liked the skirt, I went with it and I stuffed my feet into the thick boots that hit me mid-calf. They had steel toes and definitely left a mark if I needed to kick someone. It also had a sheath on the inside for a knife. I pulled out the crossbody bag with the holster and packed in my gun.

Then I went into the bathroom and gave myself a critical look. My hair was still wet, so I just braided it back. I skipped the cosmetics, cause we were going out for fun, food, and then dancing.

Ready, I left the room and scrawled a note on the whiteboard near the door to our suite. It told the guys I was heading out and I had my phone and who I was with.

Downstairs, Freddie straightened as I leapt the last three steps. "Ready," I told him and he grinned. When he held out a hand, I clasped his and then we were off.

CHAPTER 13

EMERSYN

We left the Clubhouse hand in hand, bypassing the rats who worked out in the warehouse. I didn't see any of the other guys, but it didn't mean they weren't around. Probably a good thing, cause there was a restlessness to Freddie even with his shy smile and flushed cheeks.

He pushed open the outer door that opened onto the alley. The fat, puffy white clouds above looked like they were just there to decorate the vibrant blue sky. The sunlight itself slanted down in shafts, though the alley was almost always in the shade.

It was chilly, and a little damp. The wet pavement and puddles were evidence of earlier rain. That had all blown out though. Freddie frowned and cut a look to me and my skirt. "Are you cold?"

"Nope," I promised. Was it cooler out here? Yes. The air was also fresher and the breeze carried the scents of piping hot dough, coffee, and… "Oh, do you think the funnel cake cart is back?"

It had shown up last year for a few weeks. I probably gained five pounds from running down to grab one every chance I got.

"I sense a sugar rush in our future," Freddie intoned almost playfully.

"These are the carbs we're looking for." I made a face and stuck my tongue out at him.

His laughter was exactly what I was going for. That said, his head was on a swivel and he kept checking ahead of us and behind. His hand was firm on mine, keeping me close. Not that I minded in the slightest.

"Coffee," I said. "Funnel cake if it's there. Then we can go grab donuts for everyone."

"None of that is protein," he reminded me.

I put a hand to my chest. "You sound like Mickey." After a moment of thinking it over, I grinned. "And Jasper."

He snorted. "I am thinking that someone eats a high protein diet on the road, so I don't want you over indulging on the carbs and then beating yourself up for it later."

The pragmatism of it was just so refreshing. "If you don't mind a slightly longer walk, while we eat funnel cake and drink coffee, we could make our way over to 70th and Carpenter."

"Korean barbecue?" Humming, he slowed as we reached the end of the alley where it spilled out onto the street. The sunshine dappled the sidewalks thanks to the sparse collection of trees placed at different intervals.

Foot traffic wasn't that heavy, but it was late morning. There was heavier traffic on the street. The food carts were definitely open. The coffee place I liked was a block away and the funnel cake food cart was *right* there.

I could kiss the man.

"I don't mind the walk," Freddie said, glancing down at me. "You in the mood for steak on a stick?"

Laughter swirled up through me. I bounced a little and pressed a kiss to his cheek. Instead of flushing in embarrassment this time, his smile just grew. At his bemused look, I winked. "Just wanted to say thank you."

"Uh huh."

"And now, I want funnel cake."

"That's more like it." Despite his teasing, he moved right with me and didn't let much distance get between us as I made my way to the cart. The older gentleman with his crinkled face and easy smile welcomed us.

"Two please," I said, holding up two fingers. "The big ones."

"Powdered sugar?" He was already squeezing the batter into the hot oil. Fresh and hot funnel cake was the *best*. I bounced in place.

"Yes, please. For both of us." I glanced at Freddie and grinned as he shook his head. "You don't want it?"

"No, the powdered sugar is fine, Boo-Boo. I'm just enjoying you."

"Well, then, by all means. Enjoy away." When I reached for my wallet though, Freddie made a negative little noise and he already had the bills out to pay for everything. It wasn't long before we had the hot crispy goodness bathed in powdered sugar.

I died and went to heaven right there in three bites. Funnel cakes in hand, we continued down the street. Freddie shortened his stride so I wasn't having to take two steps for each of his.

The funnel cakes survived to the coffee shop. I had powdered sugar on my top and my fingers. Freddie cleaned me up and I helped him before we went in to order. I beat him so I could pay for the coffee.

"You can buy lunch," I offered and enjoyed his chuckle. Hot coffee in hand in no time, we were back out on the street and walking down the block.

I found myself studying the area. Drenched in sunlight with sidewalk cafes opened, it was just nice. Granted, this route took us from the more industrial areas nearer the port and deeper into the city.

Quite a few windows showed signs of renovations and coming soon signs. On the corner at 75th there was a new sign proudly announcing a bookstore. There was also a date for the grand opening in just under two weeks.

We were still going to be here.

"You're happy," Freddie said when I paused to take a picture of the storefront. I wanted to make sure I didn't forget. I also wanted to show Kel. The Vandals still liked looking after the area and this would be a fantastic addition to the neighborhood.

"I am," I said, checking the image before I tucked my phone away. "It's nice to be home. It's nice to see all the changes out here." Then I tilted my head up at him. I hadn't brought sunglasses so I used my free hand to shield my eyes. "I'm enjoying being out here with you and I can't wait to dance with you in a bit. So yeah, I'm definitely happy."

"Is that the funnel cake and the coffee talking?" The teasing light in his eyes took any sting out of the words. He was never good about taking compliments.

"Maybe ten percent?" I said, scrunching my nose like I had to really think about it.

"Once we get your steak on a stick, that's probably going to get higher, huh?" He let out the most resigned of sighs. "Well, a man has to do what a man has to do."

It was silly and more than a little ridiculous, but I didn't care. Like I'd said, I was having fun. It didn't take us long to get to the Korean barbecue cart where he set up around the huge square with the fountain in the center. It was a great spot for lunch crowds to grab a bite and eat on the steps or on the wall around the fountain.

We split up briefly with Freddie getting in the line for the steak while I discarded our empty coffee cups. The pleasant buzz under my skin had me skipping back toward him.

"Hey there." A guy stepped into my path, cutting off my view of Freddie. He was dressed in a suit, off the rack and not custom, and there was a mustard stain on his tie. He wasn't that bad looking, but...

"Not interested," I told him as I went to go around him. The movement of his hand in my periphery warned me he was about to grab my arm and I got hold of his thumb, peeling his grip off and bending it uncomfortably.

"Fuck," he swore.

"Again," I said. "Not interested. Don't touch me."

"Bitch," he swore and I didn't care about that so much. As tempting as it was to break his thumb, I let him go.

Leaving him behind, I headed back for Freddie, who stared daggers beyond me. He was halfway to me having left his place in line. "It's fine," I told him as I caught his hand. The last thing I wanted was for him to get angry or for some random asshole to spoil our day.

"He grabbed you," Freddie said, his voice low, dark and dangerous.

"He *tried* to grab me," I corrected. "I didn't let him. Thumb lock worked."

"What did he say to you?" Freddie split his attention between sweeping his gaze over me and staring past me. I had maybe a few seconds to save that guy's life because Freddie's temper was already lit.

"He said 'hey,'" I said. "Then I told him 'not interested'. He didn't say much after I bent his thumb backwards."

The word bitch really wasn't much and I didn't care what he thought. Freddie scowled and I squeezed his hand.

"I'm *fine*," I stressed the last syllable. "We're still having fun, right?"

He blew out a long breath then switched his attention back to me. "I don't like anyone grabbing you."

"Then good thing for him I didn't let him grab me. I was pretty badass about it." I raised my chin, inviting the compliment and some of the anger bled out of his expression.

"You're always badass, Boo-Boo." He shifted his grip on my hand and then turned us back toward the cart. A lady waved us back to his spot. Apparently, she'd seen everything and she gave us a friendly smile.

Freddie still put me on his other side and I caught him checking the square regularly. I didn't doubt he was looking for that guy but here was to hoping he was hell and gone. Then it was our turn and we got three huge steak on sticks for me, and two for Freddie. He also got us some sweet and sticky soy-glazed potatoes.

Treasures in hand, we found a spot on the steps near some shade and settled in to eat. Life hummed around us. There were moms out walking with strollers. Businessmen and women hurrying between buildings like they had appointments—to be fair, they probably did.

There were students reading or studying. Others, just like us, had grabbed a comfortable spot in the sun and shade as the fountain switched between the single spray in the middle and the multitude of smaller ones around the edges.

All they really needed was... Before I could even complete the thought, I saw the musician pulling out a violin and left the case at his feet.

"Music," I said to Freddie. "Perfect."

He chuckled as I took a bite out of my steak. Thankfully, he'd gotten a couple of bottles of water to wash down our lunch. The violinist started out classical, but he didn't stay there. When he switched to more modern songs, I was impressed.

Tummy full, I leaned my head against Freddie's shoulder. "Is this okay?"

"Yes," he said, and the lack of any stress in his voice promised me it really was okay. Someone with a guitar had moved out to join the violinist and there was someone else with a saxophone. Whether they played together before or it was their first time, they gave us an amazing impromptu concert.

We lingered there for almost an hour, just soaking up the atmosphere and the music. When the musicians started packing up, so did we. After we tossed our trash, we swung by the musicians and gave them some bills for their performance.

Hand-in-hand once more, we began the walk back. "You know, when I was younger, I thought it would be so cool to be a street performer."

"Dancing or doing tricks?"

"Probably doing tricks. I could dance, but I never see much of that out here. Musicians yes, singers and painters... occasionally a sketch artist. So maybe I could have cornered the market. There's just something freeing about doing what you want when you want."

"Yep, that freedom also comes with a tight budget and not a lot of food."

"Don't rain on my fantasy with your practicality."

He snorted. "I'm not that practical. Remember, I've had a lot of different jobs, from convenience stores, to janitorial, to dishwasher in a restaurant. The jobs all sucked, but they paid. The guys were always making sure there was enough, but I needed to do my part."

"Did you ever want to do anything specific?"

"Like Milo wanting to be a lawyer or Jasper just wanted to work for himself?"

I shrugged. "Something like that. Kel loves his shop and Vaughn used to love doing tattoos."

"He will again," Freddie said, soothing me. "Just takes time."

It would. Trauma fucked us all up in different ways. "Yeah." I sighed. "But yes, like them. Did you ever have something you wanted to be?"

Freddie didn't answer right away, we passed a couple of blocks in silence before he finally said, "I don't know. I never really thought about tomorrow much less next week, next month, or next year."

That made my chest hurt.

"Didn't think I'd ever have much of a future when I let myself think about it. Getting high helped with that, I could get blitzed and all that just falls away." He gave me a small smile. "Being clean is a lot harder, but it's all about one day at a time."

Another block passed in quiet, then he gave my hand a squeeze.

"Sorry, I'm not much of a catch, Boo-Boo."

I smacked his arm with my free hand. "Shut up. You're amazing."

He blinked. "I meant about the future planning and stuff."

"Freddie, are you planning to be here tomorrow?"

"Yes."

"Next week?"

He let out a long breath. "Yes."

"Next month?"

"I get it…"

"Ah," I waved a finger at him. "Just tell me yes, you're planning to be here next month and next year. That's all I need to hear. We can figure *anything* out, but I need you to be here. I need to know you're not going to give up. Even if it gets hard or you need help, that you want to be here and with me."

Pausing, he turned to look down at me. "Yes, Boo-Boo, this is where I want to be and I want to be right here with you. Today. Tomorrow. Next week. Next month. Next year. I promise."

That lifted some of the weight off my heart. "I like this plan."

"I guess it is a plan," he said with a chuckle.

"Yep." I bumped him with my hip. "Now, let's head back and do your very first dance lesson. We'll play your favorite song and we'll dance together."

"Here's hoping I don't suck," he muttered.

"You're not going to suck," I told him. "You're dancing with me. I got you."

CHAPTER 14

EMERSYN

Once we were back at Clubhouse, we headed straight to the studio. Among the reasons I mentioned it to Kel was that I needed the others to let us have the time without feeling excluded, and because Freddie deserved the attention. They would never begrudge him, but he would also be less inclined to say he needed the specific time or he'd want to slip away to not "bother" us.

That whole turn of phrase *bothered* me more. Freddie didn't bother anyone. He would put himself last and had for far too long. The others saw it and so did I, but it was also why when he asked for *anything* the answer would be yes. Once we were inside the studio, I slid off my shoes next to the door, then locked it. He toed off his own shoes before following me into the middle of the room. He glanced at his socks then at me, but I waved at him to keep them on for now.

I didn't usually care if anyone came in to watch me practice or rehearse. Today was not about me though. Coffee cup in hand, I took another drink then stole a look over my shoulder at him.

Since I finished the first cup before we were even back to my favorite shop, Freddie indulged me by sliding in to get us fresh cups. He shifted in place, one hand going to the back of his neck. The nervous energy vibrated in the air around him.

Not pushing right now, I diverted to the stereo system and flipped through the CDs the guys had collected for me, as well as the ones I'd added over the past several months. At the top were several playlists from the tour. I moved them aside. I wanted something else entirely.

"I haven't really decided on a favorite song," Freddie admitted and I flicked a look up to catch him watching me in the mirror.

I grinned. "We have time." Holding his gaze, I raised one of the CDs. "Trust me to pick a couple for us to get started with?"

"I trust you with everything," he said easily. Almost too easily. A cloud drifted across the clear blue of his eyes as his shoulders drooped. "I should trust you more."

"Don't do that." It wasn't an order so much as a plea.

"But, Boo-Boo…"

"No buts. Don't diminish anything about you. You have to protect you and since that's my first choice too, I want you to protect you. You trust me as much as you can and you're working on trusting me more." Spinning the CD case in my hand, I pulled the scar tissue of my psyche taut. "You have been there for me on every step of this journey, even when being there cost you more than you're willing to admit."

Pinetree cost us both.

"You could blame me for the choices I made that forced your hand. You could have left me there." The automatic objection filled his expression and I raised a hand to forestall his protests. "I know you couldn't. No more than I could have left you in a similar place. Before you came…"

Old injuries were often delicate as they healed. But time and patience, could help the tissue to toughen up. The rigid marks in my head were much like the ones on my arms, only invisible to anyone else. Art might dress up my forearms, but it didn't erase them. Nothing could erase them.

Oddly, I no longer felt the need to remove them or even wipe them away. I could touch the marks and not hate them. Yes, they were from a dark moment in my past but they were also the marks of surviving that moment. They heralded a real beginning of the end for my uncle in more ways than one. An end to his ever being able to hurt me again. An end to his influence and control over my life. And finally, an end to him.

"My uncle always seemed to end people before they could help me. The doctors, the teachers, even the other dancers… Those who would have helped died or disappeared. Before you came to Pinetree, the only person who'd ever come for me again and again was Lainey." My best friend. She took such risks for me.

"She came for you then too," Freddie reminded me. "She answered our messages. Came to warn us where you were."

"I know she did. She risked herself even when I would never have wanted her to."

"You would do the same," Freddie said without an ounce of doubt in his eyes.

A smile touched the corners of my lips. "I would. I'd do it for you guys too. You know that, right?"

"I do, Boo-Boo," he said, his voice tight but fierce as he took a couple of steps toward me. "I don't think I'm worth near what you are, but I know if I was in trouble—you'd come get me." His smile turned a bit wistful. "You came that night with Jasper and the guys."

The night he'd been jonesing. The night he'd killed to save himself.

"We're not so bad, you know." I dropped the disc into the player and turned it on.

"You guys are the best," he countered before raking a hand through his thick blond hair. "I know I'm weak, and there are times when I make the bad calls, but Jasper has always come to find me... The others. Now you... Bodhi... So many people. I don't know if I'm worth all of this, Boo-Boo."

I hit play on the music and walked slowly toward him. "I do. When I said 'we're not so bad,' Freddie. I meant you and me."

The surprise in his eyes would never not slice at me. I knew he didn't believe in himself. Not the way I did.

"I don't..."

"It's okay," I said, holding a hand out to him as the first bars of Shawn Mendes' In My Blood began to play. "I can believe in you until you get there. Just like you did for me."

His sigh held so much wistfulness, yet beneath it all was that element of crippling doubt. He'd fought so many battles to be *here* in this moment. So this was where I would meet him. The whole time, I kept my hand extended to him because the last steps were his.

The marked hesitation extended leaving us standing there as though in a frozen tableau. I'd wait here forever if he needed it, no matter how it pulled taut all that scar tissue inside of us. When he finally settled his palm against mine, I was torn between wanting to weep and wanting to cheer. The contact was electric, and I could almost feel the tension eddying the air around him.

"Show me?" The simple request buoyed me as he closed his fingers around mine.

"Yes." The answer was just that simple. I shifted my grip under his hand then reached for his other. His hesitation was far briefer this time. We were halfway through In Your Blood when he let me put his free hand on my waist.

"Waltzing is easy," I told him and the surprise that fluttered across his expression almost made me laugh. "It's a box movement, four steps, and you lead which means I follow your steps."

"But I don't know what my steps are supposed to be?" He frowned and looked down at our feet.

"I can follow anything you do, so I'll show you then you just match me movement for movement." The Mendes song segued to another, but neither of us were listening. The CD had a lot of instrumental versions of the songs all designed for performance. What I liked about them was that they were quieter and lacked words to distract.

"Okay," Freddie said, releasing my hand abruptly and taking his hand from my waist. He shook both like he needed to get rid of the jitters. When he reached for me this time, I glided forward and his quick smile was its own reward. "Box step?"

"Box step."

I didn't verbalize the four-count step pattern, just moved. Freddie divided his attention between my feet and my face. It took a few tries but he was moving with me. His feet matching mine.

I wiggled his arm as we continued to make the passes around the room. The box step was an easy one and I wasn't going to rush him. "Tighten up the frame. You don't need to be rigid, but you want to control the motion."

"Dirty Dancing," he commented and I frowned.

"None of this is dirty."

Freddie halted in mid-step, mouth open as he stared at me.

"What?"

"Dirty Dancing," he repeated. "You know, the movie?"

I raised my eyebrows. "I don't think I've seen it. I mean, I know it came out a few years ago…"

"No," Freddie said with a groan. "The older one. Look…" He let go and held his arms up as though he were dancing with me and did a lovely box step backwards before he used his hand to swirl the air in front of him. "This is my dance space. That is your dance space. I stay in my space, and you stay in yours."

"Yes. I mean, I wouldn't have phrased it that way, but that's pretty much how it works with a basic waltz."

His smile was brilliant and he returned without any coaxing. This time, we followed the steps until he had it down. Then I moved him through a left foot change and a right. "Most of this is just the simple mechanics of it. There's a formality to waltzing—it's kind of like flirting, only in movement."

"I like flirting."

The ease in his voice relaxed the tension in me. The knot in my core eased and then we were just dancing around the room, in big sweeping motions. I almost wished I'd brought a skirt so it would swish. When he pivoted and released my waist while extending his arm, I followed the motion and did a little spin before he pulled me back.

Four more songs and then we took a quick break for water. Freddie unscrewed the cap and shook his head. "Don't tell the guys I'm learning to waltz?"

"Your secrets are all safe with me. But the waltz is just the start." Then, because I wanted him to maintain all the control, "How are you doing? Would you like to continue or call it here?"

He blinked. "I'm good. Are you tired? I mean, we're on your break."

"I'm more than good." Elation bubbled through me. "I don't want to push too much."

A wider grin pulled at his mouth when he ducked his head and for just a moment, there was a flush of crimson on his cheeks. "I want you to push."

"You're sure?" I waited for him to lift his head and for his gaze to lock onto mine.

"I'm sure."

I retreated to the stereo and swapped out the CDs. I had one that mixed slower songs with faster ones. Still no full lyrics. Not yet. The jazz feeling and the instrumentals would be enough.

When I walked to him, he was ready and his touch was light but perfect. Every step seemed to bring us closer. He didn't tense up when I had a hand on his shoulder. We moved through a promenade and then a progressive change. Eventually, we were swapping leads like we were going to some charity ball.

After our next break, I changed it up. He'd mastered the waltz. I loved his dedication and focus. It let us touch and move, but now I wanted to do something a little different. But first... "Pushing is still good?"

He emptied the rest of his water bottle before he nodded. "Pushing is still good."

It was warm in here, and the constant motion added a thin layer of humidity around us from the sweat. When he came toward me, I faced away from him. Meeting his gaze in the mirror, I curled a beckoning finger to him.

Again, he hesitated, but the smirk that took over his expression gave me a boost. "You want me to grind against your ass, Boo-Boo? Cause it's a really nice ass."

"You can grind if you want, but right now, you're going to shadow me and we're going to dance to the music."

I grabbed the remote control and turned on the music. It was a latin beat. One I liked because it made you move and it had a lot of hip swaying. Tilting my head back, I met Freddie's gaze again.

"Hands on my hips," I told him, "and follow me."

"Yes, ma'am."

CHAPTER 15

EMERSYN

Our first dance lesson was an unparalleled success. We danced on and off for a couple of hours. We moved together until we were both dripping with sweat. For nearly all of it, Freddie kept his hands on me. He gripped my hips, he moved with me, his chest "near" but not against my back.

When I switched so we were almost chest to chest, he didn't back off. If anything, he seemed to lean into the dance more. We cycled through so many songs until we were just dancing, no form, no discipline, and no expectations. We danced and had fun.

After, Freddie needed a break. Overstimulation was a thing. It had happened to me before. We'd done a lot of touching. While I let him control the majority of it, there were still moments where I'd taken over and guided his hands on me or I'd put mine on his. The best part was he followed me up the stairs and dropped a kiss on my lips before he ducked into his room to shower.

That... that had been *epic*.

Riding that high, I slipped into my own room for a shower and to change. Jasper still wasn't back, but there was a message from Mickey. He would be back in the late afternoon and volunteered to pick up our favorites from the Thai place. The fact the guys' orders ticked up on the screen just made laugh.

It was so *normal*. Our normal, and I loved every moment of it. I wanted to soak in these moments. The jokes. The teasing comments. All over dinner orders. Jasper had even sent in his own Thai order, which had prompted me to do the same. If we had to postpone our date again, we'd make it up to each other. We always did.

Still, it made me smile as I added my requests, before I ducked myself into the shower proper. After I'd cleaned up and blown my hair dry, I got dressed in comfortable clothes. The dance capris and an oversized t-shirt were ideal.

Socks were my concession to the rough floors downstairs. I had no plans to go out. The sitting room was empty as I made my way through it and out the door.

More changes were taking place throughout the upstairs. We'd converted Milo's old room and added more space to it so when he came with Lainey and the other guys, they had their own space. Theo needed his space too, but the guys had finished that before Theo arrived to stay. The last was a storage room and armory that was locked and coded.

Every change converted the place into a home. Liam still had his apartment. He had several properties. So did I, but I didn't care about them so much. Mickey had his string of safe houses, and bolt holes he could use when he was moving abused women and children into safety.

But the clubhouse had become our real home. I was

riding those warm thoughts as I descended the stairs and headed for the kitchen. I needed something to eat and it would be a few hours before dinner. If we had the frozen pizzas, I could put one of those in the oven. The guys teased me, but ever since I'd discovered a deep fondness for the frozen pizzas, they were always in stock.

Theo rose as I crossed the living area and I slowed. He had a game controller in hand and sported a pair of headphones. "Hey, she's here, so I'm going to take a break." He paused for a moment, then snorted. "I'll be back in a few, don't start without me." Then he pulled the headset off.

"Levi?" It was a guess, but he and Bodhi's younger brother had formed a bond long before we found them. The game system had arrived along with instructions for the accounts Bodhi had set up for the boys. It had amused me, we had a game system of our own, but the guys hadn't wasted any time setting this up for Theo, and he'd been in front of it as often as he could.

"Yes," he said, his mouth tightening and his chin raising. Oh, he expected me to tell him off or something.

"Cool," I said, then motioned to the kitchen. "I'm going to get some lunch. Hungry?"

I wasn't going to discipline him. That wasn't what he needed from me. Honestly, I wasn't at all sure what he needed yet, or what I did for that matter. He was my brother. A younger one. Like me, he'd been kept in the dark about the existence of anyone else, even our father. A man he was far better off not knowing and one I wished that I had never met.

"I could eat," Theo said as he followed me. Like Milo, Theo was tall. At the rate he was growing, I had a feeling he'd be as tall as Vaughn. He was already a quarter of an inch taller than Freddie. It was sometimes a challenge to remember he was only fourteen. Just barely fourteen at that.

Once in the kitchen, I poked around in the freezer and found a nice stash of my favorites. "Pepperoni okay? Or do you want Hamburger? Or Sausage?" I held up each of the boxes one at time. "There's also a little bit of everything, which is my favorite."

"Pepperoni," Theo said after a beat. "Also, can't you get pizza delivered?"

"Yes. But it's not the same." I carried the two boxes over to the stove before I started it to get it preheating.

"Yeah," Theo said slowly. "I can tell. Those are flat and kind of disc like and not at all hot, steamy and fluffy like the other stuff." It was impossible to miss the sarcasm under-lining every word.

"You don't have to eat one," I said as I stripped mine out of the plastic and set it on the cookie sheet.

"I didn't say I didn't want it, but that's... that's weird to eat that when you could just order one."

"I like them." I stripped his out of the plastic and set it up too. Now I just had to wait for the oven to beep that the preheat was done. This was one of my favorite parts. Kellan had been teaching me to cook, but I'd mastered this and I liked being able to fix them myself.

He wore a troubled expression when I glanced over at him. As if suddenly aware of my scrutiny, he folded his arms. "Sorry."

"For what?" I glanced at the temperature on the oven before focusing on Theo again.

"For—" He hesitated. "I don't know. I guess I sounded rude. So, sorry."

"Okay," I said.

"Okay?" Theo repeated.

"Yep," I told him. "Okay. You thought you were rude, you said sorry, and I'm okay with it. All good."

The oven beeped and I happily twisted to slide the pizzas

in to heat and then set the timer. It was a silly bit of accomplishment for me, but I did like that I could do it. Theo watched me with a frown like he couldn't figure me out. Rather than walk over to the table, I bounced up to sit on the counter. His scrutiny might be a bit uncomfortable, but like his earlier puzzlement, it didn't bother me.

But after a bit of a prolonged silence, I canted my head. "Is something wrong?" Because he had Levi waiting out there for his game and he was just standing here.

"No," he said quickly. Almost too quickly. Then he frowned. "Why are you hard to talk to?"

"I didn't know I was difficult to talk to." I shrugged. "You're still getting to know me so that might be it."

"But you're my sister." He formed the pair of syllables like he was examining them, trying to understand what they meant.

"Milo is our brother," I pointed out and the lines around his mouth tightened. "It's okay if you don't like him right now, I didn't like him much the first time I met him as an adult either."

The swift anger melted away. "Wait... the first time *you* met him? Didn't you grow up together?"

"Nope. Our mother died and we were put into foster care. Then I was adopted, cause I was a baby, and he stayed in foster care without me. I didn't even know he existed before a couple of years ago." I shrugged. "Pissed me off so much that this big brute was trying to tell me what to do and who I could and couldn't be friends with and was so damn bossy."

Affection swirled through me.

"He was such an ass, but... he loved me. It took some getting used to and I'd been an only child for so long. Family... family was hard for me. It took Milo and me some time to work things out. But he's the best and I adore him. There isn't anything he won't do for the people he cares about. Whether you like it or not, you are in that category now."

He huffed out a hard sigh, then leaned back against the table. "I don't know."

"You don't have to know yet. You're more than welcome to be here. You're family. My baby brother." His grimace at the description made me laugh. I rather liked it. "The Vandals already think of you as one of them."

"You think they'd let me join?"

"Join?" I raised my brows.

"Be an actual Vandal, do jobs, and stuff. I know not everything you guys do is legal. Or maybe it is, but it feels like it isn't. I think I could be good at it."

Lips pursed, I studied him. "You're a little young to be going to work. You need to finish school. Take the time to enjoy it. Play games with Levi. Text Andrea. Grow up without having to look over your shoulder."

He couldn't quite suppress his flinch. I knew something about that too. "Why is everyone so invested in school?"

"Because education is important. I never got to finish. I did get a GED but that was because I was always on the road, always performing. Who I am is an aerialist and a dancer. I love to dance. I love to fly. I could go to school, and maybe someday I will. There's lots of stuff I could study."

Scrubbing his hands over his face, he went silent. I could practically feel the agitation rolling off him in vibrating waves. "I don't—I don't want to go to some private school where I have to live with other people." Those words came out so harsh, with each syllable dragged as if against his will.

That alone decided me. "You don't have to."

He blinked. "What?"

"You don't have to go to a private school or a boarding school. You can go to public school right here or we can look into homeschooling, though I hated my tutors back when I had to deal with them. We can certainly afford to interview whoever we want for the job."

The relief on his face and in his eyes was hardly manufactured. Then again, neither was the suspicion sliding into his gaze. "Why?"

"Because you said you don't want to go somewhere that reminds you of where you were held." I could ignore his flinch or wait him out. I chose the latter and when he finally met my gaze again, I nodded. "You told me what you need, and what you want. This isn't a prison, Theo. We may just be getting to know each other, but I will never force you to do something that makes you suffer."

He cut his gaze away, discomfort radiating over him.

"You have to have an education though. You have to know how to handle contracts, how to deal with people, business, and just getting through the day. You might stay here with us for the rest of your life if you want, but you're going to be really bored if you can't figure out what *you* want to do. Then there's Levi and Andrea."

That jerked his attention back to me. "What about them?"

"They are going to go to school. Maybe a boarding school, maybe not. Boarding schools are pretty normal for families like mine was and Lainey's is. You're going to miss them, but you also don't want to feel like you're left behind either."

His stare bored into me and I couldn't really tell if he was angry, sad, frightened or maybe all three. Had I pushed it too far? I wanted to be as honest as possible. It worked for me and Milo. Even when the topics were uncomfortable. I didn't hold back and neither did he.

Even when he mentioned how he was going to have sex with Lainey. Ugh. I was happy for them, but I did *not* need details. The oven timer went off and I jumped. Fortunately, I wasn't alone in reacting to the sudden noise. The smell of the pizza hit me at the same time and my stomach gurgled.

Once I had the pizzas out, I hunted up the pizza cutter. My second favorite part about cooking my own pizza.

"I don't want them to go to those schools either," he admitted after that protracted silence. "I don't want anything to happen to them."

"Trust me, those schools will be vetted and if I know Lainey, there will be security on campus for them. Discreet, but present. At least until she's reassured herself that Andrea will never go missing again."

Theo frowned. "Are you going to send security with me too?"

"Maybe." I cut his pizza first then mine. "Depends. We protect our own, Theo. You're ours."

The explosive sigh he released made my heart ache for him. I had some ideas of what his life had been like before we found him. That made my heart hurt for him. We were also trying to build bridges over the chasms between us. Fractures in the bedrock of who we should be to each other.

If he'd been with Milo or me, we'd have done everything we could to protect him. We weren't there then. We were now.

"I'm going to go tell Levi I'm going to have lunch with you." He hesitated. "If that's okay?"

"It's more than okay, but I can always take the pizza out there and watch you guys play if you want. I don't know much about the game, but I am very good at cheering players on."

Theo laughed. It was a rusty sound at first, but it came out a little more warmly by the end. "I don't mind just eating lunch, but there were new levels that came out today and a whole new area opened up..." Animation bled into him. It was like watching the sun come out on a stormy day. "It's pretty bad ass, I can show you how to play if you want to learn."

"Maybe next time." I loaded our pizzas up on plates. "Grab some sodas and let's go see this game."

The animation remained as he stared at me. It was like he was trying to decide if I was serious, and then finally he grinned. I swore it was the first time I saw a real smile on him. While he did look like our father, it wasn't King I saw when I looked at Theo. I never would either.

"Thanks, Em—" Another hesitation. "Should I call you Ivy too? I know that's what Milo calls you."

"You can call me whatever you want," I said.

"I like Em," he offered. "But Ivy feels more personal."

I didn't disagree. "Think about it, we don't have to decide anything now." I'd caught the hint of movement outside of the kitchen before I led the way out. If I were to guess, it was Freddie checking on us but leaving us to talk. He wouldn't have interrupted unless he perceived a problem. Now he'd ghosted out, looking after us in his own way.

Ten minutes later, I was ensconced on the sofa in the living room eating my pizza while Theo and Levi devastated hordes of zombies. It was bloody, vicious, and more than a little graphic.

It was also kind of funny when the guys were shit talking each other. I think I liked that part best.

CHAPTER 16

LIAM

The plan was just this side of crazy, but it was also sexy as hell. From the first time she proposed it, I'd been curious as hell to see how she would pull it off. Not *if* she could, but *how* she would. Kellan stood three feet from me, arms folded and his expression a mask of contained concern.

"She's been practicing," I reminded him. We'd segregated the warehouse to create a stable background for her target and to give her the room for mistakes. We'd also banned all the rats during her sessions, as much to keep their eyes off her while she practiced. Particularly since most of it involved her being in leotards with lots of skin on display.

While she might not care if they stared at her, she was used to performing, it was better for the rest of us and the rats' health if they didn't indulge in any wolf whistling or other behavior. Hellspawn was gorgeous, and grew more beautiful with every single day. She had all the right curves in all the right places. Her muscle definition was back and she wore a smile like some women did a ten thousand dollar diamond necklace.

Perfection.

"I get that. I've even watched her practice." The even tone Kellan used didn't betray his opinion of the practice rounds.

"She got better." The first few rounds had been... Well, painful and entertaining are not two words that should be linked as they were. I'd winced more than once and damn near laughed on far too many occasions.

"She's—something else," Kellan admitted and I heard every definition of "something else" that he didn't say aloud. I agreed with all of them. He blew out a breath. "It's not that I don't think she can do it. I know she *can,* whether it's today or tomorrow. She *will* do it."

"It's that doing it opens doors to more challenges?" I'd seen it coming on the road with her performances. I wasn't alone in that. Vaughn, Freddie, and Rome had all said variations on the same thing since the tour began. I'd been anticipating Rome getting up there with her as a partner, and that was coming with the next run of shows.

He'd been more than ready for it, but he'd waited for her to be ready. The past year had been one challenge after another for Hellspawn. From ending Bradley Sharpe to backing Milo and the others in Prague when it came to dealing with King—the world was so much better off without either of those men in it—, she'd come into herself and cemented the ties between all of us. She'd helped us as much as she'd let us help her, sometimes I thought more.

The tour? The tour was just her reclaiming another piece of her own life, making her mark. It had taken her time, sweat, and effort, but I'd watched the joy bleed back into her. Reclaiming the stage let her take back another piece they'd tried to steal from her. She was getting back every damn piece she wanted and more besides.

"She can handle it," I said when Kellan hadn't responded to the question. Hellspawn was setting up the bow and the arrows while Vaughn rechecked the targets. Freddie had claimed a seat on one of the crates with Jasper standing there, arms folded and looking like tension vibrated around him in a cloud.

Rome appeared to be perfectly relaxed. Then again, little worried my other half, particularly when she was directly in front of us. Nothing would touch her that we didn't allow the privilege and he was within arm's reach should she require anything.

"Doc is on his way," Kellan said after he pulled his phone out of his pocket.

"He had new arrivals today," I said, more stating it than asking but I glanced at Kel for his nod of confirmation. The safe houses offered shelter and protection to abused women, teens, and children. They kept Doc busy and he thrived on being able to do something. "He take Theo with him?"

Kellan nodded. Doc's schedule meant Theo didn't always get to hang with Doc as often as he wanted. It also meant we made time for him. Another reason I respected Doc's work, his devotion to it didn't take a damn thing away from any of us, not Theo, not Hellspawn, hell not Freddie.

It was also why I was more than happy to invest. I had my accountants already setting up a cash stream so Doc could access it at his discretion. Not everyone could do the work he did. So it was better to make sure he had all the resources at his disposal.

"He'll be here," I said, then folded my arms as I fought the urge to go over and sweep Hellspawn up and steal her away for the night. We were all giving her and Freddie a lot of space for the dance they were doing. Didn't mean I didn't *want* the time with her too, but I could be patient. Freddie *needed* her attention and fuck knew, I wanted it to work for them.

"Yep," Kellan said, tucking the phone away. Jasper drifted over to stand on the other side of Kel.

"I know she described this, but am I the only one feeling a little tense at the moment?"

"No," I said in the same moment as Kellan. In front of us, Hellspawn was in a hand stand and she was using her *feet* to pick up the bow, along with the arrow she had set up to have it notched.

Every controlled motion elongated her legs and showed off the muscle definition in them. More, the lines of her arms stood out in sharp relief as she maneuvered on her hands. The problem was the angle. How the hell was she supposed to see her shot?

I wasn't the only one canting my head to track her movements. "She's been practicing," I repeated the earlier phrase, more as a reminder to myself than to them.

"Yeah," Jasper said, rubbing a hand over his mouth as though masking his response. "That's not really making me feel better at the moment."

"No," Kellan said slowly. Hellspawn had the bow and arrow aimed at the target.

"Clear," Vaughn said as he moved away. She had the arrow nocked, but she wasn't drawing back on the string.

"Why is she doing this again?" For some reason, sweat gathered at the back of my neck and slid down my spine. I knew all the reasons, I could tick them off easily. At the same time...

"Challenges," Kellan responded.

"Pushing herself," Jasper added.

"She's good," Freddie said and I hadn't even realized he'd drifted over to join us as she got into position. The guys weren't saying anything so I assumed this was part of the process. If she was essentially aiming at the target she didn't have to correct anymore?

There was no fucking reason to be this nervous. Hellspawn could do this. She could do any goddamn thing she set her mind to. The mental castigation only got me so far, I still held my breath when she pulled back on the string.

Without hesitation, she fired and the arrow thwocked against the target, but outside of the ring and it bounced to the floor.

"Dammit," she swore.

"Three degrees to the left," Rome told her as he crossed over to set another arrow in place for her. The whole time, she maintained her position, upside down, on her hands, back arched with her legs angled so she could grip the bow and arrow.

"Got it," she murmured, the softness of her voice underscoring her concentration. She shifted her position and it was just a gradual one. Three degrees to the left.

"Clear," Vaughn repeated.

Good plan. Make sure she knew she wasn't going to accidentally shoot one of us. The next five seconds ticked by almost endlessly as she pulled back on the string and then the arrow flew.

This time it struck the target, and inside the ring. I wasn't alone in cheering even as Jasper whistled.

"Another two degrees," was all Rome said and I shook my head. She needed a break from that angle but she took the next arrow and had it set up.

Vaughn called clear and the arrow flew. This one struck the inside ring, right on it, but still inside.

"Nailed it," Vaughn called and she lowered the bow slowly, setting it down before she rolled the rest of the way and to her feet.

Jasper had her up and swung her around. "That was amazing. You're also absolutely crazy."

Her laughter was the perfect response. Sweat soaked her face and left her hair damp. She hugged Jasper and locked gazes with me over his shoulder.

"Looking good, Hellspawn." The compliment only made her smile widen.

"Water break," Vaughn said. "Then we'll reset."

"Her arms are going to fall off," Kellan muttered as Jasper rejoined us. I wasn't so sure about that, currently Hellspawn fisted a bottle of water and she didn't even show a sign of trembling.

"She can handle it," Freddie said, absolute confidence underscoring every word. "Touring with her taught me a lot."

He had all of our attention.

"She doesn't quit and she has endurance for days. The harder something is, the more she'll push. Each time I think it's too much, she proves to me it isn't." He shrugged. "It's wild."

Frankly, I couldn't argue with that. "Once we got into self-defense training, she was a lot like that too." Get past her reserve and she was tenacious as hell.

"I don't know why any of us would be shocked by that," Jasper said, his tone far more self-deprecating than judgmental. "If she wasn't this stubborn, she wouldn't have survived."

"You guys doing okay?" she called as she swung her arms and stretched them a little while pacing around her mark. She tapped a spot on the floor and Rome moved to add a small X with the chalk.

"We're doing just fine, Sparrow," Kellan told her. "Enjoying the view."

She grinned.

"I like an easy audience."

"Keep it up, Hellspawn," I teased her and earned another of her laughs.

Rome said something to her and she turned to him.

"Can I ask you guys something?" Freddie said, shifting to face us rather than Hellspawn.

"What's up?" Jasper asked, taking point like he always did with Freddie. The bond between the pair had always made Jasper a natural for Freddie to reach out to when he was in trouble.

Instead of answering immediately, Freddie glanced over his shoulder to where Hellspawn was counting off the paces between her mark and the target.

"I... Just, you know Boo-Boo and I are dating?"

"Yep," Jasper said easily. When Freddie glanced at Kellan and me, though, we both nodded. The dating had become a little more formal, but they were spending dedicated time together.

Freddie didn't follow-up his question with anything more. Worry raked its claws across my belly. The past few months had been good for Freddie. The time on the road, he'd been sleeping better. He wasn't using, maintaining his sobriety seemed to be working and he just—seemed happier.

He was, right?

"Going again," Hellspawn called. "Going to nail it on the first shot."

"You can do it," Freddie replied immediately. "You got this, Boo-Boo. Or you know, you could always do strip shooting, lose a piece of clothing for each arrow that doesn't land."

I snorted. Jasper groaned, but Kellan just shook his head.

"You wish," was all she said before she rolled back up into her handstand. There was just something deeply sexy about how aware of her body she was and how much control she could exhibit.

"I want to do more with Boo-Boo than just date," Freddie said abruptly, his voice pitched low and his attention on us. "I want... I want a real relationship. Like you guys have. I want to be able to have sex with her and not freak out."

"Have you freaked out?" I didn't think he had, but I still wanted to ask.

Freddie frowned. "No, but we also haven't done as much as I would like...I mean..."

None of us prompted him. We let him sort it out. This was not a conversation he needed to worry about having, no matter how long it took him.

"Clear!" Vaughn said, though his attention was divided between us and Em. I had to wonder if Freddie had already had this conversation with them.

It was possible.

"She's been teaching me to dance." Freddie wasn't looking at us. "It means she touches me and I touch her."

Made sense.

"How is that going?" Damn, sometimes I forgot how easy Jasper could be and how gentle.

"Good, I think." Freddie paused, then shook his head. "No, I know it's good. Sometimes it feels like my chest is gonna explode, but she always seems to know and backs off."

She probably did know. Her reaction the first time I'd teased her ass. Yeah, she had her own triggers. Her own wounds to heal.

"I hate that she knows and at the same time..." Freddie blew out a breath. "I'm so goddamn grateful for her."

"Agreed," I echoed the same sentiment as Kellan and Jasper. Then, Hellspawn fired and the arrow landed inside the second ring, but it thwocked into the target neatly.

I put two fingers to my lips and wolf-whistled. She laughed but Rome was already bringing her another arrow.

"How do I know though?" Freddie said abruptly, facing

us. "Like dancing is great. Touching her is great, but—how do I know when I'll be okay with the touching and the naked?"

None of us could answer that. None of us had Freddie's experiences. The fact it happened to him long before we'd ever known him didn't make me hate what happened to him any less. Or wish we'd been introduced sooner.

I'd love a list of names. I'd love to scratch them off.

"Shrike," I said when Kellan and Jasper both seemed to be taking their time. "The only one who can answer that is you. But the one piece of advice I can give you is trust her. No matter how fast or slow you want to go, let her be your partner. She can do it." Then because I needed the reminder as much as they did, even as she let the second arrow fly and it hit the bullseye. "She's a hell of a lot tougher than she looks."

"I know she is," Freddie said before he whistled and applauded. But instead of taking a break, Hellspawn had Rome bring her another arrow.

We were going to be here all night.

It was fine, nowhere else I'd rather be.

CHAPTER 17

FREDDIE

"Are you serious?" I could not have heard that correctly, but Boo-Boo just grinned at me.

"Yes, I'm serious. I told you about the water jet that Rome took me on." At the moment, she was going through different items she'd had delivered today. There were batons and boots. Some of it looked like costumes, but...

"You want to set yourself on fire?" How was I supposed to wrap my head around that?

Pivoting, Boo-Boo faced me. "Yes." Then she tilted her head to the side before adding, "And no."

"Thanks for clearing that up for me." I folded my arms as I stared at her. It kept me from indulging in my urge to take the stuff out of her hands until she explained this to me.

"I want to fire dance," she said. "It's not about setting myself on fire, it's about dancing *with* the fire. While I get that it probably sounds like a lot, if you do it properly, it's very safe."

Eyes narrowed, I studied her. Was she yanking my chain right now? "Most of the things you do have to be done properly, but if you make a mistake with fire—you get burned."

"Yes." The response wasn't flippant nor was she ignoring me. She set the boots and baton aside before closing the distance between us. "Freddie, if I miss a twist or I lose my grip on the silks, I can fall. I'll get hurt that way too."

"Except you know how to fall," I said, not that I cared for the idea that much. She rarely used a net when she practiced or performed. The stronger and more confident she became, the less inclined she was to ask for the net, even when testing a new routine. "Then again, depending on how high you are…"

"Exactly," she said, then held her hands out to me. I gripped her hands in mine. "Freddie, I get it, all the new routines are a little scary. The bow and arrow is still a little clunky. I need to work on that. But the fire dance? That could add a little magic to the performances. I wouldn't want to do it inside, probably safer to reserve it for outdoor performances."

"You don't do many of those." I squeezed her hands. I couldn't quite shake the nightmare of her getting burned or worse, actually catching on fire. "Have you actually talked to the others? Doc?"

Maybe throwing Doc out there was a bit of a low blow.

No, definitely a low blow.

"Fuck, sorry, Boo-Boo."

"You don't have to be sorry," she said, tightening her grip on my hands. "I will talk to all of them but first, I need to know if it's even doable. Sully and I discussed this a few times and he reached out to some other fire dancers for ideas."

"Wait, so what are we practicing if you don't know how to do it?"

"Well, I wanted to start with twirling the fire baton for the heat and before you yell—" She let go of me and raised a hand as if asking for patience. After retrieving the baton, she held it up. "I want to practice with the baton, then the ribbons. Once I have those down, I add fire."

"Then you add the fire." I sounded like a parrot, yet I was rubbing a hand over my face. "Boo-Boo, you remember that I'm the red hot mess in this relationship, right?"

Her wide smile didn't settle my heart down nor did the way her eyes softened. "Trust me?"

The guys were going to kill me.

"What do you need me to do?"

A week later...

"The whole block?" This was about more than just adding new challenges to the shows. Rehearsals for the next leg would begin in just a couple of weeks. Vaughn, Rome, and I had sat in on her video call with Sully. I wasn't sure who seemed more stunned by the long list of changes she wanted to the routines.

No, correction, Sully was definitely the most stunned. We'd at least had front row seats to what she was planning and practicing. But now? She wanted to buy this whole block?

"Yes," she said, pivoting to face me. "I know it's a lot. Okay, it's really a lot. But I'm pretty sure I can afford it and I want to do something good with the money."

All of my earlier objections blew away as I stared at her. "Boo-Boo, you didn't do anything wrong."

"But the Sharpes did. I was a Sharpe for a very long time."

Old pain and darkness coated those words. "I know that I was a Hardigan, and that I was adopted. That I had no choice in who raised me."

"Who abused you."

She sighed. "Yes, who abused me. That I can say that aloud without fear of reprisal is a good thing, but at the end of the day, I wanted to be proud of being Emersyn Sharpe. Even when I was hiding all the ugliness."

"That's not your fault," I protested. "Boo-Boo, your uncle was the monster. Your father was a weak, spineless man who deserved so much worse than we did. Your mother—" Here, I hesitated. We knew the story, we knew she'd also *suffered*. But she'd left Boo-Boo with that monster even knowing what he was capable of.

Maybe Boo-Boo could forgive her. I wouldn't.

"I know what she did," Boo-Boo said with a sigh, arms folded as she hugged herself. I hated being the one who made her defensive. "But that's the thing, all of that money, all of those holdings—Liam has been cleaning them up, from the money to the companies, to everything, but nothing erases where it came from."

"You don't want it."

She shook her head. "Liam took control of all of it because he thought someday I might want it. He's made me learn about it because he never wants me to be dependent on anyone. Just like he taught me to fight or Kellan taught me to shoot and drive, and you taught me how to use a knife."

"We want you safe." No arguments. Even if she couldn't win every fight, we wanted her to be able to survive long enough for us to get there if we weren't already.

"You also want me to *feel* safe." The emphasis on the verbiage had emotion clawing at my throat. "All of you do that for me. You make me feel safe being who I need to be, whether it's taking my show on the road, doing stunts that terrify you—"

I frowned but the way her lips quirked promised it wasn't a complaint.

"You let me be me, even when I'm trying to figure out who that person is or can be. Maybe especially when I'm evolving." She turned to look down the length of the block. The buildings were decrepit, old trash, leaves, and broken bottles cluttered the gutters.

Beyond the tagging on the doors and the broken windows, there was just an air of sadness. Sagging roofs, and crumbling facades as well as cracked pavement with grass fighting its way up to split it further were all testaments to the abandoned area's decline.

Hardly something new in Braxton Harbor. Sadly, more and more of it was beginning to look like this.

Sliding an arm over her shoulders, I tilted my head to meet her gaze. When she leaned into me, some of the tension in both of us eased. "You want to evolve with this particular block?"

"Maybe," she answered, not dismissing the question. Instead, she just leaned her head against my shoulder. "Braxton Harbor is my home. It's *our* home. I want to give back to it."

"Okay... still think that buying a block might be overkill."

She lifted her shoulders in a suggestion of a shrug. "Maybe it is. But then—it wouldn't be taking a risk, if it wasn't?"

"Boo-Boo?" I frowned down at her. "Tell me something?"

"Anything. What do you want to know?"

"The stunts, the new routines, the dancing with fire..." I wasn't sure my heart was really ready for that to become a regular reality, like ever. "Now buying this block... Why? Why now? Why push so hard on so many different things?"

I wanted to understand.

"Is there something else wrong?" I got a little crazy when I was using, but I didn't think that was an issue here. She didn't have the problems with drugs I had. Though she'd admitted to using at one point, not in a long time and I didn't think her life meant she needed to run from anything.

What the fuck had I missed?

Boo-Boo turned toward me, and pressed a hand to my chest. The nearness used to make sweat prickle along the back of my neck. It still made my heart race, but not from fear. I liked the way she felt against me. The softness and the curves. I liked even more that she would lean on me like I could take care of her and wasn't the one who needed fixing.

"Freddie." There was just a way about how she said my name. "You've been pushing yourself to step outside of your comfort zone. You are taking new risks with me every single day. Kisses... which I really like by the way—" the swiftness of her smile and the warmth blossoming in her eyes sent a wave of raw affection through me. "—the dancing, the cuddling, even letting me rub your back a couple of days ago."

My back had been sore from something, hell I didn't even remember why and she'd scooted over on the sofa to sit right behind me. I was damn near a puddle when I realized she'd started relieving the knots in my spine and slid past every single defense I had.

The moment that occurred to me though, I'd tensed and she'd backed off. No comments or complaints. She would have moved away, but then I'd leaned against her leg and she'd stayed there for the rest of the movie.

"You're taking risks because I am?" Wonder unfurled in me. "You don't have to do that... Boo-Boo you took all the risks when you told me what happened to you. When you asked the guys to push you, you were amazing... I want to be *more* like you."

A shyness crept into her eyes as she ducked her chin. It was a shyness I'd never seen before. "And I want to be more like you."

CHAPTER 18

EMERSYN

$\mathcal{A}$ ll too soon, our break was over, and we were back on the road. Unlike the first weeks of the tour, this relaunch seemed to pulse with its own energy. The other members of the company had shown up for the introduction of new material. Their enthusiasm had been immediate and right in the forefront for our first round of rehearsals.

The fire dance was still out—for now— I wanted more time to work on it and practice. Maybe for something special near the end of the tour. Rome and I had worked out a full set that he could join me on right in the middle of the show, then he would retreat and come back out for the grand finale.

While one of our dances had originally been choreographed with Eric in mind, we'd amended it until the only person I thought of on that stage with me *was* Rome. The Vandals had shown up for debut night for the new tour. All of them, and Milo too. Theo had even been out there in the audience.

Theo seemed to be the only one who really was captivated by all the stage lights and sounds. More because he couldn't fathom this life. Well, that and probably all the boobs on display when he'd come backstage after the show. Mickey and Milo kept him moving though.

The next ten weeks passed in a blur of activity, including two trips home. One to sign off on the paperwork for the block purchases and renovations. A second to let Vaughn talk to the contractors about what he wanted in his shop.

The fact he was ready to open a studio again was everything. Everyone healed differently and at different rates. Still, the best part of our family and my guys, we were all committed to supporting each other.

SIX MONTHS LATER...

It was spring again in Braxton Harbor, the cold wintry weather gave way to the cold, rainy spring. I loved it. My birthday had been a wonderful celebration with all my guys. Even Freddie pushed himself. We discovered new layers of intimacy, though he hadn't been able to get as far as he'd wanted.

Still, further than we'd managed before and every inch he stole back for himself was a *win*. The weather had been raining on and off, so I took the car to the dance school rather than walk. I had hired two new instructors and they would be starting over the next two weeks.

We'd been discussing another tour but I didn't want to leave my kids without their classes. In addition to background checks and vetting, Jasper had the rats follow the teachers for weeks in their normal lives to make sure they weren't hiding anything.

Honestly, if it were about anything else, I might think it was overkill. In this case, however, it was about my dance kids and I didn't want anything to touch them. The school was a safe space for them and I intended to make sure it stayed that way.

Freddie leaned against the front door of the school waiting for me when I pulled in. He had his hair pulled back into a leather tie. The look was equal parts casual and fierce. He straightened as I climbed out of the car.

"Hey there, good looking," he said with a slow smile. "Are you busy?"

"I could be," I said, bumping the door closed with my hip before locking it. "But I have to warn you that I have a boyfriend or two. They don't always like when guys try to pick me up."

"One or two?" He scoffed. "I can handle one or two."

Chuckling, I headed toward him. "Can you handle seven?"

"Seven?" He pressed a hand against his chest. "You need seven boyfriends?"

"Absolutely," I said, pushing up on my toes to meet him as he dipped his head for a light kiss. "Need, adore, and want, every single day."

He grinned. "Fine, fine. I can take a hint."

Snorting, I nudged him to the side as I used my keys to unlock the door. "Good. Because I expect an ice cream date on our first sunny day."

It took him a beat and then he laughed. "Yes, you're right. I did lose the last game of pool." He followed me inside. "But I forgot we bet on ice cream."

"We didn't," I said as I entered the code to disarm the system. "I just decided right now you owe me ice cream on a date."

Still chuckling, he followed me in and swept the place with a look. I let him prowl through. The dance school wasn't huge. We had three dance rooms, a dressing room, a storage area, and a bathroom. There were also lockers up here in the front for the kids to store their stuff when they came for class.

While Freddie did his sweep, I settled in behind the desk and booted up the computer. I wanted to print out the schedules before the new instructors got here. Once we went over everything, I'd be here with them to facilitate the meeting of the classes and to get the kids used to the new faces.

I'd been split on hiring new teachers, but I also enjoyed the touring and the guys were wildly supportive of it. I liked being able to dedicate the time to fund raising, and to giving new dancers and performers their first break.

"All clear," Freddie said as he wandered back into the front.

"Thank you for checking." As the pages printed off with the class rosters and schedules, I glanced at him. "You okay?"

There was a nervous, kind of jittery energy around him despite the playfulness from earlier. "I am," he said, doing a little drum against the countertop. When I raised my eyebrows, he blew out a breath and grinned. "I really am, Boo-Boo, I promise. I just… I have an idea and I've been kind of stuck on the idea for a while."

"Okay," I said, stapling the two sets of pages into separate sets before focusing on him. The stapler at the school was a duplicate of my stapler, and a gift from Freddie. The corner of his mouth kicked up when he saw me use it. "Do you need to talk to me about it?"

Need. Not want. Sometimes we could want to say every-thing and still not get the words out. Need, however, need meant we had to find a way and sometimes we could use help to get there.

He paced away from the desk and then back again before he stripped off his leather jacket. The black t-shirt he wore was untucked from the similarly dark jeans. He cut a nice figure. I'd noticed the muscle he'd been putting on the past few weeks, but he hadn't brought it up so I left it alone.

"When we were on the tour," he said, halting his pacing and focusing on me. "I scored."

My stomach bottomed out.

"There was a guy selling outside the venue, and it had been a tough week. It—you know, that part doesn't matter. Every day can be a tough day, I don't want to make excuses for myself. I got the drugs, paid for them from the petty cash I was keeping in case you wanted coffee or a fast sugar hit from donuts."

His smile was a little sickly.

"I didn't plan it, but it was there and I had the opportunity and I just…" He spread his hands and my heart broke for just how miserable he looked. "I flushed it down the toilet before the show was over that night."

Relief spilled through me and it took everything I had not to blow out that ragged breath. Freddie needed to tell me so I needed to listen.

"I told Vaughn," he said, then raised a hand. "Don't get mad at him for not telling you. I begged him not to."

"The week you came back here, when Liam came to hang out at the show with us. You said Jasper needed you here."

Had they all been in on it? Of course they would be and that was fine, they were his brothers, his friends, and his family.

"Yes." He grimaced. "I needed to talk to Doc and to Jas and to just… I needed to level out because even though I flushed it, I was back to thinking about it and I didn't want to slip,

Boo-Boo." He planted his hands on the counter and leaned forward. "I never want to slip."

"I know," I said, accepting him at his word.

"I almost did." He pushed off the counter and paced around the room. "The guys have wanted me to go to rehab for years, but…"

I made a face. Rehab was far too much like Pinetree. Far too much like the places that had hurt him before.

"Exactly," he said, meeting my gaze. "Doc has been great. All of the guys have been. When I need to talk to them, all I have to do is pick up the phone. I've gone to a few of Doc's support group meetings with some of his rescues."

Rescues. I hated that term and at the same time, it fit.

"I don't always say anything, I just sit in and I listen. I listen to their stories and… they resonate, you know?" Hands on his hips, he ceased his pacing and stared at the toes of his shoes. "When you came to me about the boys in your dance class a few weeks back, I made the time to talk to them. What I didn't tell you was that it scared the shit out of me to do it."

I opened my mouth, but Freddie held up a hand.

"Let me finish and whatever you do, don't blame yourself. I wanted to help you. I wanted to help them. But, I mean look at me, some days it feels like I can barely help myself. How was I supposed to help them?"

It took everything I had to not respond and to let him tell me in his own way. That was how it worked with us, we let each other slide on little things, but never the big ones.

Never when we needed to be heard.

"Thank you," he said in an almost hushed whisper. Steeling himself with a deep breath, he focused on me. "You asking me for help was a big step to me. Me *wanting* to help was another big step. At the end of the day, when I was standing in front of those guys, all I could do was talk to them the way I wished someone had spoken to me. Only…"

My nerves were stretched taut, but I bit down on the inside of my lip and said nothing.

"Only the words wouldn't come. Then I remembered Ms. Stephanie and how she would just sit down next to me and be there. She'd ask, but she didn't push. If I didn't want to talk, she'd say that was okay, she could just hang out with me."

Tears burned behind my eyes at the depth of emotion in his voice. The longing and the affection.

"She used to make me crazy. Why wouldn't she just go away? But she never gave up on me. Jasper was the same, but you know how Jasper is. He's aggressive in looking after you."

We shared a smile. He wasn't wrong. Jasper could be very aggressive in his need to protect us. "We love him for it."

"Yes," Freddie said with a nod. "We do. But Ms. Stephanie was different. She never gave up, but she never crowded me. She never *forced* anything from me. If I confided in her, it was always my choice and until that moment, standing in front of those kids, I hadn't realized it. I hadn't *understood* how much power she gave back to me every single time."

Or how much it meant to him. I swallowed around the lump of emotion in my throat.

"So, I leaned on Ms. Stephanie and I listened with my head and my heart, just like she did. I asked the kids, neither were really ready to talk. So I just hung out, I was just there. It took them some time to trust me, and you know, that was okay. I played basketball with them at the court down the street. It wasn't a fast process, but they came around and then they told me what was happening. They told me so I could help."

The wonder trickled back into Freddie's voice.

"Me, Boo-Boo. But more importantly, *them.* It took me so

long to really hear what Ms. Stephanie had been telling me forever, but I heard her and I was able to do that for them."

He scrubbed a hand over his face, as if suddenly becoming aware of the tears on his cheeks.

"I know you're planning to go back on the road. I said I would go, but I don't think I can be there full time, not this time."

"Okay," I said, accepting that immediately. If Freddie needed anything...

"What I mean is, I'm going to enroll in school. There's a social work program offered at the state university. I want to help kids. I want to do for them what Ms. Stephanie did for me. I want... Sobriety is always going to be a lifelong fight, but I can do that and I can help others too."

I pushed the chair back and circled the desk as he tracked my movements.

"I still want to be there with you too, but classes might take up a lot of time."

"Please say I can hug you," I said as I closed the distance. He answered by opening his arms and I practically threw myself at him.

"Is that okay with you?" The question came out in a hushed whisper. "I know I said I would always be there, but I want to do this too."

"Freddie," I said, pulling back only far enough to meet his gaze and I didn't try to slow my own tears. "It's more than okay. If you want it, then I want it for you. I want to support you, and if that means classes, or study buddies, or nude pics to encourage you when I'm out of town—you got it."

"Boo-Boo, I love you," he said, then canted his head to the side. "Nude pics for only when you're out of town?"

I burst out laughing. "Maybe you get something special for starting a new challenge."

"Oh, I like incentives," he said, then lowered me to my feet. "I haven't told the guys yet."

My heart fisted.

"I wanted to tell you first."

"Thank you for telling me," I said. "I can be there when you tell them or you can just do it, but I guarantee you they are going to want to support you."

Freddie sniffled and then laughed. "Liam's probably going to want to send me to some fancy school."

"Probably, but you should let him pay for part of it, even if you want to earn your own way." He'd earned money on the tour, not that I think he'd ever touched it. But they all had, the tour had paid them for their time. "He likes being your big brother."

Pressing his forehead to mine, he sighed. "I know he does. It's kind of funny when he and Jas argue about who is the best."

Yes, it was. Even more so because it showed Freddie how much they loved him.

"When do you want to start?"

CHAPTER 19

EMERSYN

*W*aiting until after I spoke to the new instructors and went over the class schedules with them, as well as student assessments, just added an edge to my own impatience. Freddie's news was incredible. I couldn't remember the last time he said he *wanted* something for himself.

As soon as we wrapped though, he climbed into the passenger seat of the car while I drove us back to the club-house. I'd sent a message to the guys earlier and asked for family dinner tonight. There would be some schedule juggling, but they all said they would be there.

"Theo might be there too," I reminded Freddie. "I can take him out for dinner if you need the time." It would mean not being there for the discussion, but I didn't want Freddie to be remotely uncomfortable.

"I don't care if the kid is there," Freddie said. "I kind of like the punk."

The punk.

The description fit Theo so much.

"For once, I'm not the youngest and I actually get to give someone else advice." He shrugged. "He's family."

I was going to poke him about not being the youngest when I was there either, but I loved that description. Theo had become something of a baby brother to all of them.

He played tough so much. We got it, all of us. I saw it in Mickey's eyes and in Jasper's. None of us got to be kids. Maybe our experiences were different, but we recognized it in each other. So, if Theo needed to play tough, we could support it.

But he *deserved* to be a kid too. He deserved those days in the sun. If I did nothing else, I was going to make sure he got that. Seeing the smile in Milo's eyes now, and the difference in him since I'd first met him?

I wanted that for Theo too.

"Hey," Freddie said, settling his hand on my thigh as we idled at the traffic light. "My turn. You okay?"

"Worrying," I admitted.

"About me?"

"No. I mean, yes. I always worry about you guys, but not specifically about *you*. Not right now." I blew out a breath as the light changed and I put my foot down on the accelerator. I loved the car. I loved the freedom of driving myself. Didn't mean I didn't love riding with them too. Like now. "Truthfully, I hate that you felt the need to score. At the same time, I am so damn proud of you for flushing it and reaching out for help."

He gave my leg a squeeze. "Thank you. So if not us, what are you worrying about?"

"Theo. The tour. What comes next. How to hold onto all of this." The words tumbled out of me. "It feels like this has been our normal for so short a time and I'm *happy*, Freddie.

Really happy. I want to keep being happy with you guys and I want you to be happy."

"You're worried it's going to slip through your fingers?" He stroked a slow circle with his thumb against my leg.

"Yes," I said, shaking my head. "I know it's stupid but…"

"It's not stupid, Boo-Boo. We don't take being happy for granted. We don't take having the people we want around us for granted either. Honestly, I don't think we take anything for granted."

When I glanced at him, I found him watching me, head against the seat. "No, we don't." I had to agree. "I never want to take it for granted either."

"You won't," he said. "In fact, right now, we're making a pact. Neither of us will take it for granted. If you think I'm slipping, I expect you to poke me."

"Well, the same goes for you if you see me doing it."

"Deal."

The offer, and the agreement, helped. It helped tremendously. Liam was just climbing off his bike as I pulled into the garage. Kellan and Jasper were there and Mickey was right behind me. We were all arriving at the same time.

Laughter bubbled up through me as Jasper strode over to open my driver's side door before I'd barely parked. He unsnapped my seatbelt and tugged me out for a hug.

"Called it," he said. "I win. She's mine."

Liam snorted. "Five bucks on Hellspawn."

"Ten," Freddie called as he climbed out. "Boo-Boo has skills."

"Hush," I told them, but the warmth of having them there was like a balm for my soul. I never realized how much they insulated me until they were all around me. I dropped a kiss on Jasper's lips before he passed me over to Kellan. Then it was a round of kisses, one from Kel, then Liam, and Mickey.

Vaughn, Rome, and Theo were inside with the stacks of

pizza, garlic bread, and sticky cinnamon treats. Theo made a face when Rome and then Vaughn gave me kisses. Despite the PDAs, he hadn't really asked me anything about it and I was fine with not explaining.

It just sounded like a wildly uncomfortable conversation to have. Probably better if the guys addressed it all around, though it wasn't until I was settled with pizza on a plate in my lap that I realized that half of Theo's face was blue, not bright blue but like he'd scrubbed a lot of it off but his skin was still stained blue, blue.

"Did you fall into the paint or something?"

Rome chuckled, the pure merriment a magical enough sound despite Theo's grumbling.

"Translation," Liam said. "Theo didn't listen to Rome."

"Not true," Theo argued. "I did listen."

"Not immediately," Rome said. "Or you wouldn't be blue."

Laughter rippled around the room. Theo made a face, but he seemed more flushed from embarrassment than any real discomfort. The humor reflected in his eyes and he shot me a grin. "I paid attention after," he said. "I promise."

I wasn't the only one who snuck a look toward Rome who only shrugged. Jasper eyed Liam who chuckled. "Translation, eventually."

More laughter and I shook my head. "Will you listen to him in the future?"

It was Theo's turn to lift his shoulders and Freddie piped in with, "Translation: *theo*-retically."

I almost inhaled my pizza. Kellan had to pat my back when I choked on the cheese. Rome high-fived Freddie and even Theo grinned widely.

"Children," Jasper said, wiping away an imaginary tear. "They do us proud."

Freddie answered him with a single middle finger, but the air of mirth remained. I indulged in a soda in between bites of pizza as the conversation shifted from ribbing Theo to asking him about school.

Instead of arguing about classes or growing more sullen, he actually answered with some animation. We'd found a school that allowed him to do some classes remote while the hands-on subjects, including science and mechanics, required in-person classes.

"We're starting our first engine rebuild next week," he said, eyeing Kellan. "Are you still okay with me working on some of it at the shop? I'll have to bring the three others on my team." From his grimace, I wasn't sure that Theo was okay with bringing them.

"Fine by me," Kellan said. "You can't be there during closing hours, and you need me or Jasper on site while you're there."

Rome cleared his throat and Kellan gave him a look.

"You sure?"

Rome shrugged.

"Okay, so when Rome is in town, then Rome can chaperone."

"Is that a test to see if I'll listen?" The dryness in Theo's tone earned an equally dry look from Rome.

"You'll listen." He didn't even have to add an or else, because Theo just spread his hands.

"I'll listen, but thank you all. I know we're supposed to do some of the work in the shop at the tech school and that's fine for the basics, but I'd rather build the new engine in a more controlled environment."

That led to a few more questions about the style of the engine, the rpms, and more items that I really didn't understand. Mickey had a hand wrapped around my nape and had begun to massage the tension there lightly. I let my eyes fall half-closed, just enjoying the flow of conversation.

Liam and Jasper had kicked off a joint venture with the

launch of five new trucks to handle transport for the clothing stores and more. Liam had been looking to expand for a while. Between Mickey's safe houses, the reclamation projects here in the city, and Jasper growing the transport business, it seemed a good time to combine them.

"It also means we can dedicate more trucks to the tour so you don't have to shift the schedule as much," Jasper pointed out. "Unless you want to change it, and we're always fine to make it work."

"But it will be easier on everyone when *or* if you need to do it," Kellan said, then dropped a kiss on the top of my head. "I approve."

Tilting my head back, I smiled up at him. Mickey was going to knock me out at this rate. I was melting into the sofa. Kellan wasn't helping by rubbing my thigh. It was just... *nice.*

"Speaking of tours," Freddie said. "I'm going to need to step out of the next one—maybe not all of it—and I already talked to Boo-Boo about it."

"What's up?" Jasper asked as he focused on him. I caught Freddie's gaze and winked. His smile relaxed some of the tension in his face.

"I want to go to school." He leaned forward, capturing the attention of everyone. "So hear me out..."

He laid out his plan and his reasons. Mickey's hand stilled on my nape at the mention of Ms. Stephanie. It was my turn to reach for his free hand and he gripped it in return.

"I'm okay, Little Bit," he murmured, brushing a kiss to my temple. "Just a surprise—but a good one." I squeezed his hand. I was so proud of Freddie, he didn't hold back, even bringing up his near slip. While the guys had known about it, I think it was as much to confirm that he'd told me as to lay out where it fell in his reasoning.

When he finished, Freddie spread his hands.

"It's a lot, I know, but... I really want to do it. I never realized how much I was looking for something more in my life until this idea hit me. Boo-Boo asked me to talk to those kids and I couldn't think of a worse person. Then I did and it took time, but I got through to them. Maybe I won't be good at it..."

Self-doubt crept into those last words.

"You'd be good." Rome rose from where he'd been seated and flipped closed two of the empty pizza boxes. "I would talk to you too."

Freddie blinked, disbelief and shock vying for supremacy on his expression.

"What he said," Vaughn agreed as he stretched. "What do you need? Like—school wise? Besides the downtime, which I'm sure Dove already approved enthusiastically." He grinned at me and I answered with a smile of my own.

"Absolutely, in fact I'd sign up and go to school with you if you wanted." Granted, I'd been out of schools completely since I was eight and all of my education came through tutors.

"Hmm... do you have a list of schools?" Liam asked, his phone out. "We need to find the best options for you, particularly if you don't want to head out of state or live near the campus in another state."

"No," Freddie said, swiftly. "The state U here has a social work degree."

"That's a good start," Mickey said. "Once you get licensed, there's always continuing education courses, and some of those are online as well. But a lot of what you need to know you do, this would be more about expanding your knowledge base."

"State U here has entry requirements. Assessment tests..." I could practically hear Liam's thoughts whirling.

"I hate tests," Freddie admitted. "Hopefully that's not a sticking point."

"I can help," Theo offered and I flicked a look to where he was leaning forward. "Like you guys did with me. Turns out I'm really good at testing strategies. According to Ms. Franklin at the center, she said I have a good way of approaching them. So if you want, I can walk you through it to see if it helps."

"If you don't mind," Freddie said. "I heard they had classes on how to study, probably something I should consider too."

"Yeah, that shit was annoying," Theo muttered, but at Jasper's side eye, he raised his hands. "I said it was annoying, not that it wasn't useful."

"Better," Jasper said, then looked at Freddie. "Whatever you need."

"Well, it's going to cost—" Freddie started and it was his turn to swallow his words as Liam glanced at him. "Liam, you can't pay for all of it."

"Why not?" He raised his eyebrows.

"Because…" Freddie spread his hands. "I have to do some of this on my own."

"Why?" Kellan asked, not an ounce of judgment in his voice.

"You have to do the classes," Mickey said. "You'll have to take the tests, do the work, and make the time to study. You'll have to face your own demons on the way. All of that is something you have to do. Why can't we help you pay for it?"

Freddie seemed at a total loss.

"When Milo went to law school, he used loans and we pooled resources. We did that to buy the first truck," Jasper said. "We did it again every time we expanded here at the warehouse—whether it was the business or the clubhouse itself."

"Same with my investment at the first shop," Vaughn

added. "Kel at the mechanic's shop, he needed to get certified and trained. We've always pooled resources."

As if seeking help, Freddie looked at me and I smiled. "I want to help with anything you need, and if that means making sure you have no school loans to worry about? Then why can't we do that? You're the only one who can do this for you Freddie, but we want to be a part of it. We want to be there for you—just like you guys have all been here for me."

"Basically," Liam said. "But also, you're my baby brother. You want to go to school, you get to go to school. I don't want you worrying about bills, classes, or books. That's a luxury we can afford."

"Don't fight him," Rome said. "He'll just do it anyway, then you'll fight. But it won't stop him."

Rolling his eyes, Liam stared at Rome.

His twin just shrugged. "Am I wrong?"

The silence held sway for a moment, then laughter exploded through the room.

"Fine," Freddie said, still laughing. "You guys can pay." At the same time, his eyes shone and his face was flushed. When he stole another look at me, I just grinned at him. We all wanted to help him.

Satisfaction blew through me like a desert wind, because he was going to let us.

CHAPTER 20

TEN MONTHS LATER...

EMERSYN

The Christmas tree looked fantastic in the downstairs living room. The guys had to shift the pool table over along with the new gaming system to make room for the nine-foot tree we'd picked out. We'd actually chosen several trees. One for the school, one for Vaughn's shop, another for Kellan's place, one for down here and another one for our suite upstairs.

The whole place was going to be hosed down in Christmas. Lights, decorations, and more. We were even planning a huge Christmas feast for us the night before so we could devour leftovers on Christmas Day *after* we delivered meals around the area.

We'd adopted over a dozen local families. I was excited about the fact we were going to play Santa's Vandals rather than his elves. Making the holidays about other people and making *their* wishes come true was *fantastic*. I even had a surprise planned for Theo, not that he'd asked for anything.

His first Christmas with us had been full of surprises. I hated learning that he'd never truly celebrated before. In so many ways, we'd had such radically different lives. In others? We were too much alike.

The fact we'd tried to spoil him last year hadn't gone over well. Mickey and Rome caught his discomfort, so we'd dialed it back. This year, though? I had a plan.

It started with a little ski trip that Liam was *surprising* me with, between Christmas and New Year's. Theo was going as Liam's "cover" and when we got there, Bodhi and Lainey would just happen to be there with Levi and Andrea.

I was ridiculously excited with the sneakiness of it. More because Theo *missed* his friends, but he wasn't comfortable with their lifestyle. Or at least, that was what he kept saying. I suspected it was something else, but he wasn't trusting me with more information.

Hopefully he trusted someone else. Maybe Mickey or Jasper or Freddie. Until then, I would just have to stealthily smother him with affection and make sure he got time with those he cared about in safe for *him* locations.

My phone vibrated in my pocket and I tugged it out to silence the alarm before pivoting to head upstairs. Everyone had somewhere to be tonight, even me. Though tonight was about a date and I needed to take a shower before he got here.

I'd come straight from the school and I'd actually done my own training there after the kids left for the day. Once upstairs, I grinned at our tree in here. The whole room sparkled with lights. They'd swapped out all the white fairy lights with colored ones. Then added an attachment that would shift the light colors in time to whatever music we played.

It was absolutely magical.

I paused on the way to my room and pivoted to study the

decorations. Something had... Then I saw it. Someone had wrapped the stapler and the axe in Christmas lights and tinsel.

A snort of laughter escaped me. It was absolutely ridiculous and perfect. I would have to figure out who did it later. Maybe. Then again, maybe I could just enjoy the surprise. I had a few for the guys I'd been secreting away.

I hurried into the shower, the last thing I wanted to do was be late because I was just swooning over all the decorations. Then again, it was hard not to. The guys had gone all out and I loved it so much.

With that in mind though, I got the shower going, stripped and jumped in. If I lit a fire under my ass, I could get my hair washed and blown dry before Freddie got here. I'd just ducked my hair under the water to rinse the shampoo when there was a knock on the door.

"Hey, Boo-Boo," Freddie said as the door opened. "You decent?"

"Nope," I told him cheerfully. "Hot, wet, and a little soapy at the moment."

He chuckled. "I thought I'd heard you come in."

Crap! "I didn't realize you were already back, didn't you have tests today?"

"Yep, finals were this morning. Knocked them all out and came back early." The door closed but he didn't retreat and that was fine. "Not going to lie, I'm glad they are done."

"Yeah?" I reached for the conditioner. "Do you feel good about them?" His first semester had been tough. He'd wanted to give up more than once, but the summer had been much better. Last time we'd talked about it, he'd liked the classes for the fall semester much more.

"Actually... I do." A moment later the curtain slid back and a very naked Freddie eyed me. "Mind if I join you?"

Conditioner ran into my eyes as I stared at him. The sting

had me turning into the water to rinse them and helped stop me from staring. "Not at all." Then because every daring moment should be applauded, I added, "This is new."

"I was standing out there thinking about doing it, imagining it..." The heat of his chest brushed against my back. The presence of him was just there, not quite touching but unmistakable. "I wanted to be able to just get naked and slide in here like it was normal as hell."

"So you did it." I let out a happy little sigh of satisfaction. "You just got naked and joined me."

"Yeah." A measure of disbelief rippled through his voice. Then his hands came to rest on my hips. "What do you say to a change of plans for tonight?"

His naked body against mine had me thinking about a lot of things and none of them had anything do with our original plans. Honestly, I wasn't even sure what those plans were. I tilted my head so I could look up at him.

"What did you have in mind?"

When he slid his arm around my middle and tugged me to him, I wanted to close my eyes. Freddie and I had experimented a lot over the past few months.

Blowjobs had taken a while, and he still preferred the dark for them, and I was okay with that. I'd be okay with anything that gave him pleasure.

"I was thinking," he said, nuzzling a kiss to my ear. The weight of his erection was against the seam of my ass and his hand spread over my abdomen. The act was asking me to lean on him, so I did. "I was thinking I want you to push me tonight."

"Freddie..." We had pushed it a couple of times in the past six months. The last time hadn't gone well at all. I didn't want him tearing himself up about it. Not again.

"I know," he said, resting his chin on my shoulder as he began to rub slow circles with his palm. The water left us both slick, but he was drifting down toward my cunt and then away again. It was a delicious tease, and a relaxed one. "I know what happened last time. I think I know what happened then, and I know how to face it now—or at least..."

He released such a harsh breath that I turned so I could meet his gaze. This close, it scraped my nipples against his chest. The scars on his skin were visible. Some from fights. Some from cutting. Others so old, he couldn't remember when he'd gotten them.

The scars were another reason he didn't want the lights on when I touched his cock or when I swallowed him. He didn't want me to see. "You don't have to do this," I told him. "We have all the time in the world."

"But Boo-Boo, I want *more*. I want to be able to do more with you. We've been so close so many times and I don't freak out... last time, it was because I hadn't shown you the scars."

We hadn't turned off the lights. It just hadn't occurred to me. We'd been playing and pushing, then his shirt had come off. He'd kissed me and when I ran my hands over his back, he'd frozen.

It had taken a moment for the rigidity to register, but it was too long. Too long before I'd pulled my hands away...

Freddie cupped my face in his wet palms. "Boo-Boo, it wasn't you. I know I rabbited. Not my proudest moment."

"I just never want to be what hurts you." It had been hours before he'd come back. The only thing that had kept me from going after him was Jasper's message that he'd found him.

"You weren't," Freddie said, searching my eyes. "I promise you, it was definitely me. Not you. I panicked..." The words stuttered for a moment, like his breath coming out in little hard pants.

He gripped one of my hands and pressed it to his chest, just over his heart.

"I panicked because I'd never told you about some of the scars. Then I remembered how bad some of them are and that I don't know where they came from. Especially..."

Eyes closed, he deepened his breaths as we stood under the spray of the water. Bit by bit, the wild pound of his heart began to slow to a more even tempo. When his eyes opened again, he seemed calmer.

"Been practicing breathing exercises. Learned them in one of my trauma groups."

Group sessions. He still didn't like them, but he'd discovered that they were useful. That had happened over the summer as part of one of his therapy courses and dealing with troubled youths. He'd attended at first for understanding. Then stayed because he actually learned.

"I'm still really proud of you about that," I reminded him.

His smile was sheepish and his face flushed. But that could just be the hot water in here. "I kept thinking, okay just one more and now..."

"Now you're starting to help lead them."

He lifted his shoulders. "The kids in these groups, some of them are a lot like me. They hate themselves so much. They blame themselves for everything that happened and I thought that was kind of bullshit. I mean, I didn't hate myself except..."

I raised my brows and waited.

"Except you know, I did." That confession had come a month earlier. Was it possible to be so desperately sad and happy at the same time?

Probably.

"I get it."

"I know you do," he murmured. "You're the biggest help

of all. You listen. You ask questions. But you've never judged or looked at me differently."

"You don't with me," I said. "Confession is our thing."

He chuckled. "Yeah, it is…"

"But you were saying," I pulled him back to earlier before his breathing had grown so ragged.

"You also don't let me get away with shit," he said, this time his grin was pure open joy. "A fact I deeply love, but don't tell the guys or they'll think it's something I want them to do."

I laughed as he dropped a kiss on my lips. "Stop stalling," I nudged him.

"We're having a moment here," he teased before he pressed another kiss to the corner of my mouth. "Working on having a lot more."

"Hmm-hmm. Go back to the scars, Freddie. You want to tell me something so we can push past the freaking out."

"I really do love when you get bossy, Boo-Boo." His low groan was a decadent little stroke of sound. "But, you're right." Shoulders squaring up, he locked his gaze on mine. "Especially the scars around my dick. They aren't pretty. I used to think it left me a little deformed, but it's just places I was burned or they did whatever they did."

He shrugged like it didn't matter, but we both knew better.

"I panicked because I thought it would upset you and I couldn't explain them and I hadn't said anything. Then it was just…blind panic."

When I raised my arm to show the feather decorated tattoo on the inside of my forearm, he nodded.

"Yeah, just like those. Mementos of ugly moments. Only, I can just speculate for most of them on what they are from. I've never wanted anyone else to see. Always avoided being naked around anyone else. Even the guys. When I couldn't avoid it, they always made a point to not look at me."

"It helped." That wasn't a question.

He nodded once. "It's why I could rub myself off on your ass. Or why I liked the lights off when I would feel that beautiful mouth on me. I could pretend that I was normal."

He was killing me.

"But I don't want to pretend anymore." He dropped his hands back to my hips and took a step back. "I never want to pretend with you again."

I licked my lips. "So it's okay if I look at you?"

"Please?"

CHAPTER 21

FREDDIE

My heart locked up in my chest. It wasn't physically possible to stop beating altogether, but I swore it felt like it had. The whole time I'd opened my soul to her, Boo-Boo had stood there and let me pour it out. She'd pushed only when I'd tried to distract her from the pain and the darkness.

The simple truth was, my darkness didn't scare her. As much as I wanted to protect her from it, I didn't have to. She had her own darkness. When she'd faced it down, I'd been right there with her. We'd done it together. She could handle me and mine.

I just needed to be willing to do it *with* her. Not for her. Not because of her. But *with* her, cause she wouldn't let me fall and even if I did, hell, she'd be right there to help put me back together again.

Instead of dropping her gaze to look at me immediately,

she kept her attention fixed on my face. "You have seen my eyes before," I reminded her.

"Could be that I'm just enjoying looking at you, you know," she said. With her dark hair soaked and slicked back, it highlighted her high cheekbones and the air of fragility that was always present. Everything about her was so masterfully put together, sometimes, she was so beautiful it made it hard to breathe.

Then she'd crack a joke or tease me, and she was just Boo-Boo. Ethereal, perfect, and absolutely the best.

"Could also be that you have lovely eyes," she said, pushing up on her tiptoes before she kissed my jaw. "And that I like it when you blush too."

My face went hot and I glared at her. Granted, I wasn't really annoyed but no one could make me *flush* like she did. "Enough of that, Boo-Boo. You can have fun picking on me later."

"Fine," she said, the single syllable riding out on a huff of an exasperated sigh. "I'll make sure I memorize everything about you later."

Rolling my eyes, I shook my head, but she took another step back and looked at me. Really *looked* at me. The prickle of unease shivered over my skin, but it was there and gone again. The laughter didn't give it much purchase.

"Freddie..." She pursed her lips, contemplating me for so long I thought she'd forgotten . "I'm afraid that I think you're even hotter now than I did before."

My mouth fell open for a moment, I'd been ready with a sarcastic comment. Yet, the last thing I expected her to say was the first thing that came out of her mouth.

When she made a little twirl motion with her finger, I snapped my mouth closed with a click of my teeth. She wanted me to turn around.

This is Boo-Boo.

The mental chant reminded me that I trusted Boo-Boo. She would never hurt me. Oddly enough, the unease I worried about didn't manifest at all. If anything, her playfulness entertained me. I did a little spin for her, slowing so I faced away.

There were scars on my back. Most of these I'd earned as an adult. A couple from knife fights. Another from doing a wipeout when I'd been learning to ride a motorcycle and gotten cocky.

"I'm going to touch you," she said.

"Okay." I waited for the resistance to rise up. I waited for the tension to lock up my muscles. Neither occurred.

The feather light contact of her fingers on my skin sent a ripple of goosebumps over my skin. Closing my eyes, I savored the sensation as she explored my back. It was almost like she was petting me.

Maybe she was.

Then she pressed a kiss to my shoulder. "How do you feel?" Her voice wrapped around me like a siren call, beckoning for an answer.

"Really fucking amazing," I told her, almost afraid to give voice to it and jinxing it. "I like you touching me."

"I like touching you too." She slid her hands around me and pressed her naked body against my back. I covered her hands on my stomach, aware of my dick straining. I'd been hard just thinking about her in the shower.

An erection seemed a permanent state around Boo-Boo. I was so used to it at this point, I noticed more when I didn't have one than when I did.

"Still good?" Every word was an open door to tell her what I needed. If I wanted to stop right now, she would. Fuck knew she had before and I'd left her frustrated and unsatisfied.

"Yeah," I exhaled. "Real good. I want this to last, Boo-Boo."

"Want to know a secret?"

"Hmm?"

She dipped her hands lower and she gripped the base of my cock, I closed my eyes. The slow glide of her caress had my balls dragging up and I swore I was ready to blow. So not ready to be done right now.

"We can do this as many times as we want," she murmured. "Fast or slow. Whatever you're ready for."

She was right. She was absolutely right, but I wanted *her*. I wanted to love her the way I'd imagined from the first time I'd seen that pretty pussy standing there naked, bruised, and proud.

Boo-Boo was a fighter. She was our fighter.

I covered her hand and she released me at the contact. "Out of the shower." Fucking against a shower wall sounded good. So did the counter, the floor, and even the door—but we had a bed. Boo-Boo's bed, and I wanted to do this right.

In no time she shut off the shower, and I snagged a towel to pass to her before I ran one over me. Heat raced through me and my skin was so tight. The fact my heart raced had me doing a breathing exercise.

It wasn't until I hit a full minute that I opened my eyes again. Boo-Boo stood right there, waiting. Her soft brown eyes held me captive. That air of fragility was there, vulnerable and open. It was easy to forget sometimes just how tiny she was compared to us, and she always made me feel taller, bigger, better.

"Still good?" She lifted her chin.

I cupped her cheek. "You shouldn't have to ask me that." I had my breathing under control.

"But I did ask. I'll ask for every single step we take. I want to know you're okay. I want this to be good for you."

"It already is," I promised her and when I dipped my head to kiss her, she met me halfway. The tease of her tongue against mine was an offering to a dying man in a desert. Or maybe the starving one who'd been hiding in the city forever.

Not hiding anymore.

Not hiding *again*.

The longer the kiss went on, I almost forgot the plan to move. Then she dug her nails into my shoulder, the bite of them penetrated the lust-fueled haze drowning me. I lifted my head. "Bed," I said belatedly and her smile was everything.

I had no idea which of us moved first or if we just moved together. One minute we were at the door and the next at the bed. Then I was collapsing down against her, but not falling on her. I didn't want to squash her. Then her mouth fused with mine again. When she wrapped her legs around my hips it just let me glide against her. The rocking of my hips against hers threatened to blow my load before I had my first feel of slipping inside of her.

It took effort to break the kiss and lift my head, but Boo-Boo was right there. Her lips glistened, her cheeks flushed and her eyes were dark. There was a breathlessness to her.

"One last thing...since you came here, I haven't touched another woman. Even the ones I tried to fuck before, it was always away from me. I got off, then left. I've never been a very good lover. I never wanted anyone to touch me."

She stroked her hand through my hair. "I know."

"Now I never want anyone to touch me who isn't you." I sealed that declaration with a kiss. Our hands met on my cock and I don't know which of us lined me up, but once I was there, she went still. This was for me, it was my move.

Pulling back, I raised up enough just to see her eyes. I wanted to see them as I sank into her.

"It's your turn," she whispered. "You have to push."

"Yeah," I said. "I do." As much as I meant to ease in, I surged forward and she took every inch of me. It was the sexiest, wettest, sweetest grip ever as her cunt wrapped around me.

"Oh…" Her gasp was a boon to my ego, but I didn't need that so much as I wanted to just drink in her responses. Then I was moving, the pound of my hips against hers was a wild rhythm, but she met me stroke for stroke. I braced my hands above her head.

I didn't want to send her up the bed or lose contact from her anywhere. The lightest of caresses when she slid her fingers between us and touched where I slid into her and then I recognized it. She teased her clit and her smile grew wider.

She'd meant it when she said we had all the time to get this right. Then her cunt seemed to tighten and ripple around me as the first wave of her orgasm hit. It was enough to detonate mine. My spine went liquid and my balls dragged up. I came with a shout.

It was like losing myself, I came in sharp, fast spurts and she held me in that velvet glove of her body. Then she was wrapped around me and holding me tighter. I had no idea how long we lay there, but I couldn't quite get past the wonder of it.

The wonder of her.

I buried my face against her throat as she stroked my hair and cradled me with her body. An eternity passed before I raised my head and she was right there, waiting for me.

"All the time, right?" I whispered and my voice came out rougher than I expected. "And anything?"

"Yes," she said.

A shudder went through me and I closed my eyes for a moment to savor all of this, to savor her. I was already stiffening again. I'd say it was a first, but I always had this reaction around her.

Just worked out really well for us at the moment.

"Good, okay," I said as I eased away from her. "Now I need to know everything."

"Everything?" The puzzled note in her voice made me grin.

"Yes, Boo-Boo. Everything. I want to know how you like your breasts touched and how you like to be eaten out. I want to know what turns you on and what makes you scream. Cause your next orgasm is definitely coming from me."

"That could take some time."

The lightness made me smile. "That's what I'm planning on…"

EPILOGUE

FIVE YEARS LATER...

FREDDIE

I checked my watch after I parked in front of the house. I had a welfare visit to perform. The family here was fostering two boys. Both I'd placed, and the foster parents expressed an interest in adoption, particularly because the boys were brothers and they wanted to keep them together. The Thompsons were a gift, because that was what I wanted too.

Their parents, however, were still alive. Dad in jail and Mom about to do a stint there herself. Terminating their rights would take time, but I wanted to see how the boys were doing. I'd come by weekly at first, then once a month after the first six weeks since placing them. The pair of shadows with their big bruised eyes and gaunt faces had filled in.

It was a trend I wanted to see continue. As I slid out of the car, the front door opened and a pair of whirlwinds came racing out.

"Mr. Freddie!" Ryan, the younger of the pair yelled as he raced down the walk to meet me. At five, Ryan still had a lot of fire in him. He'd come out of his shell faster. Warren, all of eight, maintained a deeper reserve. He was too used to stepping between his brother and abuse.

I got it. It was what brothers did.

"Buddy," I said, greeting Ryan as he gave me a hug. The first time I met them, Ryan wouldn't even look at me. "I keep telling you it's Freddie."

"But you're Mr. Freddie," Ryan said, looking up at me with all the trust in the world. "It's powite."

Polite. I smiled. "Politeness matters." Of course it did. "Fine, you win. Mr. Freddie it is."

"Hey, Mr. Freddie," Warren said as he reached us. "Mrs. Amy said to bring you in when you got here."

"Yeah?" I said. "How are you doing, Warren?"

"Not so bad," he told me. "Got an eighty-five on my math test."

"Hell, yes," I said, then held up a hand to high-five him. "Also, we're going to forget that I just cursed and go with a high energy enthusiastic congratulations."

Warren laughed. "It's okay, Mr. Freddie. Mrs. Amy is making cookies."

"Oh, I like cookies."

"Me too," Ryan announced, gripping my hand as I walked with them toward the front door. "Do you wanna know what I learned this week?"

"Tell me," I said. "I want to know everything."

SAVAGE VANDAL BONUS SCENES

ABSTRACTION (ALTERNATE POV)

ROME

The rubble of the playground faded as did the sounds of the cars in the distance. The grind and rattle of the unit on the roof of one of the older buildings jerked to life as their furnace kicked on. The old elementary school, or the remains of it, were less than a half-block away to the south.

I didn't look in that direction because you couldn't see it from here, anyway. After the city shut it down and started bussing kids from the neighborhood to a more affluent section, the meth heads, the deadbeats, and the squatters had moved in. We'd cleaned them out a few times. But like vermin they kept coming back...

Thoughts of the school faded away as the beach continued to take shape. The lines and cracks were rougher here, I needed to texture them more. The scent of the paint filled my nostrils, it soothed even as I switched out cans. The knots in my neck from stretching my arms up didn't really register nor did the burn in my arms.

The heat of the sun kissing the sand burned my back as I added new layers and added extra bits of detail until I uncov-

ered the shore. The moment the ocean rolled in, foamy caps—
it erased everything that had been there before. Beauty from
decay. I could never quite make it new again, but I could hide
the darkness beneath the color.

A cheap imitation?

Maybe.

My neck cracked as I took a step back. The sand had
different depths and textures. Higher up, away from the tidal
edge, I'd written Starling. I didn't want that to wash away.

"You do really good work." The starling's voice always
surprised me. It had so many different textures to it. Like the
cracked wall behind the painting. There was strength and
sturdiness, but damage had left its mark. The huskiness that
kissed the underside of her voice told me how much she
didn't use it.

Definitely not out of fear. She could and had branded
with her words. But she didn't speak. Not that it bothered
me too much. Still, it took me a moment to adjust from
focusing on the wall to focusing on her. I hadn't forgotten
she was here and yet...

"You're still here." I smiled. She could have taken off. At
any point while we were out here, she could have left. I
would have let her. Not that I wanted her to go and not that I
didn't want her safe. Jasper seemed convinced there were
more threats against her than the creature chained up in the
fridge. Liam wouldn't let me go see him. He had, but he
didn't want me in there.

I'd rather be with my starling anyway.

She gave a little shiver and I frowned. The temperature
must have fallen. The sun had moved over the buildings and
now we were in shadows. Part of why I stopped painting. We
were losing the light. "But it's cold."

I packed up my stuff on autopilot. I collected even the
empty cans. I was trying to paint over the decay and not

leave more signs of the disuse and disrepair. "You should have told me it was getting colder."

"You were the one without a shirt," she reminded me in that tone that bordered on taunting, but never quite crossed the line. Particularly since her stomach rumbled. "Even your nipples are on point." She might seem demanding to some, but there was an exactitude to her. She wanted her routines. She wanted things to be the way she expected them to be.

I couldn't fault the desire. I wanted things to be in a certain order.

But she didn't leave when she could have.

I glanced down at my chest and yes, my nipples were in sharp relief and paint spattered me. Not all that unusual. I had paint permanently on my skin in some places. I yanked on my shirt, then the hoodie and glanced at her after I had everything back in the bag.

"I've survived worse."

For a brief moment, she met my gaze and held it. I didn't like looking people in the eye. Not like this. If I did it growing up, it usually led to fights. Older kids would get pissed. Liam wasn't always there to intercept the hits.

I learned how to dish out my own.

But I didn't want to hit anything while she stared at me. "I've survived worse." For a moment, her eyes shadowed and she looked away before I did.

"So have I."

I searched for a way to ask her about what she'd survived. I didn't talk about my past. Maybe she didn't want to talk about hers. She hurried away from me though, not running. No, more like owning the cracked and broken pavement of this abandoned playground. The grace in her movements made me smile.

"You coming?" She called after she reached the top all on

her own like she'd just climbed velvet red-carpeted stairs rather than crumbling cement.

My smile widened and an inescapable feeling fluttered in my chest.

The smash of a bottle punctured it and the dark voice saying "Well, well, well, what have we here?" smothered what escaped.

The flutters turned to rage.

They didn't belong here.

They didn't belong near her.

The world turned to sharp relief of shadows and light soon to be painted with red.

DISTRACTION (BONUS POV)

LIAM

*H*aving the bed kicked to wake me up was not my favorite, particularly when I'd had less than two hours of sleep. As it was, I ignored the bullshit flying around the room and the glares they hurled at me. Fuck my life, I'd been on the go for two solid damn days and I'd had time in the ring the night before. I didn't have time for the posturing or the egos.

"Sleeping beauty didn't even notice she'd left her room, and he hadn't locked the door." Vaughn wasn't happy.

Too bad.

I shrugged and headed for the fridge for a beer. If I had to deal with all of them this fucking early in my day, then I deserved a beer.

"Where the hell is Rome?" Jasper demanded. "Why did he leave you watching her?"

Man, Jasper never changed. I kind of hoped he never did. I smirked as I pulled out the beer. "You're welcome that I came over to do a favor. I didn't have to show up, you know."

Jasper's expression had turned thunderous, and Kestrel let out an aggrieved sigh. "Where is he, Liam?"

"I didn't ask," I told them and flashed a grin at the object of Rome's obsessions. She was a lot prettier up close. A lot tougher too. Surrounded by all this angry testosterone and she didn't flinch. Rome worried about her, to the point he'd asked me to help. A request he knew I wouldn't refuse. "You don't look so fragile and scared to me."

Little vixen blew smoke in my direction and I wanted to laugh. What did Rome see that had him so concerned? Jasper, Kellan, *and* Vaughn were all glaring at me.

What the fuck ever. Rolling my head from side to side, I cracked the vertebrae and took a long slug of beer before saying, "I don't know where he had to go. Just said he had something he was working on. Man, you know how he gets when he has a project. He said the squirrel didn't do much and I just needed to be on hand until you got back. I was fucking tired, so I slept."

The squirrel comment just rolled off her but she still flicked her gaze to me like she was trying to figure me out. Good luck with that one, princess. Oddly enough, the last appellation fit her. She was a princess, regal even while she bled down the inside of her leg.

Maybe it was being too hyped up from the fights, but you couldn't miss the distinctive copper note in the air and I knocked back more beer. And these three hardasses were too busy glaring at me to notice.

Fuckers.

"Vaughn..." Jasper started.

"No. I am not going to look for him. If Liam doesn't know where he is, I'm not wasting hours hunting all over town. I have appointments booked all afternoon. I'm eating, then I'm out of here."

Never said I didn't know where he was. Just said I didn't ask or where he had to go—you know later. Absolute and total semantics. They were too distracted to notice.

"Don't look at me," Kestrel said. "I've got Sparrow duty."

"Sparrow?" I snorted. "She's not a sparrow." I took the opportunity to study her, openly, and maybe to tweak the rest of them a little. But she was obviously uncomfortable even if she'd done a damn good job of hiding it so far. "You're quiet, but you're tough. Or you wouldn't be sitting there bleeding without an ounce of complaint."

Jasper jerked to his feet. "What the fuck do you mean she's bleeding?"

Kestrel yanked her chair around, and Vaughn shoved me to the side to get to her. And just like that, they forgot all about me and I settled in to watch. The guys were crazy for her and that made a certain amount of sense. In some ways, she was the missing piece.

In others, this was not the place for her. She shouldn't even be inside this warehouse much less the clubhouse. Vaughn took off to grab Doc as Jasper and Kellan asked her questions.

She got her period. It was hardly the first time any of us saw period blood, but you'd think she'd been shot. I downed another swallow of beer as the chaos surrounding her pulled them in.

Emersyn Sharpe was a serious damn distraction. Serious enough, they forgot I was here. Serious enough that Jasper was snapping at Doc, Kellan looked like he wanted to punch Jasper, and Vaughn stared at her like she hung the moon.

Rome would die for her. All of them would.

But she was a distraction none of us could afford, least of all my brother.

And he'd *asked* me to be here.

Asked for my assistance. Rome never had to ask me for a damn thing. There wasn't anything I wouldn't give him. He didn't have to ask me for this, either. Doc, Jasper, and Emersyn headed upstairs in a happy little clutch. Yeah, that looked like about as much fun as shooting myself in the foot.

The little minx glared at me. Definitely not a squirrel. The others had forgotten me.

She hadn't.

I dropped the empty beer bottle into the trash. The sound of the bottle clinking yanked Vaughn and Kellan's attention toward me.

Yep. She was going to get them all killed.

None of us needed this distraction.

Fuck.

"Don't say it," I told Kellan. "I'll grab my shit and go as long as you're here now."

"Yeah," Kellan told me slowly. "Rome shouldn't have asked you."

I shrugged and headed out. We weren't going to have this argument again. I had my reasons. They had theirs.

It was what it was. Snatches of conversation leaked through the door separating the princess from Kellan's room and I shook my head. Jasper had all but peed on her to mark his territory. Doc was not one I would have suspected as falling into the orbit of her allure.

I could see why though.

I just had to make sure it didn't happen to me.

Yeah, I'd help keep an eye on her. I'd protect her if necessary.

But I wasn't about to let her distract me.

Distractions got you killed.

EXPECTATION (BONUS POV)

KELLAN

The flight landed only fifteen minutes behind schedule. I kept one eye on the board and the other on my surroundings. It wasn't like I had reason to come to the airport often. With the exception of one summer job and the time Milo had wanted to drive to see his sister, I'd never left Braxton Harbor. Those trips didn't really count, one was for work and technically one was for business. Family business, but still business.

Waiting gave me plenty of time to study the passengers exiting through the automatic doors. Without a ticket, you couldn't get back there. Some came out in business wear. Others were dressed in sweats and t-shirts. There were plenty of travelers wearing jeans and sweatshirts. Every one of them had a story.

Was this a vacation for them? Business, for sure, for a few of them. Were they coming home? Where had they gone? One of the reasons joining the army tempted me so much once upon a time. I'd get to leave. See the world. Be somewhere else.

Be someone else.

I shook off the malaise and depressing thoughts. This wasn't about bloodlines or family legacy. Well, at least not *mine*. Milo's, on the other hand, would be strolling through those doors any minute and I would be closer to her than I had been ever. The ride we'd given her when she'd been drunk and likely roofied didn't count.

In all honesty, I doubted she remembered Milo, much less me. Totally fine. We got her to her hotel, safe and sound. The doors swept apart to let out another wave of passengers. I didn't catch sight of her right off. Her slighter build proved harder to see behind the other passengers. She didn't stay with the pack though.

Dressed in dark leggings, an oversized sweater, and furry boots, she looked like a pixie playing dress-up in borrowed clothing that was too big for her. Her hair was pulled up into a single ponytail that bobbed as she walked. Instead of pulling at her features and making them severe, the hairstyle just made her look painfully young.

Too young.

She glanced around carefully as she slowed. Belatedly, I lifted the sign I'd brought with me. A single placard that read Sharpe. Walking up to her without introduction would probably be weird, so I waited for her to notice me.

Slipping her arms through the straps of her backpack, she did another scan. I swore I could almost feel the caress of her eyes as she passed me and the zing when she locked on to the sign. Without hesitation, she strode straight to me.

Lithe and slender, she moved with purpose and the oversized sweater dwarfing her couldn't minimize the attitude swirling around her. It hadn't been but a few years since the last time I saw her in person, how the hell had she grown up and managed to still strike me as painfully young at the same time?

"Hello," she said. "I'm Emersyn Sharpe." The soft contralto

was like a caress all its own. My dick straightened like he'd been called to salute. Fucking thing had no sense. Hadn't since the first time I'd gotten hard staring at Callie Timmins.

Yep, all brawn, no brains. That was my dick.

Really not the time or the place.

I offered my hand. "I'm your driver, Kestrel. If you want to point me to your luggage. I'll collect it for you."

"Actually," she said. "I've already requested the airline send it directly to the hotel. Is your car close?"

Apprehension wrapped around my spine. "Close enough. Are you ready to go?" While she didn't look behind her, I glanced past her. She wasn't *nervous* but there was something off about her.

"That would be great," she told me. "I do need to see your driver's and hack license."

The directness surprised me, but it also impressed me. Tucking the placard under my arm, I reached into my jacket pocket and pulled out the folio wallet that had both my driver's license *and* my hack license. Granted, the second was only a few days old, but it wouldn't raise any eyebrows.

She studied both cards intently, then pulled out her phone and took a picture of them. Curiosity flooded me. Flicking her gaze up at me, she smiled. "You can never be too careful. And thank you."

"You're welcome. Can I carry your bag for you?"

"I'm good," she told me, before pocketing her phone. "Where to, Kestrel?"

"This way." I shifted as we walked and kept one arm slightly behind her without touching. I also drifted a step behind and over. In this case, if she didn't want to be seen or to linger, then I'd make sure of both. While she hadn't offered up any other reasons, I still kept an eye out all the way to the car.

The fact she let out a deep sigh of relief as she sat down had every alarm bell ringing. What had her so worried?

She didn't sit right behind me, and that was fine. It meant I could glance back at her more easily. I waited until we were out of the parking garage. "You're staying at the Beauregard, correct?" That was the hotel information the service had given me.

"No," she said. "There's been a change of plans. I am going to be staying at Harbor North Hotel." That was several miles from the other hotel. "It's on…"

"I know where it is." I had to change lanes because we'd need to get on a different road once we were out of the airport. "I'll get you there."

"Thank you," she said, then slumped back into the seat and turned her head to look out the window. It was a gray and dreary day with rain spitting. It was also chilly.

The desire to ask her how she was burned on the tip of my tongue, but I was the driver. Not a friend. Not a brother to her brother that she didn't know existed. I was a stranger. I had a job. My only job for the next few days, be available to get her around and shadow her so no one bothered her.

The ebb and flow of traffic meant we ran into delays. Her phone rang and she lifted to stare at the screen. Then she silenced it. When it rang again, she turned it off.

"You're probably gonna get a call in a minute," she told me. "The chaperone is going to want to know where I am. She'll have gotten your number from the service."

"Chaperone?" Wasn't she over eighteen now?

"Don't ask, it's about as horrible as it sounds. But I'm not a minor anymore and I don't want her to know where I'm going. I don't want *anyone* to know where I'm going."

"No problem, Miss Sharpe." I smiled at her. "No problem at all."

Sure enough, my phone rang. It wasn't one of the guys so

I sent it straight to voicemail. Like her phone before it rang again and again until I just silenced the phone.

"You're not going to get into trouble are you?" The barest hint of concern for a stranger.

"No," I promised her. And if I did, well bring it. I could handle whatever they wanted to throw at me. "Customer's always right."

Another flicker of that smile and then it grew. "Thank you."

"Not a problem." Then because I couldn't ignore the faint grumbling of her stomach especially since we were stuck in a backup getting through the interchange, I asked, "Can I stop somewhere to get you something to eat?"

"I'd kill for a cheeseburger," she admitted. "Like legitimately kill."

"Well, you won't have to go that far. If anyone needs killing, I'll take care of it and we'll get you a cheeseburger."

She laughed. That was my intent.

"Now tell me," I continued. "Do you have a preference?"

Burger. Death. Whatever. I was good. She was nothing like I expected, but I was going to enjoy the next few days. If I had anything to say about it, so would she.

PERSPECTIVE (BONUS POV)

FREDDIE

*J*t was late when I got back to the clubhouse. Juggling two different jobs had seemed like a good idea at the time. Paying off debts while not hitting up the guys or having to listen to anyone tell me to go to college was the goal. The problem with two jobs was they paid shit for wages, bored the fuck out of me, and meant I got like no goddamn sleep.

Lack of sleep, in turn, meant that when I got pulled over for losing lane position on my way home—bear in fucking mind no one else was on the damn street—I'd forgotten my wallet with my license in it and I'd borrowed one of the extra cars and there was no insurance in the glove box.

Instead of cutting me a break, the pig made me get out and walk a straight fucking line. Like I was drunk or stoned. I wished. Apparently, wrong thing to say. Who knew the dude didn't have a sense of humor? Which was the round-about way the car got impounded and my ass ended up in jail.

A place the pricks I call my brothers fucking *left* me. Asses.

Of all the fucking people to bail me out, Liam had been the last one I pictured showing up. He didn't even say anything. Just ordered me to get in the car and follow him. After he bought me dinner, he sent me back to the clubhouse.

That was that.

Well, that and he told me I needed to shower cause I smelled like shit. Three days in a fucking jail cell would do that. I made a beeline for my own room as soon as I was back. Granted, I didn't usually care what most people thought but when I was beginning to offend myself, there was definitely a problem.

A shit, shower, shave, and shampoo and I was damn near a new man. I even shaved back the sides of my hair. The dye I'd thrown in it to cover up the purple I'd fucked around with had left it this dull ugly ass brown. Maybe I should shave the whole thing off.

I'd just finished brushing my teeth when doors slammed down the hallway. Hawk's roar was not an unfamiliar sound. At least it wasn't *me* on his shit list. I mean, I probably *was* on his shit list, but it wasn't my door he slammed open. Curiosity, however, had me wandering out and following the snarled sounds of Hawk ripping into someone.

The thump of fists and the sound of bodies crashing into a wall weren't that unusual either. We all fought. Some of us more than others.

Some of us a *lot* more than others. A headache brewed behind my eyes and my stomach growled. They didn't know I was here yet. I could just go back and eat my food and crash out to some music for a few hours. Pretty sure I had a couple of downers hidden away. They'd make sure I got some sleep.

"Don't fucking touch her." Definitely Hawk.

"Are you trying to hurt her?" Holy shit. Doc? I frowned at

the answering growl in Doc's voice. Doc never snarled at anyone.

Well, Hawk did cause Hawk could be a dick to just about everyone. Except me—for the most part.

"She's all skin and bones and bruises. I don't want to do anything to her."

Wait—*her*?

Jail had meant I'd missed going to the show and I hadn't been there to back Hawk up nor had I gotten to see her. Was she here? No, they wouldn't bring her here?

Would they?

I followed the sounds of the fighting into Kellan's room. The door to the little room between his and Rome's was open.

"You want to think about that, Jasper," Doc said in a calm voice as I nudged the door a little wider. Oh, Jasper had a gun tucked under Doc's jaw.

That was bad.

It could be worse. He could have fired the gun already. Then I glanced past the two to the gorgeous girl standing in the doorway. Bruised. Battered. Pale as a ghost. Dark hair and huge dark eyes.

Holy.

Shit.

It *was* her.

"Did I miss the party invite?" I asked, the grin as automatic as breathing. Get everyone's attention on me and maybe they wouldn't kill each other. Still, I didn't look at the dick measuring contest. Jasper was the biggest prick of us all, dick size notwithstanding. If he wasn't distracted and soon, he might actually shoot Doc and that would suck for all of us. So I latched my gaze on the bruised beauty. Why was she so fucking hurt? "Well hello, gorgeous. I definitely missed the party invite, or I'd have been right up to see you. You're looking a little rough. The guys do like to throw their girls around, get all dominant and shit. Now me? I'm a slow and easy ride, I'll take you real gentle like."

I kind of wanted to wrap her up in a blanket and just cuddle her. Maybe give her an aspirin. Why the fuck were they fighting over her?

"Freddie, fuck right the hell off," Jasper snarled. "She is not here for your entertainment."

"Well, no shit, Boss, I can see that. Though I think you should be a little easier on the ladies. Just 'cause we pay 'em don't mean we need to slap them around."

Yep. *That* got their attention. They both whirled on me and I grinned. Seriously, assholes, she was shivering so hard she looked almost blue under the bruises and her poor little nipples were puckered almost painfully. The fact she had that smooth pussy was sweet, but again, why weren't they looking after her?

What the fuck could be so important they were fighting while she looked like that? Maybe I should take her back to my room. I could at least feed her half my sandwich.

Maybe all of it.

"Out of curiosity, do you laser or wax?" I asked when Thing One and Thing Two didn't do anything but glare at me. "I mean, that's the smoothest pussy I've seen in a long time."

Some of the fear in her eyes vanished and she stared at me like I'd sprouted a second head. I could have, I supposed, but I kind of objected to hitting on women who looked like they'd been through hell.

Besides—she was—she was her.

"Put some fucking clothes on," Jasper snapped at her. Wow, he sucked. Or maybe he was just horny and hating himself. Either way, dick move bro. Dick move. She gave him a look that made me grin. Oh, there was a fighter in there.

I liked her already.

"Yeah, you do whatever you want, Boo-Boo," I told her, still grinning. "I don't think I'd want to put on clothes over any of that, either. If you want, I can just shuck my clothes, then we can be naked together. Solidarity."

Her laugh was a goddamn gift. Still she wasn't that steady on her feet and I started forward. So had Doc, but Jasper cut us both off.

"For fuck's sake," he snarled as he grabbed her bag and tossed it on the bed before giving me a shove. "Get out. You too."

"I think I'll wait." Doc told him coolly. "I still need to rewrap her ankle and she needs help…"

If looks could kill, these two would have obliterated each other already. "I could help," I said just as Jasper shoved me back into Kellan's room. The other two were glaring at each other. Vaughn appeared in the open doorway to the hall and he glanced at me then the door.

When I made a face, he rolled his eyes but he didn't slow down as he strolled in there. I blew out a breath as Vaughn just took over and ignored all of them. Boo-Boo took all of his focus and I sagged. Fuck me, I was gonna go eat. Then I'd sneak back in and see if she needed anything.

I barely made it to the hall before Jasper and Doc came barreling out. The two of them glared at me, but Jasper at least gave me a once over and just muttered later before the two of them took their argument somewhere else.

Fine by me.

Back in my room, I closed the door and walked over to the bed. The burger and fries were both cold when I opened the wrapping, but I didn't care. Food was food. I ate it as I lay there on the bed and I stared up at the poster on the ceiling. It was one of her flying in silks. I'd gotten it from one of the gift shops by the theater. I'd planned to save it for Raptor, but I'd pinned it to my ceiling instead.

No matter how long I stared at that ethereal girl on the ceiling, I couldn't reconcile it with the bruised and battered Boo-Boo in the other room. Nor did I like how much of myself I saw in her eyes. I shoved the food into my mouth and reached over to the nightstand. There were a couple of pills in a little envelope taped up against the lid. Harder to find.

I popped them both.

I'd need them.

The last thing I wanted to see was where that darkness went. Right now, I'd take whatever escape I could get.

SUSPICION (BONUS POV)

LAINEY

*G*randfather was late, but his secretary called thirty minutes earlier to let me know a meeting had run long. She offered to reschedule our lunch or I could wait for him. Honestly, I didn't have anywhere else to be and I was very fond of the seared scallops and creamy spinach stuffed salmon in the perfect garlic butter that Jacques served.

I didn't eat at the club that often, but it was my favorite when Grandfather and I were able to steal away. Without hesitation, I'd ordered them along with the honey roasted duck that my grandfather preferred. They wouldn't bring the meal out until he arrived, in the meanwhile, I enjoyed the sparkling water and nibbled on the charcuterie they'd brought me out to tide me over.

The combination of cheeses, smoked meat, and nuts with different jellies and compotes definitely teased my palate. So much better than school food. With a sigh, I checked my watch. In all likelihood, Grandfather would be another—

The chair across from me moved abruptly and I glanced up to find Adam sliding into the seat.

Really?

"I'm sorry," I said, keeping my voice even. "I'm saving that seat for a man I actually like."

"Well, when your grandfather gets here, I'll excuse myself."

I did not roll my eyes. "You can do it now. I'm perfectly fine sitting here in this lovely establishment, drinking water and eating cheese." Not to mention I hadn't invited him nor was I interested in having this little tête-á-tête. "Thank you for your concern."

"I'm not concerned," he replied in a droll tone, but his attention wasn't on me. The waiter approached but he didn't give the man time to speak. "Schloss Reinhartshausen Erbacher Markobrunn Riesling Trockenbeerenauslese, Rheingau, 1959. Two glasses."

"Right away, sir." The waiter obeyed the crisp instruction just like most people in our lives obeyed Adam or his father. They spoke with a careless kind of ease. They expected to be obeyed. They didn't throw their weight around or yell. Most of the time, they didn't even have to raise their voices.

"What?" he asked as I continued to stare at him. The problem with Adam was he knew he was in control, he thrived on it, and everyone around us always rushed to obey him.

Everyone except me and maybe Ezra.

"Nothing," I said, demurring from the fight. This was a chance to eat at my favorite spot with one of my favorite people. I would not let Adam spoil it for me. So, I opened my purse and pulled out my phone.

As social faux pas went, this was quite rude. However, he started it when he invited himself. His soft chuckle rankled but I refused to let that show. Instead, I checked my messages, then my email. Tally was on holiday with her latest conquest and she'd sent me photos from the slopes in St. Moritz.

There was only one photo of her with—oh, what was his name? He was just the latest in a string she'd collected since the beginning of the fall term. Since I somehow doubted he would make it much past the winter break, I didn't worry about it.

Emersyn's messages were quiet still. Nothing from her since she'd gotten to Braxton Harbor. There were only a few stops left on the tour, she couldn't wait to be free. But she was going to take advantage of the break to rest and work on her routines.

Going quiet while she had performances wasn't unusual, but I missed her. The waiter returned with the wine, he took the time to open the bottle and presented a taste to Adam before he filled the two glasses and set the bottle into the ice he'd brought for it.

As soon as he was gone, Adam moved the second wine glass to me.

"You know I'm not old enough," I reminded him.

"No one is going to say a word to you, enjoy the wine. Your grandfather will probably not make lunch at all."

I frowned. "Why would you say that?"

"Just drink the wine, Lainey. We'll order your favorites. Then when we're done, I'll take you home." The patience in his voice just roughed over me like sandpaper.

"Why do you think my grandfather isn't going to make it?" I studied him. Adam's attention still didn't seem to be focused on me. It would be a mistake to think he missed anything. Still, I picked up the wine glass and shifted so I could follow his line of sight.

Ugh.

I almost wished I hadn't. Turning, I found Adam's cool, assessing eyes locked on me and seeing almost too much.

Too bad I'd noticed Bradley Sharpe. The man made my skin crawl and Adam loathed him.

"I had no idea he would be here," I said rather than ask why his presence irritated Adam.

"Of course not," he said almost dismissively. "Drink your wine, Lainey. Have you ordered your salmon and scallops?"

"Have I mentioned how much I hate you?" Damn him, the wine was good. The first sip was crisp and swirled over my tongue like a good mystery on a cold night.

"Not recently," he said, his tone damn near indulgent. "I've almost missed your acerbic wit. You keep hiding at school. Would it help your appetite to say something now?"

I snorted. I hadn't been hiding at school, I'd simply elected to forgo coming back for the holidays. The last time Adam and I had any kind of a conversation—it had been not long after his mother's funeral.

That sobered my reaction.

"No," I answered before my phone began to vibrate with a mad number of messages. I wasn't alone. Several patrons seated throughout the dining room were reaching for their phones. I'd barely silenced the buzzing when I spotted the first headline.

Missing Heiress Sought in Disappearance of Dance Partner

Missing heiress?

My stomach sank even as I clicked on the message to open the article. A glass smashed across the room and I shifted in my seat. Adam was already rising and he moved around to block me and my view.

"Where the hell is she?" Bradley Sharpe's harsh, cold words were like little stabbing bits of ice burrowing into my flesh. A hail storm raining down too fast to escape the stings.

I rose, but kept my distance. Not that I needed to worry.

"Elaine has no idea, Mr. Sharpe," Adam said in a tone that

bordered on threatening. "I suggest you withdraw and mind your tone and manner when speaking to her."

"I wasn't speaking to you." Flecks of spittle left his lips as he went to sidestep Adam, but Adam was having none of it and this whole scene had the riveted attention of the restaurant guests.

"You're not speaking to her, either," Adam cut him off and I took a step back to give Adam the room to stay between us. I wasn't afraid of Bradley Sharpe. But I didn't like him.

And I definitely didn't trust him.

He pinned those pitiless, dark eyes on me. "Where is Emersyn? I know you won't leave her alone. Where is she? What did you do?"

Honestly, I was at a loss.

"I told you," Adam said, this time he gave Sharpe a hard shove back. "She doesn't know. Come at her again or try to speak to her again—"

Bradley threw a fist. Adam let him.

He. Let. Him.

Adam's head rocked to the side. It was more of a slap than a punch, but the fist he returned knocked Bradley Sharpe down on his ass and I caught his arm before he could continue the assault.

The manager, the waiters, and even security were converging on us.

"Mr. Sharpe is clearly disturbed," Adam said in that same superior tone. The muscles of his arm flexed under my grip, but he didn't pull away. "Please escort him to his vehicle and away from here."

"Of course, Mr. Reed."

"Right away, Mr. Reed."

Then in a matter of moments, the scene was over—Sharpe was gone, the other guests returned to their conversation and Adam turned his hand over under mine.

"Now," he said, the calm so depthless it was eerie. "Let's have our wine and order your food. Then if you want to tell me anything about Emersyn, we'll take care of her."

Tell him anything?

I swore my heart crumbled as I shook my head. "I really don't know."

It wasn't until he helped me back into my seat and took his own that I saw something in his eyes that disturbed me to my soul.

It was pity, not suspicion.

That made me reopen the article.

Emersyn Sharpe was missing and my heart sank all over again.

Missing.

VICIOUS REBEL BONUS
SCENES

CLASH (BONUS POV)

RAPTOR

I didn't say a word when I checked out where they were going to be. The next show was clear across the country. But I could make the drive in a couple of days. I'd get there the same day they did. Gas money and a few hundred dollars socked away for a rainy day. Her birthday was coming up. Well, the birthday she celebrated anyway. And I wanted to see *her.* I was also being selfish as fuck.

For the first time in a long time, I didn't care. I just— needed the break. A break from everything. I needed to see her and have a breather. Leaving a note for the guys, I told them I'd be back in a few days. It was better to slip away unseen or someone would take it upon themselves to follow me. Or just climb in the car.

Once on the highway, I exhaled a long breath. The agitation in my blood cooled. The tension in my spine unknotted. Music cranked, the cool wind blowing through the windows, and my foot on the accelerator as I left Braxton Harbor in the rearview mirror. I didn't run away. Didn't think I was now. Just—this damn urge to see her. I trusted my instincts. When I ignored my gut, bad shit happened.

With every mile I put on the car, I relaxed more. This was the right call. The guys would be fine for a few days. They could handle it. If they didn't—well, I'd deal with it when I got back. The drive took took just under two days, a little over thirty-seven hours including a four hour nap I took in the car at a rest stop.

I made it to Orlando in time to see her walking into the hotel. It was pure luck that I guessed the right one. Well, luck and the fact I knew their troupe had used that hotel before. She looked dead on her feet. The bitch walking with her looked like a bitch. I didn't know who the cunt was—wait— yes I did. The chaperone. Okay, maybe a chaperone should look like someone smashed her face with a brick to create that expression.

Still…not a fan.

I followed them inside, made a show of checking the wall with all its pamphlets of local attractions while they checked in. Ivy looked so damn tired, but then it was still early and they'd been traveling.

"Since the venue is tied up with the riggers," she said while they waited on the hotel desk clerk to sort out their rooms—multiple. So, Ivy had her own room. How—lonely. Then again, maybe she wanted privacy. Having grown up with the guys all sharing the same room most of the time, I craved personal space but it could also be too damn quiet. "I'll just do stretches and use the gym here."

The chaperone nodded. "Do not go down to the gym without me."

Ivy rolled her eyes.

I bit back a smile. I swore she gave the woman a look that just radiated "bite me." Kind of bratty, but I appreciated it. Rules were there to chafe, but also to protect. Or so Miss Stephanie often reminded us. The rules were also there to be bent carefully with just the right amount of pressure.

Pre-law had given me a lot of insight on that one.

As soon as they had their rooms and keycards, I made a note of which floor and let them disappear into the elevators before I asked the clerk about whether they had a room available. Unfortunately, my plans had been blown at the last minute and the girl behind the desk blushed when I smiled at her.

I got a room on the same floor with Ivy and the clerk's phone number. Maybe I'd make this a vacation of my own. She said she'd be off the clock at three. Good to know. She also worked nights sometimes. Even better. The credit card I used wasn't the best idea, since it was for emergencies only. But I'd make do for now.

Instead of going straight up to a room, I went out to move my car and grab a bag. The hotel nightly fee included parking—thank fuck. Even with Sarah Jane's discount, it was still pricey. On my way back through the lobby, I winked at her on my way past. Her smile grew and mine might have made an appearance as I stepped into the elevator.

Getting laid hadn't been the original plan, but what the hell. It was still *really* early. I was just stepping off the elevator when the battle axe said, "Stay in the room, order room service, and catch up on your assignments from the tutor. You have my number." Then she was bustling up the hall.

"Whatever," Ivy called after her and the door slammed. I sidestepped the woman as she got to the elevator. She was on the phone before the doors opened.

Our gazes met briefly as she said, "Yes, three days—it's about time I had a break from the brat." Her look practically screamed fuck off as she jabbed the elevator button and the doors closed behind her.

What. A. Bitch.

She was just *leaving* Ivy here? *Alone?*

Irritated as fuck, I made my way to my room which was just up the hall from hers. I glanced at her door, probably staring a little too long. We weren't directly across from each other, more caddy cornered. But when I checked through the viewfinder, I could see her door.

Well, the desire to be *here* fueling my blood made sense. The cunt and I were going to have words. Closing my eyes, I took a deep breath. Violence needed to serve a purpose. Carelessness was one thing. The woman was a chaperone, not a caretaker. She probably saw nothing wrong with leaving Ivy secured in a hotel room.

She was almost twelve by her standards with Emersyn's birthday the following week. Even if she didn't look much older than eight. I was here. Here I would fucking stay, the guard dog at the goddamn door.

Every time the elevator dinged, I got up to check the door. The first was room service. Ivy opened the door, but she didn't let the delivery person in. Just asked them to leave the tray and she'd get it in a minute like she needed to get dressed. At least the sound carried from the hall easily enough. The minute the elevator dinged that the guy was gone, she pulled the door open and wedged it with her foot.

Dressed in a t-shirt and shorts and apparently having showered since her hair was wet, she looked even younger. She picked up the tray and grinned. Really grinned. The door closed before it occurred to me I should have taken a picture.

Fuck, I was creeping on my own sister. Shaking my head, I returned to the bed and dropped on it. I was a light sleeper. The doors opened and closed in the hall. The sounds of families passing by, running kids, murmuring parents, even the occasional crying baby. All of this registered, but none of it was Ivy or a door close to mine.

The sudden fierce knock on a door had me upright and across the room before I'd even processed I was moving. A young girl stood outside Ivy's room. What the fuck? The door opened and Ivy stared out, her mouth fell open in shock.

"Lainey!" I hadn't heard that squeal in *years*. It catapulted me back as Ivy threw the door open. The girls gripped each other in a tight hug, all but dancing before Ivy dragged "Lainey" into the room. "What are you doing here?"

Whatever the answer was, the door closing cut it off. Fuck me.

Adrenaline flooded my system. After emptying my bladder, I splashed water on my face and brushed my teeth. Every hotel room came with its own coffee maker so I brewed a cup. It tasted like ass, but caffeine was caffeine and I'd had way worse.

I'd barely downed two swallows when the door across the hall opened again. The girls were coming out. Ivy had put her hair up in a ponytail and wore sneakers. She also had a purse strung crosswise across her body. Where the hell were they going?

"I still can't believe you're here!" Ivy's excitement punctured my anger so deftly, I damn near forgot why I'd been annoyed.

"I'm so fucking grounded," the other girl said with a laugh. "Worth it."

Then arm and arm they headed for the elevators.

Son of a bitch.

I stuffed my feet into shoes. I was still in jeans and a clean t-shirt. It would have to do. I snagged a baseball cap out of my duffle and shoved it on my head. Wallet in my back pocket, I downed the rest of the scalding coffee in one swallow and headed for the stairs. I made it to the lobby in time to see them spill out of the elevator in a mini-crowd of people. It didn't take them long to separate over to the concierge desk.

The two girls, both possessing an unnatural poise, kept breaking up into giggles that had me grinning. Tickets to the parks purchased, they followed the concierge's directions to head out the doors. Why did the guy just sell them tickets? Then again, I hadn't heard exactly what they said to him.

I crossed to him and handed him the credit card. Fuck the cost. "One ticket to the parks."

"Hopper?"

"Whatever."

The guy opened his mouth to ask me another question and I just fixed him with a look. This wasn't a social call. "Of course, one moment." It took two, agonizingly long minutes. "Here you go, the hotel offers a shuttle to the—"

I didn't wait for him to finish that part. I'd already caught the bus idea. Relief swarmed me when I got outside and found the girls waiting with a group of others for the bus. It was easy enough to drift into the crowd. I surged on behind them, sunglasses keeping my eyes hidden. They sat together, still giggling and as much as I wanted the seat right behind them, I took a couple more rows back.

At the park entrance, the thronging crowds worried me but they also provided camouflage. I was just another kid on his way to the park. I didn't have a bag, but I also didn't set off the metal detectors. I'd left my knife back in the room. And I hadn't brought a gun. To see Ivy? I didn't think I'd need one.

For the next few hours, I soaked up both the park and the girls' reactions to it. There was no artifice. They laughed. They played. They bought each other t-shirts. Ate ice cream. Rode the rides. I did actually manage to land in the same conveyance with them more than once. They never noticed me. They didn't pay attention to anyone. I even managed to get a picture or two when they found a couple of villains including the wicked looking chick from Alice in Wonderland.

They made no move to leave as the park segued into evening. There was a huge Halloween party and you needed a special ticket. Turned out, I'd gotten one from the dick at the hotel. Go me. They trick or treated around the park, laughing and playing madly. When the parade came through, they were right at the edge of the curb. The darker it got, the closer I drifted.

By the time the fireworks lit up the sky, I'd forgotten about the driving need to be here and just enjoyed their pleasure at it all. Then it was closing time and we were all leaving the parks. The lines to get back on the buses were long. It didn't look weird at all to be standing with them and about a thousand other people.

I didn't let anyone jostle them and this time, I parked my ass right behind them on the bus. Maybe I was being selfish, but I'd already figured out this was a birthday present from Lainey to Ivy. I hadn't realized she had such a good friend. Stupid, right? Of course she had friends. But she'd been constantly traveling the last three going on four years. I wondered if she had anything "normal" in her life.

They planned together in laughing giggles everything they were going to do back at the hotel. More food, then a movie, and a sleepover. No adults. Just them. Perfection.

Good, once they were tucked into their room, maybe I'd give Miss Sarah Jane a call and —

"Oh, you've got to be *kidding* me." The snarl in Lainey's voice snapped me out of my plans and I narrowed my eyes at the two men standing between the girls and the hotel door. They weren't small, but they were pissed. Ivy was already cutting in front of Lainey like she was going to take them on.

Fuck that—

"Ignore him," Lainey ordered.

"Who is he?" Damn good question, Ivy.

One of the pair glared at Ivy briefly before transferring that look to Lainey. Personally, i was about to pluck his fucking eyes from his head. "Do you have any idea how long it took me to find you?"

"Not long enough," Lainey told him. "And this is my mother's lover's son, or as I like to refer to him the human version of period cramps."

The guy behind him burst out laughing and Mr. Period Cramps glowered. My lips twitched because that was a damn good nickname. In fact, little Miss Magpie there just started forward like she was going to plow through.

"If you wanted to come see your friend," Crampy said finally. "You should have just said something."

"Adam... I don't have to tell you anything. ....let me be clear, you're like a cloud. A big, dark, ugly storm cloud and when you go away, it's a beautiful day. So, buh bye." Lainey's voice kept dropping like she was fighting for the poise they'd abandoned all day.

Awareness of the pair kept my muscles coiled. I was gonna draw attention just standing here staring, but I sure as fuck wasn't leaving them behind. The girls almost reached his laughing friend when Adam whatever the fuck said, "We came all this way and we're not leaving until your ass is in the car with us and on the way back to school."

"Sorry, my ass doesn't detach—unlike your personality. Maybe you should put a bag over it or something." With that, she stormed past them, Ivy in tow. The pair shadowed them all the way to the elevator and I was right behind them.

"Six in the morning," he ordered. "Meet us down here and don't try to sneak off somewhere."

"Six?" Lainey snorted. "Too bad your brains don't match your looks. I'll be down by ten." She waited until the elevator doors almost closed and for a split second her gaze locked on mine and then she added, "Maybe."

As one, the pair pivoted to face me.

"What the hell do you think you're looking at?" the laughing man asked.

"Good question, been trying to figure out why two jack-asses are harassing little girls. Only pervs do that."

"What the fuck did you just say?" Adam the period cramp demanded.

"I said," I told him as I stepped right up to him. "Only pervs harass little girls."

"Dude, you're asking to die," his friend warned, but I ignored the laughing idiot and kept my gaze on the guy right in front of me. Anger rolled off him like a storm.

"Go send them a cake," Adam ordered. "Tell them they don't eat enough. You—outside."

I chuckled. "Oh, what's the matter big boy? Did I wound your pride?"

"Adam—"

"Fuck off, and do what I said." Then Adam went back to glaring at me.

It'd been a while, but this was a nice place—with cameras —so I just stepped to the side and motioned for him to take the lead. No way was I giving either of these assholes my back. Adam McDouche tried to shoulder check me and missed. His friend groaned, but he cut away from both of us toward the hotel desk. I followed Adam right out the doors.

He didn't slow until we were on the far side of the building and half in the shadows. I expected the next move and avoided the hard drive of his right fist. His left came up damn near as fast and I took a glancing blow from that. The dick had moves.

So did I.

A hard uppercut slammed his teeth together and I took

the next blow on the shoulder and the kidney shot that followed it but he took an elbow to the face for his trouble. Blood sprayed the pavement and the scent of copper filled the air. More familiar than mother's milk at this point. His fierce expression showed zero signs of giving up.

Our next clash was just bare boned bashing. Fuck, I took one shot to the eye that was gonna sting like a bitch, but the clap I delivered to his ear sent him staggering. The swift flow of feet was my warning that his buddy had arrived and I barely moved my head in time to avoid the fist he would have caught me with. As it was, it slammed him into his friend.

And I laughed.

They went down like some bad physical comedy.

When they got up. They were pissed.

"Come on pretty boys," I told them. "Let's see if you can take me two on one."

The laughing idiot charged me like a freight train. I took the blows, blocking a couple and then had to fend off Adam as well. It was like fighting the twins, only without the coordination. When I head butted his friend, I saw stars for a split second then Adam caught me in the jaw and I stumbled backwards, falling over a goddamn curb.

I rolled, managed to not hit my head or leave myself to get curb stomped when there was suddenly a little girl between me and them.

"What are you doing?" Lainey shrieked.

Fuck.

I backed off, panting and shot a look around for Ivy. But only Lainey.

"Get your ass back in the hotel," Adam growled at her, but like me, he kept his distance. Even the idiot had slowed down. We were all bleeding and bruised. I hurt, but they were going to be hurting worse even if I could barely see out of my right eye.

"No."

Arms folded, Lainey glared up at him.

"Excuse me?" He growled at her and took a step forward and I went to meet him. At my motion, he froze. For one long second, we just glared at each other. If he took another move in her direction, I'd kill him.

His expression promised much the same.

"You heard me," Lainey yelled at him. "Have you lost your mind? Fighting out here? Why are you guys beating this guy up? Do you want to get arrested? Cause if you want that, I'll call the cops. Right. Now."

The laughing idiot started laughing—again. "Fuck me, Lainey don't be such a little bitch."

Adam swung around, only this time, his fist slammed into his friend and knocked the asshole down. He didn't say a word to him, just looked at me then at Lainey.

"Fine. Get back in the hotel," he said.

"Not without you two. I apparently can't trust you and I came down to thank you for Emersyn's cake. I was going to actually ask if you wanted to join us but you're not going up there all bloody and gross."

A half-laugh escaped me.

That snagged me the angry bird's attention and she glared at me. "I don't know who you are or where you came from. But now is the time you go—*while* I have them distracted." She paused. "Oh my god, what did you do to his pretty face?"

Adam snarled when she would have taken a step toward me, halting her in place. Smart man didn't touch her though. "Lainey. On the count of three, if you aren't moving in the direction of that hotel, I'm throwing your ass in our car and going home. One…"

She made a face. "Jerk." Then shot me an apologetic look. "Sorry, I never get to see my best friend." Then she turned.

"Two."

"You really are period cramps," she snapped.

The asshole looked right at her, pulled out some bills from his wallet and tossed it at me. They fluttered into the wind and scattered around us. "For your trouble," he said, then looked at Lainey. "Now. Go."

She went and he grabbed his friend, hauled him to his feet, and said, "Don't ever let me see you again, Mister."

I chuckled. "Or what?"

He stared at me.

"And keep your money, dick. I'm not for sale."

With that, I walked away from them, awareness of them keeping me on alert. I made it back into a side door of the lobby, avoiding the main portion. Last thing I needed was cops coming after me. I made it back to my room pausing only long enough to hear Lainey's laughter in there along with Ivy's before I let myself in the room.

Fuck, my bruises had bruises. I stopped dead when I found Sarah Jane lying on my bed.

"Oh my god, are you all right?" She sat up, concern all over her face.

"Getting better," I told her and threw the security lock on the door.

DETACHMENT (BONUS POV)

KELLAN

The first time, I'd been heading down for coffee. It was early and I had a long day at the shop. Someone had brought in a car with a bad transmission. If I had to rebuild it, I'd be there until late. Work like that was good. It helped keep my mind focused and detached from obsessing about a certain someone. The door between her room and mine had been open, so I half-expected that she was already down here and in the dance studio or in the kitchen with…

The smell of smoke pumped adrenaline into my system and I raced for the kitchen. The ventilation in the clubhouse was decent, but only if we turned on the big fans. The one drawback to the construction that we hadn't quite gotten around to fixing.

Fortunately, I could flip one of the master switches on my way in. Freddie probably stuffed pizza in the damn toaster again. Why had he done it the first time? "Well, I wanted to see what would happen? Crispy pizza sounded good."

It might have been funny, if he hadn't been strung out at the time and bouncing back and forth between hyper and depressed. The smoking pouring out of the kitchen was white, thankfully and not black. So something was burning, just not likely to burn the clubhouse down even if it asphyxiated us.

The scene waiting for me was not one I could have prepared myself for.

Emersyn stood in front of the stove with an oven mitt on one hand and spatula in the other. Batter had spilled on the counter and over onto the stove top, spreading to the burners where it was burning and bubbling along with...

"Sparrow, what are you doing?" Okay. Tact was my strong suit. Not entirely sure where mine fled but I was hard pressed not to laugh my ass off when she jerked around to look at me. There was dusting of white powder over her face and definitely a splotch of batter on her nose. Wisps of hair escaped from her pony tail and the t-shirt she had on was slipping off one shoulder.

The blackened remains of the substance formerly known as a pancake stuck to the bottom of the skillet. But one glance back up to the tears in her eyes and every bit of my humor dried up.

"I'm sorry..." she began and I swore the sound of a sob catching in the back of her throat made me homicidal.

"It's fine, Sparrow." Damage control mode engaged, I reached around her to brace her gloved hand on the pan and we took it off the heat. "Not a problem. I'm guessing you haven't done this before." And lest she think I was mocking her, I added, "Trust me, the first time I tried cooking, I was pretty sure my foster mom at the time couldn't figure out whether to laugh or yell at me."

We got the pan to the sink and I flipped on the water.

"Let it soak." I gave her arm a gentle squeeze then retreated to turn off the burner.

"I made a horrible mess..."

"Well, I'm pretty damn sure you didn't fly up into those silks the first time you did it. That probably took a lot of practice."

Burner off, I got most of the batter cleaned up. The bits that had burnt to the top would have to wait until that was cooler. I checked the time, but fuck it. If I had to work late, I'd work late. If Sparrow wanted to learn how to make pancakes, then she was going to have a successful experience to base her next attempt on.

She swiped away the tears before they could spill—thank fuck.

"Let's clean this up and start from scratch. I'll walk you through every step and then we'll make some fluffy pancakes."

"The whole point was I was going to do it for you guys," she admitted, so damn crestfallen it was adorable.

"Well, on the upside, you didn't scorch the wall." I gestured to the backsplash on the stove.

Her eyes rounded. "You?"

"Oh yeah," I said, kind of proud. "I was grilling hot dogs on these wooden sticks, didn't think I'd have any trouble cooking them over the open flame and then boom. The sticks caught on fire, so I kind of threw them."

Emersyn clapped a hand over her mouth, but her eyes danced with merriment instead of misery.

"See, you're already doing better than my first time."

Between us, we made short work of the mess. Now she'd followed the instructions on the box, but I told her the secret, I always add a little bit more of the water than what the recipe suggested. Otherwise the batter was too thick and the pancakes too dense.

New pan out, I sprayed it down with some of the cooking spray and she frowned.

"I did that."

"I believe you," I soothed again. "Now, we preheat the pan."

Her brows drew together and her concentration was so intense, I swore she memorized every step I was taking.

"We start the temperature on the pan at high, then turn it down." I had her adjust the flames, then moving behind her, I paused. "Is this all right?"

"Yes," she murmured and I took her hand holding the spatula and she relaxed her muscles so I could stir with her hand, stir, fold, stir, fold until the batter was a hint close to runny.

"Now," I instructed. "We could use a measuring cup so you can learn how much to pour out, but I always do it by eye." Together we turned to the pan, carrying the bowl and she moved with me. It kind of rattled me how easily she moved under my guidance like all I had to do was shift my weight and her body followed mine.

My dick perked up at that thought, but I steadfastly ignored it as I poured the batter. "Count with me, one, two—"

"—three," she finished and we stopped pouring there was a perfect four inch diameter pancake in the pan. It would be easier to make a mess of them on the griddle, but one at a time would do it.

"Watch for the air bubbles," I told her and this close there was no way to miss the sweet way she smelled or how those wisps of hair tickled me.

"There," she said with growing excitement. Grinning, I grabbed the spatula and then wrapped her fingers around the end, together, we slid it under and flipped it.

One golden face up at us.

"It doesn't take long to cook at all!"

"Nope," I said as I reached over to flip open a cabinet and

pulled out a plate. "We can make a whole stack of them real quick if you're up for it."

She cast those dark eyes up at me and every bit of the oxygen in my lungs evacuated faster than the smoke had with the ceiling fans. "You don't mind? I mean I was going to make this for all of you."

"Then we'll make it for us," I suggested, thank fuck my voice did not crack. I swore, I felt thirteen and hitting puberty all over again.

"What about everyone else?"

"They can make their own." I bopped her nose and she grinned. With her attention on taking the finished pancake out of the pan, I could breathe again.

Detachment.

That was what I had been going for. Staying detached. Keeping us all even. Getting us through this mess to the other side.

She held out her hand for me to take it, it was time to pour another pancake.

Yeah, detachment my ass. She was too damn adorable. We made nearly a dozen pancakes and she was just as excited about the twelfth as she had been about the first.

They were the best damn pancakes I'd had in a while.

I was also hella late to get to the shop, but I really didn't give a fuck. I wouldn't have traded that hour alone with her for anything else. When I got back that night, she popped out of her room and into mine.

"Can you show me how to make eggs tomorrow?"

"Yeah, Sparrow...I can show you anything you want."

DISORIENTATION (BONUS POV)

FREDDIE

a fist caught me in the side of the head and I rocked in the chair. Laughter bubbled up inside of me as I blinked through the watery eyes to find the pair of 19 Diamonds who'd jumped me glaring as bits of blood and spittle hit them as I laughed. Now they looked like speckled diamonds and that was funny as fuck.

I was high.

"Have you ever felt like nobody was there?" I asked. Granted it was a mostly rhetorical question.

"Shut up asshole." He backhanded me and more blood flew from my lip. It sprayed across the tile and the girl who'd offered to suck my dick let out a squeal. I wonder if this was what they meant by spotted dick. Another laugh escaped me.

"I told you to make him talk," another voice intruded. That dude sounded like a real asshole.

"You said get him here," the spotted dick responded and there were tears in her voice. This time when flesh struck flesh, the spotted dick let out a cry.

"You know I'll be found right?" I said. Hitting chicks was so fucking lazy. Besides, I was right here.

"What?" The guy whirled on me and he got right down in my face.

"Have you ever felt forgotten in the middle of nowhere?" I asked, blinking away the fresh wave of tears his Shrek-level onion breath dragged out of me. "And have you ever heard of a breath mint?"

He snarled, sadly exhaling more of that nasty breath into my face, and hit me square in the stomach. I would have puked, 'cept I didn't have anything in my stomach so I laughed.

"They want answers or pieces," a new voice said. Yeah I couldn't see that one cause they'd knocked my chair over and I was lying on my side on the floor. This was kind of nice. Spotted dick rubbed her face and threw me an apologetic smile. Yeah, I knew better than to chase free pussy.

Still…shit, I tried to smile but all I could taste was blood so it probably came out some gruesome Freddie Krueger shit —Freddie Krueger.

Oh shit.

I laughed.

The air wheezed out of me.

"What the fuck are you laughing at?"

The chair was yanked up and the world swayed as it righted itself.

"Have you ever felt like you could disappear?" I asked, I was flying. At some point, this shit was gonna hurt, but not right now. This was awesome.

"We're not gonna get shit out of him like this. She gave him too much."

"Like you could fall and no one would hear," I said with a sigh. But they weren't listening. Nope, they were arguing and fuck that, I closed my eyes to shut them out. I didn't need to hear that shit when I liked people, sure as shit didn't want to listen to a bunch of spotted dicks fight.

You know—unless they were gonna beat the shit out of themselves…that would be sweet.

The minute I closed my eyes though, I saw Boo-Boo's face. Fuck. I was supposed to get Boo-Boo something to eat and I'd totally gone to get her something special and then… yeah, then I got lost cause that was what I did.

The song burned in my chest cause the louder the fight grew the more it harshed my buzz. I needed the buzz. The buzz was the good stuff.

Yeah I was high.

Flying high, like Boo-Boo.

And yeah, when the dark came shining in—I'd be found.

The lyrics didn't make much sense, but I loved the fucking song so I just sang it for all I was worth. It warbled and bounced off the walls. I got popped a few more times, but it just made me sing louder.

"Fuck my life, *shut him up!*"

Okay, I cackled at that. Funny as hell, but even as they hauled me out of the chair and dragged me next door and up some stairs, I kept singing. I even gave the big bruiser hauling me a smacking kiss on the cheek.

He all but threw me in the room and rubbed at his face like a maniac. So fucking funny. Taking a deep breath, I wheezed and coughed and waited—where was I with the song? Shit. I forgot.

Oh, I knew—I channeled my inner Anne Hathaway and sang about when I had a dream and it wasn't long before the guys with me slammed the door on their way out. Head back, I stared at the cracked ceiling and tried to picture Boo-Boo doing that silk dancing to the song.

That would be cool.

I could fly with her like this.

But the song had one thing right—they tore our hopes apart.

INKED (BONUS POV)

VAUGHN

*D*ove's harsh breath and the slam of a door knocked some of the glorious haze off my release. Hers too apparently because one moment she was wrapped around me and the next she pushed those tiny hands to my chest to get me to move. With a groan, I dragged myself to the side. Leaving her slick cunt was not my idea of something to hurry, but she slipped out of bed and hurried to the door.

Dammit.

I hauled myself up, but she was already out of the room naked with my cum dripping down her thighs. No way in Hell was she rushing out there alone so I got my shit together and was a half-step behind her.

"Easy, Sparrow," Kel said as he caught her. While he didn't drag her back, he did pick her right up off the ground and turned her from the door.

"Jasper—"

"I know." He used his soothing voice, one he would rely on when Jasper was too close to the edge but Dove's crushed expression shredded my fucking heart. Yeah, I came to apologize and yes, we'd had sex. None of that was something that should ever make her feel bad. "Let him go for the moment."

"He's right," I told her and ignored the brutal look Kel shot my way. Yeah, he blamed me for some of this. While he wasn't wrong, I didn't actually care what they all thought right now. Dove was the important one. Those doe eyes cut to me and a glimmer of tears flashed in them. Yeah, I couldn't handle the crying right now. Especially if we were the ones making her cry. "C'mere, Dove."

"Vaughn..." That was misery. Pure and simple. I hated hurting my brothers too, but Jasper needed to calm the fuck down. His possessiveness had gotten out of control.

"I know, c'mon."

When Kel set her down, careful of where he'd put his hands, I just scooped her up. Ignoring Kellan for now, I carried her right back into her dark room and kicked the door closed. First, she was already shivering from the cooler temperature out there. Or maybe it was just a reaction to the overwhelming emotion.

We needed to dial this shit back before we really scared her off.

"Put me down," she ordered as soon as I had the door closed.

"I will," I promised, but I didn't set her down until we reached the bed. Then I turned on the light. Because some conversations were meant for the dark. This was not one of them.

"I need to get dressed," she told me before she scooted to the end of the bed.

"I wish you wouldn't." I could pull a Jasper and order her, but I wouldn't. As it was, I took a seat on the bed and got out of her way. Her reaction down in the warehouse over the fight said a lot more about her strength *and* her fragility than anything else. The urge to wrap her up was right there, but we couldn't smother her.

No matter how much we wanted to do it.

"I have to go after him…"

"No," I said. "You don't."

Whirling, she glared at me. "You didn't see his face."

"I don't have to have seen his face," I told her, focusing on the fire in her eyes. "I know him, Dove. I know how angry he probably was."

"Then why are you so calm?"

"Because he's Jasper. Anger is his love language, some-times." I sighed. "That sounds bad. He's very possessive where you are concerned. Finding you here—with me? Probably drove home the point that he doesn't get a say in what you do."

"Or who?" The dry challenge there pulled a reluctant smile from me.

"No, he doesn't get to decide that Dove. If you want me, I'm right here. I'm not going anywhere."

"And if I want him?"

"I won't deny you what you want." I spread my hands, but at least she wasn't trying to get dressed anymore. She just stood there with the t-shirt in her hands. "Or who."

Shock rippled over her face. "Why?"

"Why won't I deny you?" Cause I wanted to be sure what she was asking.

Something frustrated and helpless flickered over her face as she spread her arms. "I don't understand you guys."

"Come here, Dove." I held out a hand to her and curled my fingers in invitation. For a moment, she hovered there—suspended between action and inaction. The need to help her was a knot in my gut. But she needed to reach out to us. The shirt fell from her fingers as she crossed to the bed.

When her palm glided over mine, I wrapped my hand

around hers and gave her a gentle tug. She came right to me and I pulled her onto my lap. She framed my thighs with her own as she straddled me. The dampness from earlier left us both sticky, but I didn't give a damn about that.

With light fingers, she explored my chest and the ink on my shoulders and my arms. "I don't like that I'm the reason he's hurting."

"You're not," I told her and when she kept her gaze on my chest, I slid a finger under her chin and lifted her eyes to me. "*You* are not the reason. Jas has his own issues. Those aren't on you to fix or to apologize for."

"But—" She broke off and went back to staring at my tattoos. When she moved to the shield, I shifted my arm so she could run her fingers over it. "But he looked so hurt."

"I imagine he did. He wants you a lot. He wants you to want him." I took a breath. "I think he wants you to want him only."

Those dark eyes lifted to mine.

"I want you," I told her. "I've made no bones about that."

"Well…" The barest hint of a smile curved the corner of her mouth.

"Bone, Dove," I teased. "Not boner." She bit her lip, but it didn't keep her smile from flashing over her face. "My point is—I want you. I'm okay if you want him too. Jas will be—eventually. Just let him get out of his own way."

"Vaughn…" There was no mistaking the troubled note in her voice. "This is all very—different for me."

"So we figure it out." Because while I'd never been opposed to sharing with the guys, it was definitely different for all of us to want one girl. We did. Whether they owned up to it yet or not. We all wanted her and we'd wanted her for a long time. Maybe that level of intensity was too much for her.

Yet.

But Jas—we needed Jas to get to this realization on his own. She needed him. Hopefully it wouldn't involve me having to knock his head in to get some sense in there.

"Just like that?"

"Just like that," I confirmed. The brush of her fingers dancing over my tattoos pulled my attention to my chest again. "Do you want me to tell you the stories of these?"

"Yes." No hesitation.

I grinned. "Before or after, I make you 'bone'-less once more?"

It was a gamble, but the tension vibrating off of her made the spot between my shoulder blades itch. When I cupped her cheek, she leaned right in and then her mouth was on mine.

Good answer.

INTOXICATED (BONUS POV)

JASPER

*H*omes didn't always mean happy.

The sweet length of her back was visible in the firelight. We'd fucked. We'd talked. We'd fucked some more. We drank beer. We fucked. We had a snack and talked. Then we fucked again. My cock was already struggling valiantly to come back to life. I wanted to fuck every inch of her skin. I wanted to feel her come around me again and again.

Twice she'd tried to go down on me with her mouth, but I was in no way prepared to be gentle with her yet. While she kept telling me she didn't need gentle, I wasn't going to choke her with my cock because I couldn't control how badly I wanted her. Fuck, just the image alone had my dick stirring.

I traced my fingers down the smoothness of her shoulder and along the length of her back. She was so deeply asleep, she didn't even react to my touch. The level of trust alone humbled me. Swan was such a complicated mixture of vulnerable and fierce. Determination filled every inch of her fragile little body and as fragile as she seemed, she wasn't.

Maybe I hadn't wanted to see it before, but it was unmistakable now. The world had beaten her over and over. Tried to subdue her. Threatened to break her. But she never conceded the fight. She kept moving. One foot in front of the other.

Even that bastard Eric. Fuck, if I could kill him all over again, I would. The months of injuries we'd put him through until he was so broken he'd never have recovered would have to suffice. Cutting his dick off and shoving it down his throat after he admitted he'd raped her was the very least we could have done.

It was better than the alternative.

Those words haunted me. That she was safer on the road. So what did that mean at home? That money was useful, but it didn't make up for time lost with people who really cared.

More—with people you could trust.

That word carried the weight of the world.

The weight closed in on me when she'd said she trusted me. All these months of the ferocious way she fought back against us. Pushed to find a way out. Demanded to know why we'd kidnapped her and all I'd been able to say was we took her to protect her.

"What—what was your plan then?" she'd asked not an hour ago. "You took me because I was hurt. But then what?"

Hating the fact I couldn't tell her the exact why, I had to admit, "I didn't have a plan. I just had to protect you. To keep you safe. To heal all those wounds you had." I brushed the hair from her face as I spoke and the corners of her lips turned up. Her flushed skin looked almost rosy in the firelight and the puffiness of her lips just made me hungry to kiss her again. This was how she should always look and feel. Replete. Happy. Free to ask for whatever she wanted.

And fuck, I'd give her everything.

I'd meant it when I said I hadn't brought her here for sex.

Sure, I'd thought about it. But after she had that moment before, I was determined to take my time.

"That doesn't seem like you," she murmured and then tapped my nose. "You like being in charge."

"No," I admitted. "I really don't. I like getting things done. But I'm more of a kick in the door kind of guy. I see the short-term gains, the defenses, the offense. The bigger picture, the long-term? That isn't my specialty."

"And yet you are so determined to protect the others. You plan for them."

"I do my best," I told her. Even when my best wasn't enough. I'd pressed my forehead to hers. "Are you still mad at me for taking you?" Because she had every right.

"No." Her nose brushed mine. "I still don't understand it fully. Like how you guys were all working the show and how Kestrel was my driver. I know you took me because Eric hurt me."

Fuck I never wanted that asshole's name on her lips again and I'd kissed her then. The desire to erase him from her mind and her past was so intense, I didn't even finish that part of the discussion. When I rolled onto my back and slid her down onto my cock, it was everything.

More when she threw her head back and braced her hands on my shoulders as she controlled the pace, I would have given her everything. I surged up to meet the downward thrust of her hips, captivated by the way her nipples tensed and tightened. The drowsy look of pleasure suffusing her eyes as she tipped her head down had me straining upward until I could suck on one of those nipples.

It took an hour of lazy thrusts combined with sudden manic action, but she came four more times before I let go. We lay in a sweaty heap together and I'd cradled her to my chest until she'd climbed off to make use of the bathroom.

The fact my cum ran down her legs as she walked filled

me with such possessiveness that I had to admit it—even if she asked me to let her go now—I'd follow her. No matter where she went. I had to be there. I'd prefer if she stayed.

Even if it meant sharing her with Vaughn.

Anger flooded through me and I clenched my fists. The moment my knuckles began to whiten, I took my hands away from her. I would *never* touch her in anger. I would *never* be my father. If she needed Vaughn, then she could have him. Rome made her smile. Freddie made her laugh. Kellan guided her and in their unguarded moments, there was no denying the connection growing there.

She fit us.

All of us.

Rolling onto my back, I stared up at the ceiling. Kel was right. We had to tell her. Tell her and tell Raptor. But I wanted to talk to him *first*. He'd kept his distance for a reason and I'd dragged her back into our world for a reason, too.

Turning the ideas over in my head, I couldn't find an easy solution to all of this. Raptor would be furious. She might not believe us. Then again—she seemed happier, maybe? In the last few weeks. Happier than I'd seen her at all during the show.

The smiles reached her eyes.

The ease with which she moved around the clubhouse.

Even the threats, she'd taken them in stride.

Threats.

Those were still out there. Someone had cut her silks. Someone had tried to run her and Kestrel over in the parking garage. Then Eric assaulted her. I didn't think the third had anything to do with the first two. We'd removed her from the situation, but new threats had popped up.

The guys at the body shop had come for her specifically. Someone knew we had her or someone suspected.

The question was...

Movement next to me pulled all my attention to the present. Emersyn rolled over to face me and I moved to my side to face her.

"Hi," she whispered.

"Hey," I answered in the same quiet tone.

When she traced her finger over my forehead then down my cheek to my chin, I studied her. The stroke of her fingers against my beard made me smile.

"There you are…"

"Hmm?"

"You looked so angry. I worried I'd done something wrong."

Guilt hit me like a fist. "Swan, you could never do anything to make me angry at you."

"Hmm." She wrinkled her nose, clearly skeptical. "Somehow, I bet I could. You're very hard headed and stubborn. Despite what you said earlier, you *do* like being in charge."

A startled laugh escaped, but I didn't try to haul it back. "That I do…and I suppose if you really worked at it, you could make me angry. But I will never hold it against you and I swear, I will never hurt you."

An image of my father burst through my mind and the violence he could deal out. I shoved it away. That ugliness would never touch her.

Nothing would.

Not as long as I was breathing.

"There it is again," she whispered, this time so close to me her breath teased my lips. "Stop thinking about whatever that is or tell me, so we can get rid of it together."

"I'll stop." Because telling her would let that ugliness into her world and when she brushed her lips to mine, I slid my fingers into her hair to keep her there. Long, slow, drugging kisses were just what I needed.

Emersyn Sharpe was in my blood.
My addiction.
My intoxication.
I never wanted to be cured.

RESTRAINT (BONUS POV)

DOC

"*M*ickey—short for Michael—James." Almost no one called me Michael. No one. In the military, I'd been James. Or medic. Mickey had been a rebellious teenager all too often getting in to scrapes because I could. Doc—Doc was who I wanted to be. The guy who helped, who fixed, who could take care of others. "Doc works, though."

"Thank you, Mickey," Emersyn said, the fact she exhaled my name like it was a physical touch barreled through any professional veneer I'd been trying to maintain where my fragile patient was considered. Images of healed fractures and the damage done to her bones and worse flashed through my mind. But I didn't see a victim. I saw the survivor. The strong, fierce little bit of courage and determination who stood up for herself and held herself above the hell she'd been immersed in.

As she leaned in to press a kiss to my cheek I turned and her lips touched the corner of my mouth. The attraction I'd bullied down and stuffed into a steel container to be welded shut, burst out from the restraints. Her lips were softer than petals. Instead of pulling back, she nuzzled the kiss to my mouth and my soul ripped squarely in two. The taste of her was something I longed for and I damn well knew better. She was a kid.

Wasn't that what I told the punks when they brought her to me? A kid with barely any tits and a lifetime's worth of damage. She needed care, not lust. She needed affection, not passion. The flicker of disappointment in those deep, cinnamon brown eyes jerked free the last bolt as she leaned away. I clasped the nape of her neck.

A hunger I had no business feeling flooded me as she parted her lips and I dipped my tongue in for a taste. One taste. First and last. Then let her go. She deserved to go back to whatever life they'd ripped her from, especially now that the abusive fuck was dead. Need surged through me and the sample did little to ease my desire, if anything, it left me starving and I forced myself to let her go.

"Thank you," she whispered. "And goodbye."

The final two syllables slid like a blade right through my ribs. I stared after her as she hurried out of the truck and started across the street. I told myself a dozen times to move, to pull away. I should never have kissed her or let her kiss me, but with the taste of her still tingling on my lips, I put the truck in gear and headed away.

No matter how much my brain said keep moving, my instincts had me looking back. Then I turned the corner and headed back toward her. Just to make sure she got inside. That was what I told myself. Make sure she was safe. The kid needed protecting. Only instead of going into the hotel, she hurried away from it.

Dammit.

She'd chosen the hotel so why leave it? It wasn't like she had much on her at all and it was too cold for the thin layer of clothing she wore. I jerked the wheel and turned down a side street and put the truck in park. I would probably get a ticket, but I gave less of a fuck about that than leaving Emersyn wandering around Braxton Harbor without a dime to her name.

I'd barely rounded the corner when I found some jackass lifting her off the ground, I could barely see her around him. But she was fighting even if the only sounds escaping her were muffled. Holy shit did she fight. She struck with her legs, her head, and a heated curse exploded from her assailant.

Even as I registered who the voice belonged to, I didn't slow down. She was fighting so damn hard to get away. A split second before I reached them, she stumbled forward and Liam fucking O'Connell pivoted to face me. He was a big fucker and I'd seen him fight.

Problem for him. I'd also helped train him to fight at one point and I hit him full force going for his midsection. We hit the ground, him first and I made sure to drive an elbow in under his ribs to knock the air out of him. Liam wheezed, but it gave me all the time I needed to roll him onto his side and pin him with my legs as I locked his arm back in a brutal hold. I could break it if I had to, but Liam stopped struggling.

"You okay, Little Bit?" Her pupils were huge and her chest rose and fell rapidly with the shallow breaths she took. She'd gone ashen and if she didn't answer me soon, I might do more than break Liam's arm for scaring the hell out of her. She looked from me and then down at Liam. Recognition flickered across her expression and she swayed, then staggered way from both of us.

Since Liam wasn't fighting anymore, I let him go. She clung to the side of a dumpster before she threw up. Even before I reached her, the shaking trembling her whole body was visible. "Easy Little Bit," I warned her in a soothing voice that I was near. With care, I gave her a minute to process before I settled a hand on her back. The frantic beat of her heart was a wild tattoo of pure terror. "Easy, I've got you."

"What he fuck, Doc?" Liam demanded. "You tried to break my goddamn arm."

"Why the hell were you dragging her off the street?" I shot him a look and he had the grace to look a little sheepish. But only a little, his temper was up and he was rotating his shoulder with care. That arm lock hurt like a bitch.

"'Cause she took off on Rome's watch. You think Jasper's gonna get over that shit? No. So I came to see what the fuck she was doing, and don't think I didn't see her hook up with you."

"You didn't see shit," I snarled back. The last thing I needed was him spreading that shit around. Jasper was enough of a loose cannon without Raptor around to temper him. Fuck knew, Kestrel tried but Jasper's need to protect overwhelmed his reason and there was a very thin line between defender and monster. I dragged one of the napkins out of my pocket as Emersyn began to straighten and handed it to her. She stared up at me, not totally registering yet and the fact she was letting me hold her up said a lot more. Not that she weighed anything. "You with us, Little Bit?"

"What the fuck is wrong with the little hellspawn?"

Before I could punch his rude ass little mouth, Emersyn laughed and it sounded more like a choked sob.

"Ignore the prick, Emersyn." I advised, then touched her cheek lightly. There was an imprint from Liam's hand on her face, reddened skin. I didn't think it would bruise, but for fuck's sake. "How fucking hard did you grip her?"

"She was fighting," Liam answered, all cocky defiance. "Why don't you ask if she's had her shots since she bit me."

That got her attention. "You followed me. Why?"

I wanted an answer to that myself. I should have paid

closer attention, but I hadn't noticed him following either. That wouldn't happen again.

"Why?" Liam parroted. "How about we get the hell back to the clubhouse with her before the guys realize she left?"

There was no 'we' in this argument. "She wanted out," I informed him and curled an arm around her. I didn't know if her shivering was from the shock or the cold, either way, I had no problems giving her support.

"I don't care." The disdain in Liam's voice covered for a lot of deeper worries. "Jasper will put another hole in Rome if he thinks he let her go."

"He can't do anything about her escaping," I told patiently. And as hot-headed as Jasper was, Rome was a brother to him even if Jasper's tolerance for Liam had been sorely tested. He might get ticked, but he wouldn't hurt him. "The obligation of the prisoner is to escape."

"Let me repeat," Liam said, arms falling to his side as he took a step toward us like he was a threat. "I. Don't. Care. They want her there, Rome was left to look after her, she's going back... She already got him stabbed once. I'm not letting it happen a second time."

"Wait." Emersyn's tone warbled a little as she pushed away and stood straight. No matter how much I wanted to drag her back against met, I kept that impulse in check. "What do you mean I got him stabbed?"

Liam cut a look at her.

"He was hurt."

"Yes, princ—"

Transforming from trembling, fragile and lost waif to fierce warrior, Emersyn sprang forward and she popped Liam right in the face before I'd even registered her motion. Blood sprayed from the hit and I almost wanted to applaud. Someone, somewhere, had taught her how to make a hit.

"You cunt," Liam snapped as he put a hand up to his nose.

Hell, it was hardly the first time he'd taken a blow but I tugged Emersyn back to me anyway.

"Watch your mouth," I scolded. It was an old habit, I didn't think it would go away no matter how old the boys got. They were still the boys to me. Probably always would be.

"I don't care if he calls me cunt," Emersyn snapped. "I told you, don't call me princess. You do it again, and it'll be your balls I smash."

"Noted, Hellspawn." He spit out blood, then touched his nose carefully before glaring at her. "Hellspawn fits better anyway." But the heat in his eyes had nothing to do with anger. No, there was interest there.

I wasn't going to play this game. "Look," I told her. "Let's get you out of here and back to the hotel." It was the original plan after all.

"No," she said almost too swiftly. "Not the hotel."

The ashen color of her cheeks went even whiter and she sank to the ground. The swollen pupils of hers were blown and this time I knew it was shock. Crouching with her, I rubbed the back of her neck gently as she put her head down to her knees.

"She's crazy," Liam murmured with more worry than malice.

"She's traumatized, you overbearing little shit. Stop freaking out about your brother for thirty seconds and look at this girl. She hasn't done a damn thing to any of you, and yet you're treating her like she's a damn possession." What the fuck was wrong with these boys? They'd come close to that razor edge of the line between criminals and criminal behavior before, but taking this kid? Putting her through all this?

She lifted her head and instead of Liam, she focused on me. "You're hurt."

247

It was barely a cut and I didn't give a damn. Except her touch was so gentle as she tried to dab the blood on my cheek.

"I'm fine, Little Bit. Trust me, a cut like that isn't going to hurt me." But no way in hell was I leaving her here in this condition. Shock did strange things to a body. I rose and pulled her to her feet. "Can you focus on me a second?"

She stared up at me and I wasn't sure how much of what we were saying registered. Not really. The ferocious fighter had vanished back into the fragile shell.

"You're in shock." It might be news to her, but this was a profound change from when she'd slipped out of my truck. "What happened to you?"

"Nothing," she answered in a slow, almost rote voice. As if she'd practiced the answer a hundred times. "I just—"

After the profound hesitation, I nodded. "You won't go to the hotel?" That was obvious.

She shook her head.

"I'm guessing you don't want to go with Liam." It wasn't a question. Rome's twin glared at her, but it wasn't hate in his eyes.There was want in there, too. Want and worry. Boy he was fucked, but I didn't have time to worry about him right now.

"I—I don't know," Emersyn said slowly. "I need to think."

She rubbed a hand over her face and winced. There was a bit of blood at the corner of her mouth. I'd bet she bit the inside of her cheek.

"Will Jasper really hurt Rome?"

"Fuck, I don't know," Liam said, shocking me. "If he could pin it on me and shoot me, he'd probably leave Rome alone. But they're turning the city upside down looking for fucking Freddie, and all he wanted was for Rome to make sure you were safe."

Where the hell was Freddie, now?

"They haven't found him yet?" Worry filtered into the emptiness and loss in her voice.

Liam stared at her, eyebrows up. "I have no clue. I've been following you for the last couple of hours. Then your boyfriend." The barest hint of a smirk was there to irk me, not her.

"Shut the fuck up," I ground out. "Don't even joke about that."

"Hey, Doc, just calling it like I see it. I saw her kissing you before she got out of the truck, and you sure pulled up conveniently when she was out there walking."

"Wait," Emersyn cut in. "You followed me? I didn't see you." It wasn't the first time she commented on that. I wasn't sure how much of this she was processing.

"You weren't supposed to." Liam smirked.

"I walked for a long time and you just let me go? I thought you were worried about your brother."

"Yeah," I murmured. "If you were that interested in protecting Rome, why let her get that far at all?" I had my suspicions.

"I just wanted to see where you were going," Liam lied.

"And?"

He leaned over and spat blood onto the pavement. "And I debated just letting you go. Fine? Is that what you want to hear, Pr—Hellspawn?"

"Why did you change your mind?" Good question, one I wanted the answer to as well.

"Fuck if I know." Liam glared at her, then at me. "You know what? This shit is not worth it. My nose fucking hurts —nice hit, by the way. You ever want to work on that south-paw, you let me know. You take her back, and I'm getting out of here. This side of town gives me hives."

"Hey, Mockingbird," I called before Liam even made it halfway down the alley. "You're trying too hard."

The other man flipped me off, and then he was gone. I shook my head. He could lie to himself all he wanted, I just hoped he didn't pull that shit with his brother. If I could see through it, Rome damn well could.

"Where do you want to go, Emersyn?" Because no way in hell was I leaving her in this alley or anywhere, alone.

Not anymore.

So much for restraint. I was as bad as those boys, but I would let her go when the time came. No matter how much it cut me. That was what you did when the broken birds healed. You set them free.

SOARED (DELETED SCENE)

JASPER

wo hours north of Braxton Harbor was paradise. Granted, the hotel and its outbuildings probably weren't what most people probably idealized as the paradise-like location, but it was perfect for us. Working there had been a lot of hours and a lot of labor. At the same time, it offered us the kind of freedom I'd never had before. That freedom was what made it paradise.

Whether we were bellmen, lifeguard backups, waiters, or maintenance men, I'd loved the work. The shit jobs were so much better than the group home. If not for the guys, I'd probably have ditched that fucking place the year before. Milo and I had scored jobs there the summer we were sixteen and found jobs for most of us—except for Freddie. He'd been too young.

We managed to sneak him out to stay up there with us as often as we could and when we couldn't, one of us went back to keep an eye on things for him. But today—today was going to be fun. It was my birthday and we'd all cut school. Milo, Mr. Responsible, arranged everything.

"You ready?" Milo asked, his wild grin so at odds with the

raptor personality he'd been cultivating over the last couple of years. I laughed.

"Hell yes, it's a good day to die."

Vaughn chuckled from the back seat where him, Kel, and Freddie were crammed together. Liam wasn't that far behind us and Rome had elected to ride with his brother. "Nice," Vaughn commented. "Way to elevate the mood Hawk."

I snorted. "I woke up to my warning letter, why shouldn't I embrace the warm and fuzzy."

That earned a real scoff from Kellan, but it was Freddie I checked in the side mirror. His expression tightened. That warning letter was something he'd been dreading. I'd just remind him, it didn't matter if they kicked me out of the group home at the end of the school year—the only concession they would make considering I'd literally just "aged out." Four more weeks of school, but graduation day meant get the fuck out.

Worked for me. We'd been saving every dime to get a place and we would stick close to get to Freddie if we had to. If we had to pay other kids to keep an eye on him and watch his back, we fucking would.

Our parents, the system, and life might leave the us behind, we would not. We were Vandals and he was one of us. Kid brother might know how to push my buttons on a good day, but I wasn't going anywhere.

Fifteen minutes later, we followed the long drive up and around the colonial buildings. While the resort was open year round, this was not the busy time. I was planning to work up here this summer for the extra dollars and for the bungalow we could all share. I'd probably just sign Freddie out of the group home for the summer too if they let me.

Fuck letting, I'd just say I was gonna give him a job and they would probably not complain about not having to pay for him to eat. Whatever.

As soon as Milo pulled in, I was out of the car and striding up to the cliff edge. The drop from here would be exhilarating. There were a couple of paths to get back up too so we could do it more than once.

Freddie came to stand next to me and glanced over the edge. "You're nuts."

I grinned. "That's what makes it fun."

Stripping off my shirt, I backed away from the edge. At the car, I stripped off my shoes, then my pants. I had my swim trunks on. Milo was briefing the guys with a plan. To be honest, it was probably a great plan. He'd earned the name Raptor for his fierceness in protecting us as well as his keen insights.

I was a hawk, though, so I could see everything I needed to see right now.

"Hey," Milo called as I strode away from them. "Jas!"

I laughed. "Happy birthday to me, bitches!" Then I was running. I didn't need to dive off the cliff and I still wanted to get some distance when I leaped. I heard their laughter, yells and whistles, but I was already jumping.

The air whooshed at me and there was a moment of perfect peace as I seemed to hang there suspended and then I plummeted. The icy water at the bottom was a rush that slapped reality back into me.

The tide wasn't hitting the rocks yet so nothing threw me back at the cliff. When I surfaced, my laughter echoed back at me.

Fuck yes.

I swam for shore.

I was totally doing that again.

RUTHLESS TRAITOR BONUS SCENES

CRAVING (ALTERNATE POV)

LIAM

*T*aking Hellspawn to the Blue Diamond hadn't been high on my list. Then again, Emersyn needed a break. Everyone wanted to smother her in protection. She needed it, but she didn't have to suffocate under the weight of it. Former 19 Diamonds territory might not seem like the best place to take her with a bounty still on her head. Yet that was exactly why I took her with me

No one would be looking for her here. While I owned the place, my involvement had been obscured by shell corporations and other LLCs. I still needed to figure out what to do about her uncle. He'd put the bounty on her and rather than make her—or anyone else for matter—aware, I sat on the details.

Out of the apartment, she relaxed. Not the way she did when we went to train. There she was all focused-energy and compulsion. I swore she lived for the challenge. Not that I was remotely opposed to it. The fact she pushed back when I pushed her made me push her harder.

We made our way through the club to the booth I'd chosen on my first visit. No one was allowed to sit here unless the club was overflowing. She scooted in, but her attention was almost exclusively on the dancers. The fact I had to keep getting her attention to get her moving amused me.

She was laser-focused on the dancers and I wanted to watch her. When Cathy reached our table, I had to talk right into her ear or risk disturbing Hellspawn's growing fascination with the performance. The girl on the stage wasn't bad, but she lacked my partner's lithe physique and staggering amount of control.

Cathy wanted to stay but I sent her for the drinks and food first. It wasn't unusual for one of the dancers to come straight to me to tattle about something or other. Frankly, I hadn't owned the place all that long. A few weeks at most, but they all had issues and they came to me to get them fixed.

Easily enough handled.

Through the next few sets, Hellspawn remained riveted on the stage. It wasn't until she knocked my drink over onto Cathy that I realized she'd been paying as much attention to me as she had the dancers. Not going to lie, the warmth of that acknowledgement settled in my chest. It was a stupid thing to appreciate. Though the last thing I wanted to do was leave Emersyn out here, but Cathy told me about some skimming. I needed to deal with it. An iron fist in a velvet glove was only effective once you'd proven how capable of steel you were.

Cathy rolled her hips in invitation as she led the way toward the doors that would take us into the back where the business office and kitchens as well as storage were kept. Three steps into the back and she pushed right into me. The weight of her breasts on my chest, not to mention the tight grip of her hands on my shirt were a total turnoff.

I scowled down at her, but she misread it entirely and rubbed her body against me as she pressed her lips to mine.

Yeah.

No.

Hands on her hips, I took care not to throw her as I peeled her off me and set her on her feet.

"Liam?" Her lower lip jutted out in what I was certain she thought was a playful pout. Unimpressed, I fixed her with a look.

"I don't fuck the staff," I told her bluntly. "The flirting was fine, but this crosses a line."

Shock rippled over her face.

"Try that again and I'll send your ass packing so fast, you won't know what hit you. Understood?"

Anger flashed in her eyes. Enough to tell me she was more insulted than she was hurt. When she folded her arms to hide her breasts from me, I didn't take the bait and drop my gaze. Finally, she sighed. "Can't blame a girl for trying..."

"I sure as fuck can," I said, taking a step toward her and her pouting fled even as she blanched. "If you're using this place to turn tricks, it stops. You try to fuck with anyone else on the staff, you're out. You put a hand on me again without my express invitation and you're out."

Swallowing hard, she nodded. "Yes, sir."

"Repeat it back to me. Word for word."

The shock in her eyes threatened to take a turn into mutiny, but unlike my hellspawn, the waitress couldn't hold my gaze. Suddenly, she looked everywhere but at me. We stood there for the better part of a minute before she began stuttering her way through a repeat of what I'd told her.

Close enough.

I nodded to her. "Now go away."

Bypassing her and the waste of time she'd presented, I went in search of the busboy and the cook who had been helping themselves to a portion of the profits from the till *and* the dancers. Yeah, extortion was extortion in my book.

This was my place.

It took me ten minutes too long to pin both men, extract their stuttering confessions, and deliver a beatdown I doubted either would remember. Frankly, they got off light. I might go and find them later.

Especially if they hadn't returned every dime they'd taken within the next forty-eight hours.

Oh, and they were fired. One of the other cooks helped me throw them out on their asses via the back.

"Remember," I told them as they stared, bloody and bruised. "I know where you live. Do yourselves a favor, don't make me come looking for you."

That finished, I went to wash my hands before I went back to our table. Only instead of making it to the table, all I saw when I exited back into the bar was my hellspawn, on the main stage, *working* the pole.

Every breath in my body squeezed out of me in a whoosh. While she wore next to nothing, she wasn't naked. Didn't matter. Didn't matter at all. She was more attractive in her dance pants and oversized t-shirts without an ounce of makeup than any other woman I'd ever met. But riding that pole, writhing and half dancing in the fucking air like it was solid ground.

I couldn't see anything but her.

Rome had watched her videos so much and so often, I'd obviously seen the appeal. But it had *nothing* on seeing her in person. Nothing on watching the way her muscles rippled and moved with her.

Fighting with her had given me a real appreciation for the strength she possessed. But this—this was something else. Everything in the room just faded away. The guys whistling and inviting her to come to the edge of the stage, the wait-resses weaving in and out, the other dancers at their stations.

No, the only thing I could see was Emersyn and the only thing I could feel was the wild pulse of my heartbeat slam-ming inside me to the rhythm of the music. I made it almost to her when she landed on the last note of the song. The ease with which she slid into the splits made my cock leap.

Hell.

Yes.

When she locked her gaze on mine, she gave me an almost tremulous smile. It held more pleasure than anything else she'd expressed in the last few weeks. In fact, she panted fairly hard as though she needed to catch her breath.

I totally got that. I didn't think I'd ever get mine back. Then the music cranked again, bursting the bubble and letting all the sound rush in. She was back up on her feet and moving. More guys came up to the stage and held out money or set it out for her when she gave them no notice.

As she reached the end of the next song, she arched herself over backwards and then we were almost nose to nose. Something feral moved in those eyes. Something feral and captivating. Catch me if you can, it seemed to challenge me.

Applause burst out around us, whoops, whistles, and catcalls.

Challenge accepted, Hellspawn. I dragged her off the stage and kissed her. It was the worst idea. It was the best idea.

It was the only thing I could think of to put some claim on her in front of every fucker in this place. They could look, whistle, and clap all they wanted. They'd never get this from her. Never be this close. Never taste the dark passion on her lips or how she arched into it turning it from my possession to her demand. When I clasped her hair in my fist, I had to fight against the urge to grind into her.

My erection was stiff and throbbing. All I wanted to do was throw these fuckers out and spread her out right on that stage and fuck her until neither of us could walk.

Then we'd fuck again.

As it was, I had to force myself to let her go. She was Rome's. Rome wanted her.

That voice in my head warned me I was going too far. He never wanted anything. But he wanted her. I would not get in the fucking way.

We were both breathing so ragged and sharp when I finally lifted my head. "Hellspawn, you're gonna be the death of me."

She swallowed, but the swollen lips and the hot flush to her cheeks were from the kiss even more than the dancing. It was pure torture to set her down, but I was a goddamn glutton for the agony and the punishment.

"I need to get dressed," she said, as if reminding me that she wasn't wearing her own clothes.

Yeah. I'd noticed. "Go," I whispered, still not trusting my voice. "Then we're out of here."

For once, she didn't have some smart ass comment or witty comeback. She just nodded and walked away. At least she didn't look any steadier than I felt.

"Hey," a guy behind me said and I twisted to look at him. "How much for the whore?"

How much for the—

I really didn't process the rest of it. I slammed my fist into his face and he toppled, his glass jaw not even remotely a defense. His buddy tried to come and help, but I snapped his arm and then knocked his ass out. The music cut off for just a second and the whole room froze in a near comical tableau of shock and horror.

"Anyone else want to ask me a stupid question?"

The music cranked and everyone went back to their business. No one bent down to help the assholes on the ground. One of my bouncers came over and I nodded to them.

"Wake them up, toss them out, and ban them for life."

"You got it."

I'd just finished that when Emersyn came almost floating out from the backroom. Once more in her sundress, only the faint hint of sweat on her skin betrayed her earlier performance. God, she looked so fucking beautiful. Perfect. Strong. Fierce. Determined.

And I wanted her.

I couldn't afford to want her.

Fuck me.

"What's wrong?"

"We need to go," I told her. We couldn't stay here anymore. Not when all I could think about was fucking her or killing the next asshole who talked about her that way. The assholes on the floor had begun to stir.

"Did you...?"

"Yes."

"Do I want to..."

"No."

We were almost to the door and I'd yanked it open when I spotted the car, the men, and the guns. All a split second too late to slam the door again. The first slug took me in the chest and hit like a hammer. The second was worse, even as I twisted to yank Emersyn down and under me, I pulled out my gun. Firing blind was fucking stupid.

But I'd clocked where the first guy stood and that was who I aimed to hit.

EDUCATION (ALTERNATE POV)

EMERSYN

"We're here to teach you how to drive my car. Lessons for how to ride me come later—and they're extra." The distinct invitation to play echoed in his voice. Kellan hadn't flirted with me since I'd discovered his "betrayal." Then again, it wasn't really a betrayal, was it?

"Extra?" Excitement threaded through me as if in absolute defiance to my wariness. Kellan had been the first one I'd ever been attracted to. The first to almost feel like a friend. Then—the truth chipped that away, turning everything I thought I knew into a lie. "How much was the car lesson?"

But had it? Or was it all discolored by the confusion and the pain surrounding my rather savage arrival into their world? At my question, however, Kellan unsnapped his seatbelt and reached across the divide to pin me to the driver's seat.

The fire in his blue-green eyes beckoned to me and then his mouth was on mine. The fierce kiss I'd given him earlier had nothing on this. With sweeping demand, he thrust his tongue against mine and I drank him in like he was the oxygen. Whatever reticence might have remained went up in flames as he slid his hand from my chin to my throat.

The possessiveness in the grip didn't tighten or choke, he didn't collar or chain me, but it grounded me so deep in the moment, I trembled from the violent surges of desire and need. Want burst through me. This want was so different from the sex I'd been trying to seduce from him then.

Then we were both lying.

That reality settled in my bones. We weren't lying anymore.

"How wet are you right now, Sparrow?"

I clenched my thighs together as I shuddered. "Soaking." No more lies.

"Good." He ran his tongue over his lower lip, this close, I could practically *feel* the action and then he laved that tongue over my lower lip. It wasn't all that hard to imagine his tongue elsewhere. My nipples pulled so taut they stung. "Consider 'that' the cost of today's lesson."

Lesson. Right. Car. "We haven't even started the car."

"The cost covered the whole day, whether you drive it or not."

That was probably good, I was having trouble remembering the rest of the lessons.

"Uh huh and when can I get on the highway?"

"Depends on what you're willing to pay—"

Amusement *and* annoyance struck a match and flamed right through the bone-shaking desire quivering in me. "Right...you're a fucking tease, Kellan."

"Don't worry Sparrow, I'm sure you'll find some relief. Who knows—maybe I'll send a Hawk over to find you after."

I smacked his chest. What a—wait! Had he just offered to send Jasper to me? My cunt clenched tight around the emptiness. The wildness of that suggestion was so damn provocative that it only amped up my need.

His expression gentled, the kindness I'd found there so long ago returned. He meant it. Every word. Tripping over the wonder of that, I barely heard him as he said "Let's start the car."

Giddiness swept me up. I was really going to learn how to drive a car. It was a skill I'd always wanted, but who had the time? And if I had the time for lessons—then I could have them at—nope. I pinched that thought off. He got no part of this moment.

None.

"I still can't believe you're gonna teach me to drive. "

After he'd gone over where I needed to put my hands, and more—a refresher I was grateful for because my scrambled neurons were still considering what he would feel like bare against me—he answered a question that had pinged around inside of me.

"As for why I'm teaching you, I want you to have every skill you need. Driving is an essential skill. It gives you a way out. Jasper is probably gonna take you to the range if he hasn't already. You said Liam's teaching you how to fight. The others are all trying to teach you different things, share different parts of ourselves with you."

Share different parts of themselves with me.

"Ready?"

This was Kellan offering a part of himself.

"Yes!"

Hell yes, I was ready. I cut a glance at him and his smile offered me confidence and faith. Yes, he was holding out his hand in offering, all I had to do was take it.

FOCUSED (BONUS POV)

LIAM

AGE 15

"*K*eep that left up." As if to prove his point, Jerry's fist grazed my chin. I was already moving away from him, but he was relentless in his assault. He hammered on my guard, switching up his blows, but I kept retreating. It wasn't until he tried to corner me in the ring that he saw his mistake. By then it was already too late.

Every movement had been a calculation on my part. I wanted him to pursue, I wanted him to feint, jab, and punch. I'd kept my guard up, but weak. I withdrew as though *I* was the one who needed a break. Every single choice since I ducked into the ring with my black eye and bruised ribs had been designed to get him into this position.

Ruthless in his training, Jerry didn't disappoint. When Dad approached him about teaching me, he'd promised that he wouldn't hold back. As much as Dad disapproved of bloodsports, he'd respected my request.

Which put me here, in this basic gym that smelled of

sweat, work, and probably tears. I fucking loved this place. Jerry didn't just teach boxing or martial arts. He understood several different fighting forms.

What he trained me in, was using all of them to my advantage. The feint with his left knee before he snapped out with his right leg was the moment of truth. I flowed around his motion, caught the leg twisted, struck with my weaker left toward his midsection—not to hit, but to grip—before lifting his leg up and flipping his whole body.

I didn't let go, the grapple required a close hold and we went over together. The scissor grip of my legs around him as controlled his right arm with a twist kept him pinned. Yes, he had a free arm, but he didn't have the leverage he'd need to get free before I broke his arm.

Panting, I stared at him as Jerry stared back. Neither of us gave an inch. The one thing he'd drilled into me over the last year had been—you don't decide when to release the opponent just because you think you've won. They have to accept that defeat before, or you just handed them the advantage.

He didn't relax, even when I shifted my grip on his arm to apply more pressure. Then a slow smile spread across his face and he tapped the floor. But it was just a tap and there was no surrender in his expression.

Another thirty seconds past before his smile became a genuine grin. "Yield, you strong little shit. I yield."

I released him immediately and rolled up to my feet, ignoring the burning in my chest and the pull of muscles along my back. He clasped the hand I offered him and let me pull him to his feet.

"That was excellent," he complimented me, as he gripped my shoulder. I didn't wince. Even if the heavy-handed contact sent a vibration over my aching ribs. "You have been listening, more you've been plotting. I like the fact you laid a trap and let me walk right into it. Excellent job, don't think it'll happen twice. Now that I know you're *thinking*, we're going to up this training."

Now I let myself grin as he let me go and moved off. It wasn't until he ducked out of the ring that I frowned. "We're done?"

"Unless you want to explain the ribs and the shiner," he said with a pointed look.

I folded my arms. Not particularly.

"Then yes, we're done. I told your dad I would train you and I will. I promised you that you'd know everything you needed before we were done. We'll be mixing it up next week. Come in ready to get your ass kicked, but if the ribs are still bothering you—text me and we'll skip."

I'd protest but Jerry wasn't kidding. He might be thirty years older and a good friend to my parents, but he didn't go easy on me and I didn't want him to at all.

Not when I'd learned a hell of a lot. I'd always been a good fighter.

When we were done, I was going to be goddamn unstoppable. "Thanks man."

"See you next week," he called. He didn't have to remind me about my ribs, but I caught him stretching and flexing the arm I'd locked. I grinned. It was usually the other way around. I'd just grabbed my bag when my watch alarm buzzed.

Fuck. It was later than I thought. We hadn't finished as early as I thought. I showered in the gym, and changed. The driver pulled up at the curb just as I stepped out. I tucked my sunglasses into place and smoothed down my tie before sliding into the back seat.

"Should I take the scenic route, sir?" Tom asked over his shoulder with the barest hint of a smile. "If we get there on time, you might shock your mother and ruin your reputation for always running late."

"Ha ha." Not that he was wrong. "It's good to be unpredictable."

"Of course."

Tom had been my driver for the last three years. In a few months, he'd get a break because I'd have my own license. I already knew *how* to drive. I literally just waited out the clock on our birthday.

I pulled out my phone to check for messages as Tom drove us to the restaurant. Mom and Dad always invited me to a late lunch, early dinner after my training sessions because I'd already be in the city. Afterwards, Tom would take me back to school.

Most of the time I was late.

The suit and tie would hide everything but the shiner. But it was hardly the first time I came to dinner with a black eye. It wouldn't be the last either. All too soon, Tom pulled up at Formaggio's, the Italian restaurant that was Mom's favorite.

"See you in a couple of hours. You want manicotti or ravioli?"

"Ravioli," Tom said with a grin. "Definitely the ravioli and some of those little Parmesan bread bits."

"You got it." I left my training bag in the car as I slid out. The valet nodded to the doorman who let me into the restaurant. I tugged my sunglasses off as soon as i was in.

"Mr. O'Connell," Linda the hostess greeted me with a warm smile. She had a grandmother's demeanor and always smelled like baked bread and sugar cookies. "Liam, your mother is here, it's your father who is late today."

"Always has to be one of us," I told her. "I can get to the table." I waved her off from escorting me as I tucked my phone into the inner jacket pocket where I'd feel it if it vibrated and headed across the family restaurant to the private booths. We practically owned one since Mom ate here at least once a week.

"Liam!" Surprise and delight filtered through her tone as I reached the table. "You're on time!"

"I heard Dad was going to be late and didn't want to leave a beautiful woman like you unescorted."

"Oh for the love of God," she muttered, swatting my arm as I braced a hand on the back of the booth to dip my head and press a kiss to her cheek. "You men. Both of you. As if I constantly have to beat off the suitors with a stick."

"You don't have to, Mom," I promised. "We'll happily take care of it for you."

A man would have to be blind to not see how Mom looked at Dad and while this was a fun joke, because it never failed to make her blush or smile, I was dead serious.

I'd happily beat the shit out of anyone that looked at her the wrong way. Mom had changed my life. She loved me, she loved my mirror, and she'd always made room for him even if he didn't want to be there full time.

They were family in all the right ways.

As I took a seat, a waiter appeared with my water and a glass of soda. I didn't have to order, they always knew what I wanted.

"I suppose if I ask about the shiner, you're just going to grin and say I should see the other guy?"

"I could," I offered. "Or we could skip that conversation and you can tell me how your week is going. I know you and Dad were talking about heading over to Paris for fashion week, is that still on?"

"Liam, you couldn't care less about fashion week."

"But you love it," I said. "You care a lot and that means I care about you being happy."

Her laughter was a reward all its own. "You and your father, kissed by all that Irish charm."

Sometimes. Or maybe I was just serious. I liked it when Mom was happy. She took the offer and filled me in on their travel plans. While I wasn't big on fashion or retail, I soaked up every bit of information. Some day, I would take over the business so they could just do the things they loved.

They carved out a place in their world for me and I'd damn well take it and then make sure the world left them alone to do as they wished. I had a plan and they were a big part of it.

My parents. My mirror. My brothers.

The whole damn world would have to go through me to get any of them.

It was why I trained. It was why I studied. It was why I stayed focused.

INITIATION (ALTERNATE POV)

ROME

*L*iam's message said Vaughn had picked her up. So rather than go to Liam's, I just went back to the clubhouse. Probably why he told me. I didn't bother to check with the rats working or anyone else. I wanted to see her.

Since the shooting at the club, I needed to be where she was and by extension, where Liam was often. The need had grown into an obsession, one that gnawed at me when too long passed without them. I didn't question it, just followed the lines back to where they converged with them. It was better when they were both in the apartment.

I was halfway to Kel's room to get to Emersyn's when I doubled-back to Vaughn's. The door wasn't locked, so I let myself in with a brief knock. Old habits. While not even locked doors could keep us out, the unlocked door was an invitation I accepted. The soft whispery groan that greeted me couldn't prepare me for the sight of my starling, straining upward as she sat on Vaughn's face.

The flush to her cheeks just added to the perfection as she glanced over her shoulder to meet my gaze. I didn't like looking in other people's eyes. It wasn't comfortable. But I loved her eyes.

I loved the way she moved. The soft sounds she made. I loved even more how she would look at me and how she never demanded anything.

Except my name.

She'd needed my name.

I'd give her anything really.

What was my name in the grand scheme of all that? I shut the door behind me and locked it. Vaughn left an invitation. I didn't want to leave a second. Not right now. Not while heat flooded my body and something stirred deep within.

"Hi," she greeted me on a breathy groan that stiffened my cock in a way that had grown increasingly familiar around her. Especially when she moved like she was now, her hips rolling and Vaughn's hands gripping her.

I moved to the bed and knelt on the edge of the mattress. The constant torrent of soft, muted sounds escaping her were a balm and a provocation. I wanted to hear all of them. "Starling," I said, but she dropped her head. I brushed my fingers against her chin, helping her to lift her head so I could see her. The flush to her cheeks deepened. Her eyes were huge pools of starlit darkness. I wanted to dive into them and never leave.

The transformation of her expression, as she opened her mouth and released the first notes of a keening cry, was an enchantress's song I couldn't ignore. I wanted to taste that pleasure in her. I wanted to taste *her* pleasure. The stroke of my tongue against hers sent an uncontrollable shiver through my whole body.

Her kiss was the sweetest candy I'd ever sampled, a dark narcotic that instantly addicted me. I needed more. I cupped her chin, licking, sucking, teasing, and tasting as the soft sound of her cries grew in intensity. Every single one a lightning bolt to the voracious craving gripping my system. When she clasped my free hand and moved it to her breast, I sighed against her lips.

The smooth, suppleness of her skin was so fucking soft. Her nipple was taut and beaded hard. I tested the texture against my fingertips. It pebbled even tighter, the little bumps demanded exploration. When she didn't reject my stroking, I pinched it, giving the faintest twist.

Not a stereo knob. The conversation the guys had a long time ago floated out of my memory. A disconnect from that moment and this, but it suddenly made sense. Not a radio knob. No, so much warmer, softer, and eager. She pushed against my hand, her back arching.

I had to release her mouth to kiss a path to that nipple. I wanted to feel it with my tongue and my teeth. Would it be as sweet as her lips. I sucked it against my teeth, careful not to bite and her strangled cry just made me increase the suction.

Her reaction coupled with the oddness of how it felt pushed me to suck harder. I wanted more. I wanted more of *her*.

"Shift," Vaughn ordered and I lifted my head as he pulled her from me. My objections died when he didn't take her away so much as move her to her hands and knees as he slid out from under her.

His whole face glistened. It sent my gaze to where he gripped her hips. What would she taste like? Could I paint myself with her like he had?

"Hands and knees, Dove. Look up at Rome."

"Fuck her mouth, Rome," Vaughn said. "She likes the taste of cock, don't you Dove."

"Yours," she admitted. "I like yours. I like Jasper's" Then she stared up at me. "Can I suck you off?"

I could deny her nothing and I didn't want to deny her.

The question made my cock throb with a kind of painful pleasure. The pain was familiar, I'd needed it to make my art before, but this was different. This wasn't about making anything or anyone happy except her.

And maybe me.

I slid off the bed and shed my clothes. Nudity had never been a struggle for me. I didn't care if I was naked or someone else was.

The first body I'd ever seen that I wanted was hers. And I loved her all naked and soft, the golden light of the room kissed every single one of her curves. It painted her like she was the moon, basking in the light of the sun.

I wanted to capture the whole moment. I wanted to paint her just like this. But not out in the city.

No, this would be for me.

"May I?" The whispered question feathered her breath over my cock even as she drifted her hand out as though to touch me. The fact she hadn't made me want to strain forward. I wanted *her* touch.

"For you," I promised her. I'd made that decision a long time ago. I'd painted her onto my dick. It had taken me several sessions with time to heal between each one. Vaughn insisted on the healing or I couldn't use his tools. I'd inked her from memory, there was one video of her that had been done that I'd watched so many times. After downloading it to my phone, I could watch the four-minute-and-thirty-second clip anytime I wanted.

I wanted.

A lot.

Every light caress of her fingertips sent liquid heat pulsing into my dick. I'd had to get hard to do the ink. It had never been this hard. Then she traced her tongue over the tip and I *wanted*.

The hunger struck like a fist to my senses, blacking everything out except her. Gliding my fingers into her hair, the contrast of textures just added to the need burning in my veins.

"Open your mouth, Starling—tell me if I need to stop. I've never done this before."

Her flared pupils seemed to swallow what was left of the brown in her eyes. Her lips went soft and her mouth widened. I thrust my dick against the hot wetness of her mouth and savored how her tongue glided along the underside of my dick until I made it to her throat. The resistance there slowed me. She gagged, but her gaze never left mine.

I'd wanted to dive into those eyes forever and now I plunged in. Liam had told me for years how much I needed to get my dick sucked. The idea never held any appeal.

Until now.

Her body jolted with Vaughn's pounding thrusts, but I kept control of her hair. If she gagged, I needed to be able to pull out. Then I tested the thrusts. Hard and fast. Slow and deep. Each time I pushed into her throat the sensation was unbelievable. When she added suction and stroking with her tongue, my balls tightened. I wanted everything, but I always wanted to feel everything with her mouth.

My mind splintered, thoughts fracturing like an abstract as I shifted my hips and adjusted her head. She gave me everything I asked for. The vibrations of her cries stroked over my dick with rising intensity.

She gave me everything. I'd pull out with a pop and paint her lips with my cock and then she'd open up to swallow me again. When she cupped my balls, my thoughts stuttered. I had to hold onto her with both hands. The wild need to just pump into her grew. The violence of it. Every little gagging noise, every glistening tear that fell, all of it pulled my balls tighter and tighter.

Unleashed within me, my desire had become a visceral demand. It wanted *her*. I wanted her.

"Starling," I warned as the tautness in my balls suddenly expanded to encompass everything and the pleasure-pain of release struck me. I let go and everything came out of me in a rush. She didn't pull away. If anything she burrowed against my abdomen as she sucked me down.

I swore a piece of my soul went with it. When I finished, I pulled away but only so I could kiss her. I needed to kiss her. Fucking her mouth was amazing, but I wanted to taste her. To taste us on her tongue.

"Play with her clit," Vaughn said in a guttural voice, as he peeled her away from me. He shifted until he had Starling spread wide in front of him, his dick pumping in and out of her at a speed that made me want to be the one pushing into her.

I stared at the way she glistened and convulsed. The bright pink flush had gone almost cherry red. Her clit strained out from its hood and looked like the most perfect of creations. For a second, the light played over the plastic on her belly and I spotted the tattoo.

I trailed my fingers over her nipples, testing what sounds I could pull from her. Then I kissed the edges of the plastic. The tattoo was so new, so fresh, and it was so perfect against her unmarred flesh. Our marks, not the painful bruises of before.

Then I went to her clit. Testing it, teasing it, stroking it with my tongue. I wanted to kiss all of her. I wanted to wear her on my skin as Vaughn had earlier. His cock kept thrusting, the motion hypnotic and he was in the way, but he also wore her on his skin and every lap of my tongue that brushed him brought more of her taste for me to savor.

Emersyn gave a throaty scream and Vaughn's whole body stiffened, but I kept licking. I'd thought her lips were her sweetest treat. She had so much delicate decadence here, I wanted more.

"Rome," Vaughn said in a breathless, wrecked voice. "You don't have to lick my cock man."

"It's in the way," was my only response. If he didn't want to move—and I didn't blame him—then I'd lick and kiss him as much as I did her. Every brush of my lips and tongue drew some reaction from her and from him. They both groaned as she tried to arch her hips, but I held her down and Vaughn wrapped her tight.

The pleasure was all for her and when she thrashed and came, I recognized the orgasm and the heady flavor of it rushed out of her.

More.

I wanted more.

DIRTY DEVIL BONUS
SCENES

CERTIFIED (ALTERNATE POV)

BODHI

The white ceiling bored the fuck out of me. Even if it wasn't totally white. Cracks in the drywall created imperfections in the paint. A place where it bubbled in one corner. Another where it created a kind of plateau like someone used way too much spackle to fix a crack. Either way, every imperfection showed a tint of gray to it. Like the depth of the paint occluded the light.

It was a lot like me. Gray in places. I shifted my gaze across the landscape created by lazy workmen who were either in too much of a hurry or just didn't give enough of a fuck to do a decent job. Then again, who cared? Pinetree might charge the "patients" in this wing the same as those in the more luxurious accommodations, but it wasn't like we were gonna be leaving them a review on Squawk or Squeal or whatever the hell was the trending app these days.

I could see it now, Pinetree Psychiatric Facility, a private facility offering customized solutions for your mental health issues. Fuckers would add a lot of different services like, twenty-four hour monitored counseling, "certified" professionals, "group" counseling, "private" accommodations, and some spiel about Doctor Schuitevoerder and his elite credentials.

Mengele was a fucking doctor too.

Reviews wouldn't be from the patients unless they read zero of five stars, the care here sucks. They don't give a fuck if you recover, they just want your family money. Need to get rid of that troublesome relative? Pinetree is the place for you.

A scrape in the hallway cut through my mental composition of a review. I glanced at the door. It was reinforced. All you needed was the right set of keys to get in and out of it.

They'd changed the locks since my last visit. I could be patient. I mean, I was *a* patient.

Laughter shuddered through me and I grinned. I *was* a patient. Thumping came from down the hall. Probably old Darryl running into the walls again. Darryl had been trying to take himself out for weeks. The man really sucked at it.

I could give him a hand. Offered even. He said he'd think about it.

Cool.

Another scrape in the hallway.

It was awfully late for a visit. Or early, I rarely slept so who the fuck knew what time it was.

Unless…

Excitement scraped along the nerves under my skin. Every once in a while, one of the orderlies got cocky and came down here to "beat" on the inmates.

Oh please pick me.

Please.

Ple—

The door locks tumbled against each other and then the door swung open.

Yes!

I didn't move from my spot, but the last thing I expected

was the kid from group and the bitch from the day room to fill the open doorway.

"Here. In you go." She tried to shove the kid inside, but he just glanced off the wall and staggered away. Huh. The nurse pocketed more drugs than she distributed and she sure as fuck didn't care how the patients were doing.

Pretty sure she liked banging crazy too. Too bad her family couldn't afford Pinetree.

"Dammit," she snarled, yanking the kid's arm and something hit the floor. It skittered all the way into my room. A cell phone. Look, today was my lucky day. "What the hell was that?"

Without a sound, I was off the bed and at the doorway. The dumb bitch had her back to me. Was she trying to shove the kid in here? For what? Delivering meat to a lion?

Yeah, I didn't kill on command.

Besides, the kid wasn't so bad. He actually liked my stories.

This bitch though?

Oh, I didn't like her.

At all.

She fought to drag the kid forward, not paying a lick of attention to me.

Hateful *and* stupid. What a delightful combination.

The kid yanked away from her and she stumbled right back at me. I caught her head in my hands. For a moment, her whole body stilled. The world stilled. Flash-frozen, a split-second in time. Her hair was rough against my palms.

She really needed to get a better conditioner. I applied the right pressure with my fingers and gave a sharp twist. The crack of her neck spread through me like a mini-orgasm. Profound relief as her shrill presence blunted. Letting her go, I rode the wave of pleasure in the absolute perfection of that moment.

Crumpling like the broken and discarded toy she'd become, the nurse hit the floor at my feet. Exhaling, I glanced down at her. Yes. That was much better.

So much better.

"I'm keeping the phone." It was still in my room and I glanced at the kid. He just nodded, then gave me a thumbs up.

"What are you going to do with her?" He didn't care. Not about her. It was a kind of curious question. A solid one really.

I glanced down at her again. Couldn't keep her in here. She would definitely stink the place up. Besides, I didn't like her. This space might be a shitty space, but it was *my* space.

After pocketing the phone, I dragged her up and over my shoulder. Dead weight or not, she was hardly a burden. The keys that jangled in her pocket gave me another shiver of pleasure.

This was definitely a good day. "They have drain cleaner here," I told him. It had been a while since I dissolved a body. Entertainment for hours.

After closing up my room, I headed down the hall toward the maintenance closets. They kept *all* the cleaning supplies down here. Very helpful.

"Bodhi?"

Pivoting, I faced the kid but kept moving as I walked backwards. I'd almost forgotten he was there. "Yeah?"

"Thanks."

"Not my best work." I grinned, touching two fingers to my brow. The kid didn't linger. Probably good. Dissolving bodies was a gruesome business.

At least this chick was bony, less body fat to worry about. Humming, I made my way down the darkened hallway. Phone. Keys. Dead body.

Definitely my lucky day.

STAPLED (ALTERNATE POV)

STAPLER

*N*ot much to say about my life, really. It started where most lives start—a factory. I was all bits and bobs. They put them together, then bing, bong, bam, Bob's your uncle and I'm a stapler. Made it through quality assurance, inspection, got branded with the company logo and then whisked off to a life of darkness for who the fuck knows how long.

Eventually, I ended up in some office supply store with scores of others. Most of them were my kind, but there were a few others—you know the ones that aren't industrial strength. They're more civilians. Sleek. Sweet. Pretty.

Yeah, they left faster than me, but this was my lot and I was stuck in it until a mass purchase came in. Then a whole cadre of us were shipped off somewhere else.

That was my life before the jackoff who ran this joint put me on his desk. Why do I call him a jackoff? Well, let's put it this way—I've *seen* things. Like really, bad things.

Can we leave it at that? Cause talking about it is just gonna make me ill and I'll be spitting bent staples for days.

Then someone will bang *me* on the desk like that's supposed to make me work better.

Trust me, no one banged on *this* desk ever seems better for the experience.

Right, so, been on the desk for a hot minute or year—years. I dunno, I can't tell time. Clock does that and he's a grouchy bitch that periodically just stops to make someone tickle him and put his hands in the right place. The calendar changes regularly enough that the latest one doesn't even sit on the desk.

Fact was, I didn't know where that calendar was kept. Elitist bastard.

But I digress...

I've been on this desk awhile. I've seen some shit. Kind of glad staplers don't need therapy, pretty sure no one would believe me. Cause, truth is always stranger than fiction.

Right, back to the subject. I've buried my staples in scores of papers, banged them good and hard. Secured them. Then sat there ignored for what seemed like forever.

I was there the first time she was in his office.

Then the second.

Thankfully, nothing really worth commenting on happened then. The third time though? That was enough to make a stapler wish it could be tossed out a window.

So the fourth time she showed up, I knew it wasn't going to go well. I wanted to tell her to get out, take off, just run for it. But—well, no matter how hard I bang anything or I'm banged, fuck if I can say anything.

So imagine my surprise when she wrapped that silken hand around my handle, jerked me off the desk, and swung me like a mace.

Talk about a life-changing experience. Literal. Life. Changing. Experience.

I wasn't a stapler.

I was a wrecking ball.

The delicious crunching of bone was the best fucking sound ever.

Course, it was over in a blink and I didn't have words for what happened. Like, had we really just done that? Was I an accessory? Or like—the actual accessory?

Fuck my life I was going to be stuck in some evidence locker forever. Don't get me wrong, definite step up from this gig and probably a lot cleaner, but...

Oh, dude, she was taking me with her.

Yep. Cool.

So, while I might be an accessory, I was going to be her accessory. I liked that.

Thankfully, she did give me a bath or maybe it was one of the others. Bits of flesh and brain weren't good for the hardware.

My new lodgings involve a quiet room and a companion. Not that he says much, he just hangs out on the bed and stares at the wall like it's a damn masterpiece.

Course, he's a raggedy looking fellow, his fur kind of roughed down and his eyes a little mismatched.

Right, I got pet, but I didn't get banged or have to bang anything. I was still fully loaded though. So, watch your step.

ahem

Watch your staplers, too.

We are legion after all.

wink

FLUMADIDDLED (BONUS POV)

FREDDIE

noun

or less commonly **flum·a·did·dle** \ ˈfləməˌdidᵊl \ *or* **flum·-
did·dle** \ - mˈ- \ *or* **flum·mer·did·dle** \ - mə(r)ˈ-
\ *or* **flum·my·did·dle** \ - mēˈ- \ *or* **fum·a·did·dle** \ ˈfəməˈ- \
*inflected form(s): plural **-s***
1: something foolish or worthless : nonsense, trash
2: bauble, frill

*H*itting the counselor had been really fucking therapeutic. My knuckles stung a little, but I'd barely broken any skin. Lamer than the therapy session, had been his glass fucking jaw. One solid pop and he went down like a popped balloon.

Kind of made me wish the guys had been here for this. Liam and Vaughn would have appreciated the art. Jasper would have rolled his eyes, but fuck knew, he'd have approved. They'd only been trying to teach me to use my fists rather than a knife for a decade.

To be perfectly fair, if I'd had my knife, the guy would not be waking up. He hadn't pissed me off that bad.

At least not yet.

Then the orderlies tackled me and a nurse jabbed that needle into my leg. I hadn't intended to thrash and fight, but that part had just happened. Kicked her in the face.

Oops.

Got one of the orderlies in the balls.

Yep. Not finding an ounce of regret for that shit.

Fuck. Them.

Still, I floated all the way back to my room, they kept pumping me full of the good stuff. Some part of my brain was all, not the plan, man. Not the plan. I told you to not get dead.

I flipped that part off. It sounded way too much like Jasper growling at me. Not that his growls scared me. Clearly. The dude was my biggest fucking supporter and I still had no goddamn idea *why*.

A sob tore through the silence and all the air backed up in my lungs. That sound killed me and I tried to sit up. The spirit was willing but the body fucked right off.

Oh.

The good stuff.

Right.

Okay, I'd wait. The high would come down eventually and the shakes would start. Then I'd be able to open my eyes. Hopefully I didn't piss myself in the meanwhile. Why the Hell had I gone *there*? Now I really needed to pee.

Like, seriously.

Fuck. Me.

Okay, my boy, I told myself. Get up.

Yeah. *That* was effective.

Take two.

Get. The. Fuck. Up.

Nope.

I must have fallen asleep cause Jasper was just *there*. He glared at me with those slate gray eyes that made me think of the skies right before a hella-bad thunderstorm hit. Those used to scare me too.

"What the fuck are you doing?"

"Dude, you're not even here. Don't start shit with me. I can't even win-win the argument cause you're not here."

"What?"

Right. "You're a dream or a hallucination or just like a drug trip...wait, my drug trips are usually not you scowling in disapproval. This is more like the crash."

Jasper sighed and scrubbed a hand over his face. He hadn't been taking as good a care of his beard. Someone should tell him to clip it. Cause currently it was all curly and shit. Kind of reminded me of bad pube hair.

"Why are you laughing?" he asked and I didn't tell him. I mean, he wasn't here. He wouldn't know. But I would. If I told him here then saw him later, I'd never stop laughing.

Nope, better to not say anything.

A nurse walked right through Jasper and she gave me a scowl. Oh, her.

God she was such a bitch.

"You suck," I told her.

"You wish," she commented in return. "Now shut up," she continued without slowing as she jabbed me again. "You're irritating me."

I did it! I lifted my hand and flipped her off. "Good. Cause you're a *bitch!*"

But she wasn't there anymore.

Huh.

Had she been there?

"Focus," Kellan said, from where he leaned against the wall. "You're spiraling."

"You never sit with me," I argued.

"You never remember that I'm there," he replied in a thoroughly calm tone. "Jasper never leaves, but we all come and stay when you need us."

Yeah. I don't need anyone.

Not that I gave voice to that. What a fucking lie. "Boo-Boo is here."

But Kellan didn't respond, I glanced over at the wall and he wasn't there. I scanned the room and no one was here. Well, wasn't that special.

Oh wait, my eyes were open. Yes!

I fell right off the bed as I managed to turn over. The world swayed beautifully. Oh, yeah, this was the best part. No pain. No sweats. No shakes. No fear.

Gotta pee though.

I made it to the bathroom, somehow, pretty sure it didn't take near as long as I thought it did.

The piss was like a ten out of ten where relief was concerned. Almost orgasmic. Like—fucking best piss ever.

I even hit the bowl, from where I stood leaning at the wall.

Ha. That was the secret to fighting with the knife.

Excellent aim.

Mine was killer.

Sometimes, I cracked myself up.

Or maybe, I was just cracked?

When I wandered back to my bed, the nurse was there. Ugh.

I'd much rather see Boo-Boo. Naked. Dressed. Smiling. Or just there.

Yeah, I wanted to see Boo-Boo, not this bitch.

She gave me a look, and I just started laughing at her. The bitch. Not Boo-Boo. I didn't want to see her naked. I missed my pretty pussy girl.

Missed her way too much and if I kept thinking about it, I'd start blubbering again.

Not cool.

"Let me guess," I slurred. "I take the pills or I get the needle again?"

"Hmmm."

Well, it wasn't a no.

I held out a hand. "Pills, please." See, Jasper? I even remembered my manners.

Without a word, the woman passed me the little paper cup and I dry swallowed the damn things then stuck out my tongue so she could see.

One nod and she left.

"You're welcome!" I called after her. "It's usually polite to say thank you when someone cooperates!"

Sadly, I didn't catch whatever she said in response. It would have been worth it.

I gave it another five minutes, then dragged myself back to the bathroom to pee. It took a couple of coughs, but I managed to get the damn things out of my throat as I emptied my bladder again.

Damn, how bad did I have to pee? Or how long had I been waiting to pee?

Who knew?

Humming, I wandered back to the bed and fell on it. I wasn't getting out of here today.

So, I just had to wait.

Wait and be flummadiddled.

That word cracked me up.

I'd read it somewhere and it was like the best word.

I had to remember to tell Boo-Boo.

We could be flummadiddled together.

UNHINGED (BONUS POV)

FREDDIE

"Come."

I glanced up at the imperious command. It was the middle of the day. Still early, I was waiting on Boo-Boo to get here but she was late from whatever appointment she'd had.

"Come," Bodhi repeated and I glanced to where the staff disappeared. No one was even looking at us. I pushed up from the table and went right behind him. "Grab clothes from your room."

"My..."

"Your pretty pussy girl needs you."

I stopped asking questions. I stopped worrying about anything. We left the day room and I slid into my room grabbed an extra shirt and then I was back out again. Where was Boo-Boo? Bodhi had picked up a bag, I had no idea where he'd gotten it from and I didn't ask.

"She needs to leave here," Bodhi said as he strode down the hall toward a wing I hadn't made it into before. "Today."

"How?" We needed a plan. I wasn't "ready" to get us out of

here, but I was beyond ready to make it fucking happen no matter how we had to do it.

"Leave," Bodhi said as he used a keycard that opened the heavy doors to the medical ward. Where—you know, I didn't care where he got it. He had it. "Past the cells, there's a way out down there."

Past his room.

Okay, I could get us down there. It didn't require secure cards.

"Do you know where they store our shit?" I swallowed the next question as we passed a nurse. She didn't even glance in our direction. Bypassing one open door, I caught sight of a table with restraints. Nothing in that room looked —friendly.

Or safe.

Most of the doors were closed and I wasn't sure if that was a good thing or a bad. A flickering light in one corner seemed an ominous sign.

"Yes," Bodhi said and I dragged my gaze back to him. Yes —oh, our shit.

"They took all my stuff, including phone. Can you get it and the bag I had?"

Bodhi looked thoughtful. "Maybe."

Better than no.

Not once on this whole trip had he even slowed his pace. The door he opened this time went into an office… My gaze went to the bloodied body on the floor even as movement pulled my attention across the room. Pale and shaky, she leaned against the door jamb like it was the only thing keeping her up.

Blood was all over her.

"Holy shit, Boo-Boo," I headed straight for her. "Fuck me. What happened?"

"He touched me."

I froze mid-step, then glared down at the body on the floor.

"He's dead?" I needed to know.

"Definitely dead," Bodhi confirmed. "We can do it again, though. Maybe cut the head off. I did that once. It's messy. But not as messy since he's already dead. Shouldn't gush too bad."

I almost wished he wasn't dead. I wanted to make him hurt.

"I killed him." Boo-Boo's broken voice wrenched my attention back to her.

"Well," Bodhi said. "Maybe. You weren't sure. I definitely killed him."

He'd found her in here. He'd found her. He'd helped her. Then he came to get me.

That was all that mattered.

"'It doesn't matter right now, Boo-Boo. Are you hurt?" I studied her. "Is any of that blood yours?"

Next, we needed to get out of here. Bodhi brought her pants, I had a second shirt. I nudged her back into the bathroom more for her privacy. The words "he touched me" kept circling in my head. Bodhi was a friend, but Boo-Boo was everything.

Get the blood off her.

Get her changed.

Get her out of here.

Then I wanted to kill everyone that had anything to do with this place.

"I want to go home." Those soft words dug into my soul.

"Home—home or..."

"The clubhouse. Liam's. Home."

I couldn't help but smile. We'd never wanted her to leave. I never wanted her to leave. "Good. That's where you belong. Okay. Let's get you changed."

Everything in the bathroom stayed clinical. That was what she needed from me. No jokes or stupid comments. We'd do that later. Her bare feet worried me.

"It's time," Bodhi said.

"Yeah, we need to go. We'll get you shoes out there." I didn't want her to get hurt.

Bodhi was already on the move. He was right. If we strode out of here like we belonged, we could do this. He'd come through on everything else. The guy was unhinged but he was my kind of people.

I clasped her hand. "Stay with me, okay, Boo-Boo? No running off. Trust me."

She grabbed a stapler of all things. "I promise." But I didn't ask. If she wanted it, then we were taking it.

The alarms started screaming.

Yep, Bodhi was definitely unhinged.

Thanks, man.

Now to get Boo-Boo the fuck out of here.

BRUTAL FIGHTER BONUS SCENES

APPROPRIATION (ALTERNATE POV)

ROME

"*D*o I want to know?" Starling's eyes were huge. They reminded me of a startled animal trapped by oncoming lights in traffic. I'd never let anything hit her though.

Not as long as I was there to stop it.

"Probably," Liam admitted with more than a sigh. My other half was tired. But he needed her more than he wanted to confess. It was good that we'd come here. Both for Starling and for him. "Ezra is there."

"Lainey's Ezra?"

"Yep."

I almost wished he wasn't. I'd like to keep Starling here for a while. Let them both rest.

"Does Lainey know?" Worry chased another emotion across her face.

"No," I answered. Vaughn did. I did. He was Liam's problem.

"Is he in trouble?"

"To be determined," Liam said. "Your call, Hellspawn, what do you want to do?" While my brother could be guarded and careful of his thoughts, he made no such effort at the moment.

We wanted her to know us. To trust us. She needed us to trust her. So, no more secrets. I liked that.

Liam and I had no secrets. If I wanted to know, he would tell me. The same for him. Now for Starling. She bit at her lower lip and frowned. I didn't like when things bothered her. Especially when she seemed on uneven footing.

"We need to go back then?" The question was for her, not for Liam. If Starling said no, we would stay here. He could deal with Ezra or not. The man would be fine where he was in the meanwhile.

At least, he wouldn't get shot.

She sighed. "We should." Then she glanced down at her bare feet.

"Go change," Liam suggested. "We'll wait for you." He didn't glance at me but I heard the unspoken "we need to talk too" but Starling just cast us both a smile, tremulous though it was.

"Promise?"

"You're not getting rid of me," Liam informed her. "Ever. Get used to it."

Then her grin turned real and she pivoted to head for my room. As soon as she disappeared, I went into the kitchen. If we were going back, now would be a good time to pack up the coffeemaker.

Like my shadow, Liam followed right behind me. "What happened after I left?" I unplugged the machine and removed the water reservoir. "What the hell are you doing?"

"Starling likes fancy coffee."

"And?" The testiness in that single word gave me pause and I glanced at my brother.

"She will like having this there."

He scrubbed a hand over his face. "I'll buy her one. Put it back."

"We have this one."

"We do," he agreed, taking the reservoir out of my hands. "It's mine. I like it. She'll need it when she's *here*."

That was a fair point.

"So I'll buy her one."

"Today?"

He let out a laugh, though it sounded more like a groan. "Yes, today." After he plugged the machine in, he added, "Can you look at me for a moment?"

Though he asked rarely, I didn't mind meeting his gaze. When he did ask, I always complied. "Yes?"

"You really are okay with me and Hellspawn?"

"She's ours." I shrugged. "She always has been. There is nothing to be alright with. You care. I care. She cares."

It was the simplest answer.

"The other guys?"

"They are our brothers."

Liam dropped his chin.

"They are," I repeated. "We kept the truth from them. They know now. They will forgive."

I'd never liked the lie, but I'd understood. Liam never asked me to lie to them directly, only to not explain and to keep quiet. I hadn't cared for that either.

"You have a lot of faith in them," he murmured.

"So do you," I reminded him. "You protected even when they thought you weren't. You chose this path."

"Ouch," Liam grunted and then backed up a couple of steps. He glanced out the kitchen door and I knew he was listening for her. I was too. "It seemed the right thing to do at the time. Still does."

"Then trust them. They know. They care about her too.

She's ours. All of ours. We will keep her safe." Then I spread my hands. "We will keep you safe too."

"Focus on her, brother mine, focus on her. I can watch my own back."

The door to my room opened so I brushed past him, but paused only long enough to smack the back of his head. It was a maneuver he did often when someone said something stupid.

I didn't comment. Didn't have to.

His laughter was confirmation enough.

"Ready?" she asked.

Yes. We were ready.

Coffeemaker, then Ezra. Maybe we could forget the second.

He wasn't as important as the coffee.

POSSESSIVE (BONUS POV)

KELLAN

*S*leep proved elusive, but then I wasn't particularly interested in pursuing it at the moment. I had Sparrow in my bed. A sated, sprawling Sparrow held me captive. The low light softened her features even more. What captivated me was how relaxed she'd gone.

The wariness she wore like body armor and the careful expressions meant to guard her heart were also absent. On the one hand, it made her seem painfully young and yet...

With care, I stroked a hand down her cheek and she rolled into me, tucking her head against my shoulder as I slid an arm around her. The absolute trust in her seeking me out while she was asleep shackled me in place.

I'd sooner cut off my arm than disturb her. The hush of her breathing against my skin was almost a balm for the bloodied scrapes inside my soul.

The last few months had been... brutal.

I meant it when I'd told her she never needed to trade her body for comfort. Wanting her in my bed was a no brainer, but I wanted her fully-informed and aware of the power she wielded.

Then, and only then, I would accept it if she chose to give herself to me. I didn't blame Vaughn or Jasper for their choices. Not when her fiery stubbornness merely disguised the vulnerable young woman beneath.

A vulnerable abused woman at that. No, I didn't blame them for rushing into relationships with her. She pushed and they pushed back, but she also used sex to hide. That meant we needed to be more careful.

Or at least *I* needed to be more careful. I wanted to know everything about her, every morsel she would share. The darkness didn't frighten me in the least. We'd all been forged in blood and fire, some of us more literally than others.

It made me grateful that she'd had Lainey, because friends like her—like my brothers in the Vandals—they were rare and doubly precious. So many fights Sparrow had fought alone.

Not anymore.

"Hmm...you're awake," she said with a groan and I stroked her hair back from her face.

"Shh," I soothed. "Sleep."

With light fingers, she walked up my chest and traced my lips. I caught the hand and kissed her fingers, then her palm before tucking the hand to my chest.

"Sleep," I repeated, continuing to pet her hair until her breathing slowed and evened out. Her trust was so precious to me.

Fuck, *she* was precious to me. Precious to all of us.

When she was ready to give me every detail, we would take the time to get her the vengeance and justice she richly deserved.

We would burn the world of her abusers and they would bleed for her.

They would know the fear and suffering.

Anger coiled in me like a viper ready to strike. We would take what she was owed.

Possessiveness swept through me as I pressed my lips to the crown of her head. Our girl. Our Sparrow.

Ours.

DANGEROUS RENEGADE
BONUS SCENES

CARNAL (BONUS POV)

LIAM

a soft sigh and a groan snapped me from asleep to awake. The shift of the bed next to accompanied by a low, drawn out cry pulled all of my attention. Hellspawn faced me, with Rome behind her. He had a hand on her breast and another on her clit as he thrust into her from behind.

The strain on her face, the soft "o" formed by her mouth was a gorgeous sight. Rolling onto my side, I caught Rome's gaze but he just lifted his chin before returning all of his attention to the woman in our bed. So determined to swallow all the sounds of her own pleasure, Hellspawn writhed and moved.

Every thrust from Rome had her twisting her hips. The feel of her when she did that to me was fucking amazing. I leaned forward, blew a teasing breath across her neglected nipple and her dark eyes fluttered open. I waited for her to focus on me.

Surprise flickered through her drowsy pleasure followed by delight. The delight beckoned to me like a lighthouse in the storm. I swooped in to kiss her, teasing that same breast while Rome tended to the other.

Their movements grew more frenetic as I kept up the kiss, breaking the contact for only brief seconds to gasp some air and then her cries escalated. Rome's thrusts stuttered as she gripped the back of my neck and his very sharp grunts had me lifting my head to watch as the orgasm rolled over her.

Hellspawn strained and then shuddered only to tighten her fingers against my nape. Another little sound escaped and they collapsed together. I settled on my side, drinking in the sight of her. Pink flushed her chest and her cheeks.

Even in the low light of the sun filtering through the privacy shades, she looked radiant. With light fingers, she traced my face even as she curved her free arm behind her to hug Rome.

"Good morning," I said, grinning slowly. My own erection was definitely hard as a stone. Morning wood had nothing on this.

"Hi," she whispered, her voice ragged. Her light touch drifted down my chest to my dick and she wrapped her hand around the base. The touch was almost too light, so I bumped against her palm as she began to stroke in an agonizingly tender way.

"Going to torture me this morning?" I teased, more than content to just enjoy the sight of her like this. As soon as she rallied, I planned to pin her to the bed for another round.

Who was I kidding? I wasn't planning on letting her out of bed for at least twenty-four hours.

"No," she said, laughing and it was the siren call of that lyrical sound that drew me in. "Just trying to recover…this was an amazing way to wake up."

"Compliments of my brother." The quip earned another smile, this one even brighter than the last.

"Thank you, " Rome said, without irony as he lifted his head and pressed a kiss behind her ear. "You're welcome."

Her laughter escalated. She twisted, still giving me lazy pumps while she kissed Rome. It did something to me to watch them together, the way she kissed him and the absolute unabashed openness.

My mirror loved her without reservation or demand. The fact she seemed to not only reflect those same emotions but welcomed me into that knot of affection tying them together...

When she broke from Rome she leaned forward and I met her kiss with the same firm gentleness. It turned hotter and more demanding. I dragged her to me and she gave a soft cry and a shudder. Rolling over, I angled myself and slid home she wrapped around me and indulged me in a long, slow, and lazy pursuit of our pleasure.

The sound of the shower running intruded on our carnal good morning haze. "Need to get up," she mumbled and I ran my hand down to her ass and stroked it in slow circles. That she could let me touch her was an amazing gift. Even more, that she was so boneless and relaxed against me.

"You don't need to do anything," I told her. "When Rome is done, I'll carry you in there and wash you myself."

Her swift inhale and the surprise dancing across her expression as she lifted her head satisfied something truly primitive in me.

"When I care about someone, Hellspawn, there's nothing I won't do for them."

Her smile softened as she studied me. "You know, you have given me that impression."

"Good," I said firmly. Course, when we did make it to the shower and she went to her knees for me, I forgot how to breathe.

"You should know," she told me, eyes dancing. "When I

care about someone, there isn't anything I won't do for them either."

Fuck. I forgot how to think and my legs were definitely the ones shaking when she finished. We eventually left the shower, but Hellspawn didn't bother with clothes. I turned up the heat to make sure she was comfortable and then we went to have breakfast with Rome.

An hour later, I coaxed her back to bed and I had zero plans of letting her out of it. Rome promised to be back later and that was fine.

More than fine.

"Liam…" She groaned during one sweaty break while I trailed an ice cube along her spine.

"Too much?" I'd hardly been gentle. Even when I fought to be, she fought me back and it was so damn easy to get lost in her.

"No," she whispered. "But I think you might be stuck with me. Not sure I can move."

I grinned.

"Fine by me," I promised then kissed her. "Rome will tell the boys."

Her sigh only added to my humor. "I don't know how long I can stay."

"We have time," I soothed her. "Where you go… I'm going to follow."

No more denials. No more running—unless it was to her.

TREASURED (ALTERNATE POV)

EMERSYN

"*M*ilo punching Ezra made so much sense and at the same time—

"Liam..." I didn't want any of them to fight. I was still sore, and Rome was bruised up. Even Liam sported bruises. We'd just made it safely home. I really didn't want Milo getting hurt. Liam could stop him. He had before and there was already blood dripping.

With a grunt, Liam muttered, "Fine," and stalked forward. I didn't smile, but relief still feathered through me. Liam would take care of them. Lainey frowned. She hated when any of them told her what to do and Ezra was being a bit of a dick. Then again, it wasn't anything new for Ezra. At the same time, I was getting used to the brawling. These guys were all physical and intense. They filled every room they were in and there was no mistaking the threat they offered to everyone else.

But I was safe here.

That safety resonated within me.

"Come on," Freddie said pulling my focus from the fight.

"Let them figure this out. You probably want to shower and change. Then I can watch, and it will be a much nicer show."

The last line punctured the bubble of tension and I grinned. Freddie was a master of deflection. At the same time... I liked it when he played with me.

"Lainey?" I didn't want to leave her to deal with the chaos on her own. Then again, I was pretty sure she could handle it.

"No," she said. "Freddie is right, you should go grab a shower and change. Your doctor friend probably wants to go over all your injuries."

"I'm fine," I assured her. Mickey giving me an exam was not at the top of my list. I ran a hand down Rome's arm. "You okay?"

"Go," he said, then gave Freddie a look. Even as I took Freddie's offered hand, I glanced at the guys. But even Jasper shooed me to go and Vaughn lifted his chin. They were fine.

They were fine and we were back.

Rome was safe.

Relief spilled through me as they got Milo and Ezra separated finally. So when Freddie gave me the lightest of tugs to go, I went. His fingers were warm against mine and his grip was light, but very much there.

Once we were upstairs, he headed straight for Kellan's room. Mine was still tucked in between Kellan and Rome's and the only door to get inside was via Kellan's.

"Okay, I can wait out here." He squeezed my fingers.

"Freddie?"

"Yes, Boo-Boo?"

Pivoting, I faced him fully. "Thank you."

"For what?"

"For wanting to LoJack me. I think it's really sweet." It really was. Maybe it should be more weird. But I didn't want to be lost any more than they wanted to lose me.

A flush touched his face. "I just don't want to lose you."

"You won't."

"Pinky swear?" His dare as he raised his pinky only made my smile widen. I hooked my pinky around his and drifted closer. Freddie was very much my safe space, I wanted to be his.

When his gaze dipped briefly to my lips, I made the leap. "Kiss and makeup?"

"We didn't fight," he said the words almost too slowly, but he didn't retreat and his eyes didn't show even an ounce of fear or reaction. His pupils were steady even if his breath seemed to come a little faster.

But then my heart was racing too. "Then pinky swear and kiss to seal the deal." It was an offer, but I wanted to kiss Freddie. I wanted him to kiss me. I wanted it to be okay if we did.

Then he dipped his head and he brushed his lips against mine so lightly I barely felt them. Yet, they were so soft, that barely there and gone again feeling just left me hungry for more. I leaned into him, tightening my pinky around his. I wanted to tell him touching was okay and to make sure he was okay with it.

His kiss started as just a brush against one corner of my mouth, then the other. But he didn't pull away and I parted mine half-tempted to press deeper into the kiss when he kissed me for real. It wasn't just a sip, but a full drink. The sweep of his tongue, darting against mine sent all the hairs on my body to stand on end then I couldn't breathe for the want of him.

He tugged my hand up to his chest and pressed my palm to his heart. The invitation to touch, the embrace, the slow, deepening strokes of his tongue as he sealed our lips together sent my pulse galloping. This was everything and I savored the connection. Freddie was here.

He was alive and holding me and we were both safe. Safe to explore and to feel.

To kiss.

As much as I wanted for more, I didn't fight him when he lifted his head. This was a lot of contact. A connection we both needed, or at least I did, but the intimacy took time and it took a lot to trust.

That he could, at all, with me was something I treasured.

I treasured him.

"Welcome home," he whispered and my smile grew.

"I'm really glad to be here."

"LoJack," he said firmly.

And a thrill went through me. The possessiveness and determination in that one declaration made me laugh.

"LoJack. We'll find you the best."

Lifting my hand from his chest, I brushed my knuckles against his cheek. I kept the touch light, but I wanted to feel the hint of stubble. Another reminder that I was here. We were here. "Wait for me while I shower?"

"Forever," he promised.

Another laugh slipped free. "I'll try not to take that long." Then I made myself let him go and headed into my room. I didn't close the door. I didn't need to, I trusted Freddie.

I wanted him to know I trusted him too. After I got some clean clothes, I blew him a kiss and the depth of emotion in his eyes threatened to undo me.

Blowing out a breath, I headed into the bathroom. I was so damn glad to be home.

Home.

I was home.

I was treasured.

I treasured them.

I treasured him.

MERCILESS SPY BONUS SCENES

CONVENTIONAL (BONUS POV)

LIAM

*T*he last thing I wanted to do was take Hellspawn out and expose her or Rome. At the same time, I also didn't want to disappoint Mom. Dad was right, I'd been keeping my distance. While it was on purpose, it had absolutely nothing to do with pushing them away. Telling myself that hurting them would keep them safe didn't work for me. So, Sunday, I scheduled a private table for brunch at Rodin's.

Mom's delight when I called her with the name promised it had been the right call. Hellspawn's smile when I told her agreed. So, here we were, with me dressed in a suit, sans tie while Hellspawn chose a white floral print high-low dress. The blue and green florals added to the ethereal air around her. The strappy heels added a bit of height and I eyed the bare arms but she held up a simple white sweater.

"You're too pretty to take out," I rumbled. That dress had a sash in the front and looked wraparound. I wanted to tug it and see what would happen. But she held up a finger.

"Uh-uh," she scolded. "We're meeting them at eleven. We don't have time for what you want and for me to get ready again."

I grunted. Before I could answer, Rome walked out to join us. Surprisingly, he was in a button down shirt, and slacks. No jacket or tie, but he looked more than presentable. The running shoes were not quite the right attire, but I wasn't going to criticize. "Why is your shirt the same shade of blue as the flowers on her dress?"

"Because I asked Starling to match." Rome shrugged and she grinned.

"You look wonderful."

"It itches."

Crossing over to him, she tilted her head. "May I?"

He nodded and she checked his collar, then slid her finger around. A tiny rip and she came away with the interior label. Finished with that, she smoothed it down again.

"Better?"

Rome seemed to consider the question, then he nodded. "Thank you."

"You're welcome." Turning, she threaded her arm through his and looked at me. "Ready?"

I pulled out my phone and aimed it at them, then I snapped a picture. Her eyes were bright, the cosmetics she'd chosen were simple and barely noticeable except for the faint blue around her eyes. Rome even looked pleased, though his smile was faint. When she crooked her finger, I went to her obediently and handed Rome my phone. Then she posed with me.

Finally, we did a selfie and I stared at the three photos in my gallery with a small shake of my head. The impulsive thought was more enjoyable than I realized. I liked having her there. I liked having her with us. Hell Rome hadn't even protested the photo.

Right, more pictures.

"Okay, let's go." I checked my gun. They couldn't wear one, but Hellspawn had two in her purse. It was a big bulky thing that Rome usurped before we were even a step out of the apartment. But it meant they had weapons with them. The added security around Mom and Dad should help, but I didn't want to leave an angle uncovered.

"It's going to be fine," Hellspawn soothed me. "Your mom seems really nice."

"She is," Rome said without missing a beat. "Pushy too. But always smiling and kind."

That—described Mom to a T so I just chuckled. "I know it will be fine, but they're right, I've never introduced them to a girl I liked before."

"You never had Starling before."

And that… was accurate.

I met Rome's gaze over his head. He was completely relaxed. Also not something he usually was where my parents were concerned. Dipping my gaze to Hellspawn, I found her watching me with a small smile. "What?"

"You're nervous."

I was not.

"It's cute."

I scowled.

Her laughter, however, was delightful.

They were already there when we arrived and Mom beamed as we walked into the private room, I'd requested. It was bright, filtering in sunshine from the private atrium and we were blissfully alone save for the staff.

"Liam, oh, you did bring Rome…" Mom smiled at him after she pressed a kiss to my cheek. "May I?"

I was ready to intervene, but Rome dipped his head. "One," was all he said. He'd allow one kiss and for a moment, real joy shone in Mom's eyes as she pressed a kiss to his cheek.

"Thank you, dear boy."

He nodded then Mom looked at Emersyn and my

hellspawn matched her grin for grin. "Come along with me young lady." She held out her hand. "You are officially my favorite person."

"Hey," I protested as Hellspawn took her hand easily.

"Hush, she made sure I got to see both of you today and that you didn't find an excuse to duck out. So she is going to sit next to me and we're going to have a wonderful lunch."

Dad laughed as Mom tugged Hellspawn away and Rome followed like a magnet. I got it. I wanted to go too. But Dad clasped my shoulder before shaking my hand. "Go with it, son."

"It's going to make her happy, isn't it?"

"It already has. Family, it's all she's ever wanted to give you too. A nice, normal family."

Normal was weird.

Nice...but weird.

AFTERWORD

Whew.

Returning to the Vandals was a gift. I'd missed them quite a bit, and it was so fantastic to feel and hear them again, especially as they've grown and changed in the intervening time.

One of my favorite parts of Fierce Dancer was Em driving her own car and making her way back and forth from the school to the clubhouse. It showed such tremendous growth for her from where the whole series started and all of that growth was on display here.

I hope you enjoyed them as much as I did. The next series up in this "world" is BLOOD Brothers and it begins with BURN. Be sure to preorder your copy today and visit my website and sign up for news and updates . Then don't be shy, jump into my reader group on Facebook, I love to hear from my readers!

xoxo

Heather

Website:

heatherlong.net
Reader group:
facebook.com/groups/heatherspack
Spoiler group:
facebook.com/groups/teammadatheather

ABOUT HEATHER LONG

I *love* books. Not just a little bit, but a lot. Books were my best friends when I was growing up. Books didn't care if I was new to a town or to a class. They were always there, my trustiest of companions. Until they turned on me and said I had to write them.

I can tell you that my own personal happily ever after included writing books. I've always said that an HEA is a work in progress. It's true in my marriage, my friendships, and in my career. I am constantly nurturing my muse as we dive into new tales, new tropes, new characters and more.

After seventeen years in Texas, we relocated to the Pacific Northwest in search of seasons, new experiences, and new geography. I can't wait to discover what life (and my muse) have in store for me.

Maybe writing was always my destiny and romance my fate. After all, my grandmother wasn't a fan of picture books and used to read me her Harlequin Romance novels.

Follow Heather & Sign up for her newsletter:
www.heatherlong.net
TikTok

ALSO BY HEATHER LONG

82nd Street Vandals

Savage Vandal

Vicious Rebel

Ruthless Traitor

Dirty Devil

Shamelessly Loyal (Novella)

Brutal Fighter

Dangerous Renegade

Merciless Spy

Reckless Thief

Fierce Dancer

Dirty Dancer

Bay Ridge Royals

Shamelessly Loyal (Novella)

Battle Lines

Deceptive Truce

Wicked Surrender

Violent Chaos

Desperate Victory

Blue Ivy Prep

Problem Child

Mad Boys

Party Crashers

Money Shot

Bravo Team Wolf

When Danger Bites

Bitten Under Fire

Cardinal Sins

Kill Song

First Chorus

High Note

Last Word

Chance Monroe

Earth Witches Aren't Easy

Plan Witch from Out of Town

Bad Witch Rising

Fevered Hearts

Marshal of Hel Dorado

Brave are the Lonely

Micah & Mrs. Miller

A Fistful of Dreams

Raising Kane

Wanted: Fevered or Alive

Wild and Fevered

The Quick & The Fevered

A Man Called Wyatt

Heart of the Nebula

Queenmaker

Deal Breaker

Throne Taker

Wolves of Willow Bend

Wolf at Law

Wolf Bite

Caged Wolf

Wolf Claim

Wolf Next Door

Rogue Wolf

Bayou Wolf

Untamed Wolf

Wolf with Benefits

River Wolf

Single Wicked Wolf

Desert Wolf

Snow Wolf

Wolf on Board

Holly Jolly Wolf

Shadow Wolf

His Moonstruck Wolf

Thunder Wolf

Ghost Wolf

Outlaw Wolves

Wolf Unleashed